Debt of Dishonour

Mary Andrea Clarke

First published in 2010
by Crème de la Crime
P O Box 523, Chesterfield, S40 9AT

Typesetting by Yvette Warren
Cover design by Yvette Warren
Front cover image by Peter Roman

ISBN 978-0-9550566-4-1
A CIP catalogue reference for this book is available
from the British Library

Printed and bound in the UK by
CPI Cox & Wyman, Reading, RG1 8EX

www.cremedelacrime.com

About the author:
Mary Andrea Clarke has been a regular delegate at crime fiction conferences and an active member of Mystery Women since 1998. She has reviewed historical fiction for the Historical Novel Society and crime fiction for Sherlock Magazine, Shots Ezine and Mystery Women. *Debt of Dishonour* is her third novel.
Mary lives in Surrey with her cat, Alice.

Thanks are due...

to my family, Kevin, Peter, Linda, Alice and Stephen Clarke, for all their support and interest, including passing on the word about the Crimson Cavalier. A particular mention must go to my nephew, Stephen Clarke, for his sterling work on my website.

Thank you to Lorraine Hayes for several late nights of help in typing my manuscript notes.

Derek Hampson's contribution to the name of a character is much appreciated.

Encouragement received from friends in Mystery Women, the Crime Writers' Association and St Hilda's Crime Fiction Conference has been much appreciated, as has that from my fellow Crème de la Crime authors.

There has been constant support and encouragement in my writing from a number of people which has been greatly valued. These include Amanda Brown, Maureen Carter, Kate Charles, N J Cooper, Gaynor Coules, Lizzie Hayes, Sue Lord, Adrian and Ann Magson, Brian Murphy, Ayo Onatade, Linda Regan, Jennifer Palmer, Kate Stacey, Andrew Taylor and Alison Weir.

I would like to thank Lynne Patrick for her extensive patience and useful editing suggestions. Thanks also go to Lynne, Jeff, Yvette and the rest of the Crème de la Crime team for continuing to support the Crimson Cavalier.

To Lorraine.

Thanks for your friendship and support.

1

"Much obliged, ladies." Still astride his horse, the highway-man removed his hat and gave a flourishing bow. The action revealed a thinning hairline which contrasted with the grizzled stubble on his chin. "Very generous," he said with a wink through his masked eye. "Wish all my patrons were as helpful. Have a pleasant journey, ladies."

Georgiana Grey pursed her lips. It had been difficult to resist the urge to offer the password which would have allowed them to go on their way with jewels and purses intact. Yet she dared not think of the explanations she would have been urged to offer. Georgiana glanced towards her companions, one with arms folded in serene resignation, the other anxious, her glance flicking nervously from side to side, hands rubbing together in a washing motion reminiscent of Lady Macbeth.

To make matters even more complicated, Georgiana had recognised the highwayman. Silence seemed the safest option.

As the rider turned away from the occupants of the carriage, Georgiana heard him dismiss the coachman, whose own muffled voice muttered through the air in disgruntled protest. The highwayman laughed, giving his horse the order to move. A moment later, the three ladies felt the motion of the carriage as the wheels began to turn.

"Mama will be so angry," whispered the youngest traveller, putting one hand to her throat.

"Yes, she has no tolerance for highwaymen," said Georgiana, her tone matter-of-fact.

"No, you don't understand, Georgiana," said the girl earnestly. "They were her pearls. She lent them to me. What shall I tell her?"

Georgiana glanced towards the girl. Privately, she thought Lady Winters was foolish to lend her daughter an item she treasured, knowing she would be travelling on a road where highwaymen were a regular hazard. But it would not do to be less than reassuring to her young companion.

"You must tell her the truth, Louisa. It was not your fault the pearls were stolen."

"That brooch belonged to my mother," mourned the third passenger. "It's heartbreaking to lose it, particularly after it was recovered the last time."

"Well, we must hope for the best," said Georgiana. "It is possible some inquiries can be made to recover the items."

Louisa's face lit up. "Oh, do you think so?"

Georgiana nodded. "Quite possibly. A reward would have to be offered, of course."

"I'm sure Mama would not mind that," said Louisa. "Her pearls meant a great deal to her. She has had them since she was a girl – before she married Papa." She looked gloomy again. "I don't suppose she will ever let me wear them again even if she does get them back."

"We were lucky to escape with our lives," said the third lady with a shudder. "That pistol!"

Georgiana looked towards her in some surprise. She knew her cousin was not a brave person, but she thought her sensible enough to know that they would only have been in real danger if they had put up a resistance. Selina could not have known that Harry was no cold-blooded killer, it was true – but highwaymen had no reason to shoot if travellers were compliant in handing over their valuables. Again she offered reassurance.

"Well, we are none of us hurt and must be grateful for that."

Selina tut-tutted, shaking her head in a manner which could not have irritated Georgiana more had it been calculated to do so. She gave up on her attempt to console, since her cousin seemed determined to look on the bleak side. Louisa, for her part, looked remarkably sanguine. For all her youth, she seemed relatively undisturbed by the experience, apart from her dread of telling her mother about the theft. However, this was not an ordeal to be faced immediately, and Georgiana's suggestion that a reward could procure their return appeared to have raised her spirits.

The remainder of the journey was accomplished in silence. When they reached their destination, there was no bustle of carriages arriving, nor guests being assisted to alight by a willing servant. Every equipage was already neatly stowed, horses settled. As their carriage drew up outside the home of Mrs Milton, a servant ended his conversation with a visiting coachman and broke away from the wall he was leaning against. He came forward to hold the horses' heads while another servant opened the door and helped the ladies down. If either of them was surprised at having to perform these duties so long after they were completed for the earlier guests, they did not show it. Georgiana and her party were conducted up the stone steps, lit by carefully placed lamps on each side.

As the three ladies walked through the door, a few pairs of eyes looked in their direction. Selina's face turned scarlet; it was clear she sensed in their glances a reproach at a social *faux pas*, and her mousy disposition was uncomfortable with anything out of the ordinary. Georgiana, for her part, was unperturbed at the opinions of others, and Louisa seemed equally unconcerned, merely looking curiously about her. Their hostess, Mrs Milton, came forward to greet them, a smile of welcome on her face and no indication that she noticed anything out of the common way. Georgiana took the initiative in explaining what had happened.

"Mrs Milton, I must apologise for our late arrival. I am afraid we were stopped by a highwayman on our way here."

This disclosure created something of a sensation. Gradually, the hum of conversation decreased, radiating out from where they stood, through the crowd, the quiet eventually reaching the more distant guests. Selina's colour grew even deeper.

"Oh, you poor dears," said Mrs Milton. "How dreadful for you. Is there anything I can do for you? You must sit down. What a shocking thing to happen!"

Georgiana could have done without this fussing but she could see her cousin warming to Mrs Milton's suggestions. Louisa also seemed eager to share their experience.

"Oh, yes, indeed," she said. "He took Mama's pearls." Louisa put her hand to her throat.

"How awful!" Mrs Milton looked at her in awe. "Did he snatch them from your neck?"

"No. No, he didn't do that," said Louisa. "But I didn't want to give him the chance. He had a pistol pointed at us."

"Yes, I see." Mrs Milton nodded her understanding.

"It was all quite frightening," chirped in Miss Knatchbull, wringing her hands. "Very shocking. The roads seem so unsafe, one can't travel anywhere any more."

"No, I know just what you mean," said Mrs Milton. "To lose your mother's pearls, Miss Winters, that must be so upsetting for you."

Louisa nodded. There were signs of tears stinging her eyes. "Yes, it was. It was the first time Mama lent them to me. I don't know what she will say."

"He took my mother's brooch," said Miss Knatchbull.

"Oh, no," said Mrs Milton. "Oh, how disagreeable for you."

Louisa looked a little miffed at having her share of sympathy cut short and seemed about to say something more.

Concerned about the increasing competition between her two companions for commiserations on their ordeal, Georgiana redirected the attentions of their solicitous hostess towards her cousin, and escaped with Louisa with the object of procuring some refreshment. Propelling her young friend through a crowd of concerned acquaintances, Georgiana gave cheerful assurances to everyone who accosted her that they had taken no harm; she left it to Selina to recount intricate details of the drama which had befallen them to anyone who enquired.

Suddenly she found their progress halted by a stern voice, which demanded with peremptory impatience, "What the devil happened to you?"

Georgiana paused and turned her head. The imposing figure of Louisa's cousin, Maxwell Lakesby, was bearing down upon them; his forehead bore a deep frown and the expression in his blue eyes, meeting her own emerald ones, was part severity, part concern. It was Louisa, brought to a halt just behind Georgiana, who replied.

"Oh, Max, we were held up by a highwayman."

"What?"

Lakesby's gaze left her and fell upon his cousin.

"Are you all right?" he asked.

"Yes, we are quite unharmed," responded Georgiana,

"but of course it has delayed our arrival."

"That is no matter," said Lakesby slowly. "Did he take much?"

Louisa's hand went to her throat again. "He took Mama's pearls," she said breathlessly. "However shall I tell her?"

Mr Lakesby gave a low whistle. "The devil he did."

"Mama has had those pearls ever since I can remember."

"She's had them ever since *I* can remember," said her cousin. "Well, never mind, child, it was not your fault."

Louisa bit her underlip. The girl must be seriously worried, Georgiana thought, if she failed to object to her cousin addressing her as 'child'.

Lakesby's expression softened. "Would you like me to tell her?" he said.

Louisa's face brightened with relief. "Would you?" she asked.

"Certainly, if you wish it."

"Thank you, Max," said Louisa with a rush of gratitude. "Those pearls meant so much to Mama. Indeed, I was amazed when she offered to lend them to me."

"Yes, I confess I was too," said Lakesby.

"And you know, when it comes to highwaymen, she is so – so…"

"Quite," said Lakesby. "Although you may be surprised, Louisa. Your mother will know you had little choice but to hand them over. She may be more understanding than you expect. In fact, if she were to blame anyone, it is more likely to be me for neglecting to escort you."

Louisa looked unconvinced but was saved the trouble of a reply. Selina, flushed and breathless, bustled towards them clutching a glass of ratafia.

"Oh, good evening, Mr Lakesby. Have you heard of our shocking experience?"

"I have, Miss Knatchbull. Most distressing for you. I trust you are unhurt?"

"Well, yes, thank you. But I lost a brooch which belonged to my mother. A simple design and more of sentimental value than monetary, but quite distressing."

"Most upsetting for you," Lakesby sympathised.

Miss Knatchbull was shaking her head. "The second time it has been lost as well."

"The second time?" Lakesby looked puzzled.

"Oh, yes. I was so fortunate as to have it restored to me last time it was stolen. I dare not hope that it might happen again."

"Oh, yes, Max. Georgiana thought it possible we could get Mama's pearls back, if we offered a reward," said Louisa.

"Did she?" Lakesby's eyes turned towards Georgiana. "Did you have any thoughts as to a figure for suitable recompense, Miss Grey?"

Georgiana met his eyes steadily. "Not at all. Why don't you ask my brother? I daresay his experience as a magistrate has given him some idea of these matters."

"Very true," said Lakesby.

"Yes, indeed it is," said Selina solemnly. "Of course, dear Edward will know just what is right."

"Perhaps he could also indicate how one – er – goes about advertising for such things?" said Lakesby.

"Oh, yes, I'm sure he could," Selina responded in an earnest tone. "You may depend upon it, he will know the right thing to do."

"Selina, who is that woman in that quiz of a hat? She must have been delayed even more than we were; it would appear she has just arrived," said Georgiana, vaguely irritated at Lakesby's gentle mockery of her cousin.

"Really, Georgiana! Though I must admit, it is quite a

shocking colour on her. That is Mrs Woodrow. She is a friend of someone who knew my mother, I cannot recall her name, but I must go and pay my respects. I do hope you will excuse me."

"Of course," said Lakesby.

Georgiana stood silently regarding him until Miss Knatchbull was out of earshot. "It is not kind to tease her," she said.

"I know. I beg your pardon." Lakesby turned his attention to his own cousin. "Don't look so anxious, Louisa. We will find some way of resolving this matter. I shall no doubt receive a sermon from your mother about having neglected to escort you, and then she will very likely forget the whole thing."

"She won't."

"She would certainly not expect you to risk getting shot by refusing to hand over the pearls. Was your highwayman the Crimson Cavalier, by the way?"

"No, someone older," said Louisa.

Lakesby grinned. "Poor Louisa, not even the excitement of being held up by someone dashing."

Louisa glowered at him.

"Try to cheer up," Lakesby said. "If you go about with that Friday face all evening, all your beaux will desert you."

Louisa looked even less pleased at this comment. Her face suffused with pink, and her china blue eyes flickered between Georgiana and Lakesby.

"Why didn't you escort us, Max?"

"I'm sorry, child. I should have done, of course, but I had a matter in need of my urgent attention."

"What matter?" asked Louisa.

"A private matter."

Louisa's glance flickered briefly back to Georgiana.

"A young lady?" Her tone was guileless.

"A private matter," Lakesby repeated firmly.

Louisa looked demurely up at him from under her lashes. She said nothing, however, and the challenge in Lakesby's expression went unanswered. Georgiana watched them both carefully. Was Louisa simply being mischievous, attempting to taunt her cousin, or had she struck a sensitive issue? Of a sudden, Georgiana felt she was in the way. Yet having arrived with Louisa, it would be difficult to remove herself from the conversation with anything approaching tact. She therefore waited until the mistrust in Lakesby's eyes faded away. He looked back towards her and smiled.

"Miss Grey, I'm sure you know my cousin's incorrigible nature too well by now for me to have need to apologise. However, I would like to beg your pardon for being so remiss, in failing to escort you and Miss Knatchbull and leaving you to the mercy of the highwayman."

"There is no need, Mr Lakesby. We are quite unhurt. Besides, my cousin and I are hardly your responsibility."

"Did you lose much?" he asked.

Georgiana shrugged. "A few trinkets. These things happen."

"Nevertheless, an unfortunate experience."

Georgiana was aware of Lakesby's scrutiny, as if he was trying to surmise how she could have fallen victim to a highwayman. She was more glad than ever that she had not given Harry the password. It would have created far more of a sensation if they had been held up, yet managed to arrive fully adorned and solvent.

Before either could speak again, they became aware of a stirring in the room. The normal babble of guests awaiting a lavish dinner changed its tone. Expectancy gave way to tension. Georgiana and Louisa both looked around but could not see anything beyond the crowd immediately surrounding them. Nevertheless, it was clear the mood of the room had changed; there was a sense of anxiety, and the festive atmosphere had dimmed. Something crashed, and an air of shocked uncertainty filtered through the gathered guests. Voices asked each other what had happened, their combined hum sounding harsh and uneasy. Louisa craned her neck.

One voice became audible over the hubbub. "Help. Help me!"

"Please, let us through." Mrs Milton, their hostess, spoke imperiously. "A sofa, some brandy, quickly."

The throng began to separate, in a manner which reminded Georgiana of a picture she had seen in her childhood, depicting the parting of the Red Sea. In a gesture more protective than gentlemanly, Lakesby pushed both Louisa and Georgiana behind him. However, they were near the path which was opening and Louisa had time for no more than a token protest before the origin of the disturbance was in sight.

A dark-haired man was being half dragged, half carried through the crowd, his pale face a contrast to his colourful, flamboyant garb. His coat was well cut and his knee breeches a perfect fit. The most striking feature of his ensemble was his waistcoat, a clearly unique design in its purple and gold swirls, into which blended a deep rich red, spreading from the knife which protruded from his abdomen.

The shocked silence which had fallen gave way to horrified whispers.

"Who is it?" asked Louisa.

"Boyce Polp," said Lakesby.

The injured man had sunk into a chair, his breath coming in gasps. Lakesby stepped forward, removing his coat, which he folded and put behind the man's head. Mrs Milton watched, clutching between her hands a yellow satin cushion which it seemed she had been about to offer.

"Has a surgeon been sent for?" asked Lakesby.

"Yes. I have sent the boy," said Mrs Milton. Her eyes flickered between Mr Polp's prone figure and her own hands, folded in front of her now she had passed the cushion to a servant. Her manner was one of delicate revulsion, but Georgiana suspected her main concern was for the bloodstains on her chair.

All buzz of conversation had ceased. Everyone's eyes were on the bleeding man; his pale face was clammy with sweat, his lips greying. Lakesby was on his knees by the chair, holding his folded handkerchief against the wound with one hand as he attempted to remove his cravat with the other.

Georgiana stepped forward. "Let me." Putting her own hand to the handkerchief, she held the makeshift pad in position, ignoring the shocked gasps and whispers rippling through the crowd behind her.

"Thank you." Lakesby threw her a grateful glance as he raised both hands to his cravat, dismantling with ease the intricate design of the Waterfall which he had taken such pains to achieve. His valet would probably never recover from the sight of the blood spatters which now adorned it.

"Black…guard," Boyce Polp gasped. "Robbed… me."

"I don't think you should try to talk, Mr Polp," said Georgiana.

"Took… my watch," he continued.

"Miss Grey is right, Mr Polp," said Lakesby, threading one end of his cravat behind the injured man's body. He pulled it through from the other side and hitched it into position over the handkerchief. "You should save your breath. A surgeon is on the way."

"No. Robbed and – and… and then…" Polp's voice trailed off. Suddenly he spoke again, with a burst of vigour. "Highwayman. Cursed fellow. Can't travel… any…where." He gave a lopsided smile, and a bubble of blood formed at the corner of his mouth. "Ruined my best waistcoat."

"Poor devil," came a voice from the crowd of guests. "I say, Lakesby, how on earth can you manage like that? What's to do, leaving the knife stuck in the poor fellow like that?"

Before anyone realised what was happening, a hand stretched past Georgiana and removed the dagger. Georgiana felt the edge catch the side of her hand as it travelled out. Lakesby swore. Boyce Polp's eyes opened wide. From somewhere deep inside him came a ragged, rasping noise, part gasp, part groan, greedily sucking in air that would not come.

"Where the devil's that surgeon?" said Lakesby, tying the bandage as Georgiana desperately tried to stem the flow of blood.

"Here." An authoritative voice sounded above the buzz of the crowd. Bodies moved again to clear a passage for him.

Georgiana glanced up, conscious of a figure approaching, an impression of white hair fringing a bald head. The individual stopped next to her, bag in hand, staring at the chair.

Boyce Polp was dead.

2

The party returning in Georgiana's carriage was a silent one. Even Louisa could only stare out the window. Lakesby was present to escort them this time; the absence of coat and cravat and spots of blood on the front of his shirt served as tangible reminders of the tragedy they had witnessed. The journey home was earlier than expected. Dinner had been abandoned; no one had felt able to face it. Mrs Milton's chef was known to be temperamental, and would certainly take offence.

"Highwaymen don't usually stab people, do they?" Louisa's voice broke the silence.

"I have certainly never heard of them doing so," responded Georgiana truthfully.

Miss Knatchbull shuddered. "Who knows what such creatures will stoop to?" she said.

"But if they have pistols – " said Louisa.

"There is no need for them to stab anyone," said Georgiana. "If everything of value is handed over, why would it be necessary?"

"Spite," said Miss Knatchbull tartly.

"Oh, really, Selina, that's absurd," said Georgiana, her tone impatient.

"But, Georgiana…" Miss Knatchbull began to protest.

"Your cousin is right, Miss Knatchbull," said Lakesby. "From what Mr Polp said, whoever stopped him had already taken everything he had of value. What would be the point of stabbing him?"

"But he said the highwayman had done it," objected Miss Knatchbull.

Lakesby shook his head. "I know. But he could have been delirious. He was dying."

"Oh, Max, don't." It was Louisa's turn to shudder.

Lakesby begged her pardon and the small group fell silent again. Lakesby looked from one to another of his companions.

"I think, Miss Grey, if you have no objection, I would like to take my cousin home first. I shall then be pleased to escort you and Miss Knatchbull."

"Of course. Though there is really no need for you to go to such trouble."

"Allow me. Please."

Miss Knatchbull looked as if she wanted to object to this plan but had long ago learned the unwisdom of arguing with her cousin, even if she had not been conscious of the impropriety of doing so before others. In any case, Mr Lakesby was already tapping his cane on the roof of the carriage to attract the attention of the coachman and groom as Georgiana let down the window to give them the instruction.

Their arrival at Lady Winters's house took few more minutes, and it was not long before Lakesby was springing down from the carriage, stretching out a hand to assist his cousin while the groom let down the steps. Louisa bade her friend goodnight in subdued tones, and Georgiana watched her take hold of her cousin's arm to mount the stone stairs to the front door. The two stood talking for a few moments as they waited for the door to be opened, then Lakesby bent to kiss Louisa on the cheek, and handed her into the butler's charge before returning to the carriage. He smiled at the two remaining ladies as he sprang up the steps. Selina gave him a brief glance, then lowered her mousy head and began to fiddle with the fringe of her shawl. It was Georgiana who spoke.

"I gather Lady Winters is not at home?"

"She is away, visiting some relative or other," Lakesby responded.

"Surely Miss Winters is not left alone?" said Selina. "If that is the case…"

"Oh no, Miss Knatchbull, you need not be concerned. My aunt arranged for Louisa's old governess to stay for a few days." He grinned. "I suspect she would much rather have been alone."

"Had I known," said Georgiana, "she could have come to stay with us. Could she not, Selina?"

"Oh. Oh, yes. Yes, certainly," replied Selina, sounding anything but certain.

"That is very kind of you both, but it is really not necessary," said Lakesby. "Louisa will do perfectly well. It may not be what she would like but she will certainly come to no harm – or mischief."

Georgiana nodded, and the carriage slowed as it drew up in front of her own house. Lakesby stepped out quickly and turned to offer his hand to Miss Knatchbull to help her to alight. She accepted his hand stiffly, then stood on the footpath waiting for Georgiana to join her. Selina opened her mouth to make her farewell and was surprised to hear her cousin offer Mr Lakesby some refreshment. When he accepted surprise turned to disapproval; Georgiana ignored her cousin's censorious expression and led the way up the front steps.

Her footman opened the door, and accepted Mr Lakesby's presence with equanimity. Georgiana requested that wine be brought for their guest.

"In the drawing room, please, James."

"Certainly, Miss Georgiana."

Lakesby handed his cloak to James, causing Miss Knatchbull to purse her already tightly compressed lips still further.

"I imagine you must be tired, Selina," said Georgiana. "Why don't you go up to bed? I shall not be far behind you."

Selina's eyes widened. She looked from Georgiana to Lakesby in disbelief. Georgiana's lips twitched; the suggestion that her cousin might leave her alone with a man was evidently the most shocking thing to occur in an evening of shocks.

"Indeed, Georgiana, I am not at all tired, and after all it is still quite early."

"Yes, but it has been a very trying evening. You must be quite shaken."

While Selina's face confirmed the truth of this, it was clear exhaustion was warring with her sense of propriety. Besides, what would Georgiana's brother Edward say, were he to learn of such reprehensible goings-on?

As James passed through the hall with the wine, Georgiana took the decision out of her cousin's hands.

"Goodnight, Selina," she said firmly, and walked swiftly into the drawing room with Lakesby close behind.

"I fear we have scandalised your cousin," said Lakesby, making for the tray James had deposited on a small table.

Georgiana shrugged. "It is easily done."

Lakesby glanced towards the closed doors as he handed Georgiana a glass of wine. "Aren't you concerned she will mention it to someone? These things have a way of getting around very quickly."

"And have Edward's wrath upon her? I don't think so. Selina will fear he will blame her. Of course, Mr Lakesby, if you are concerned for your own reputation…"

Lakesby ignored the comment, taking a sip from his glass.

"How is Louisa?" asked Georgiana. "She seemed very subdued."

"Yes," said Lakesby. "I think Mr Polp's death – and the manner of it – upset her more than she realised." He glanced towards Georgiana. "What about you?"

"Me?"

"Yes. It was a quite appalling thing to see. I would expect anyone to be shaken." He looked at her intently. "Thank you for your help."

"I'm sorry he couldn't be saved," said Georgiana regretfully. She sensed there was something else on Lakesby's mind: perhaps the circumstances of Mr Polp's death were not all they appeared.

Lakesby looked closely at her. "What is it, Miss Grey?"

Georgiana glanced towards him, pulled from her own thoughts. "Nothing, Mr Lakesby. I beg your pardon. I was just thinking."

"Yes? What were you thinking?"

"Nothing important, truly." She paused. "I did not know Mr Polp very well but I believe he was quite a charming man."

"Yes, I believe he was," said Lakesby. "Very well liked."

"Yes." Georgiana fell silent again.

Lakesby watched her without speaking for a moment or two, then, "Can it be that you are not convinced Mr Polp was killed by a highwayman?"

Georgiana looked at him, startled. "What?"

Lakesby smiled. "Come, Miss Grey, you have been in a brown study for most of the journey from Mrs Milton's. It is clear something is preying on your mind."

Georgiana looked towards him, considering how to

frame her words, not certain she wanted to tell him what was on her mind. Lakesby raised an eyebrow.

"I beg your pardon, Mr Lakesby," she said at last. "It is just such a distressing thing to happen."

"Yes."

"Did you know Mr Polp well?"

"Not really," Lakesby said. "An acquaintance, I ran across him at the occasional party, and at White's once or twice."

"I see."

"Do you suspect someone of his murder, Miss Grey?" Lakesby asked, his tone lightening. "Me, perhaps?"

"No, of course not," said Georgiana. "You were at Mrs Milton's. Louisa and I both saw you from the time we arrived."

"Ah, I see." The amusement left his voice. "But you don't think he was killed by a highwayman?"

"Well, it does seem a little odd," Georgiana admitted. She had her own reasons for refusing to believe a highwayman could be responsible.

"I tend to agree," said Lakesby thoughtfully.

"Do you?" Georgiana looked at him in some surprise.

"Why, yes," he said slowly. "Is that so strange?"

"I don't know," she responded. Georgiana was not sure why she should be surprised. She knew Lakesby to be a fair-minded man; unlike his aunt, Lady Winters, he would not assume highwaymen to be responsible for all the evils of the world. "How did Mr Polp arrive at Mrs Milton's?"

"I've no idea," Lakesby responded. "I had assumed he came in a carriage, but now that you mention it…"

"Would his servants have let him come to Mrs Milton's in that condition?" said Georgiana. "Surely one of them would have set off to summon help."

"Yes. Horseback then?"

"It seems logical in one way but – " Georgiana frowned, trying to imagine the scene.

"I suppose that presents difficulties of its own," said Lakesby as if interpreting her thoughts. "Stabbing a man on a horse can't be an easy thing, even if one is also on horseback."

"I suppose the servants could have run away," said Georgiana.

"When held up by the highwayman?" said Lakesby. "A poor show, Miss Grey. There's always a risk on the road. Servants are well aware of that. I'd be surprised to find that at least one of them wasn't armed."

Georgiana knew this to be true, but the entire scenario struck her as odd.

"All right," she said. "Mr Polp is travelling in a carriage, with servants who stay at their post, and he is stopped by a highwayman."

"As were you."

"Yes," said Georgiana, letting this pass. "The highwayman demands money, jewels and so forth. Perhaps Mr Polp refused."

"His watch fob was taken," Lakesby reminded her.

"It doesn't mean he gave it willingly."

"True," said Lakesby, looking thoughtful.

"So he was stabbed in a struggle."

"Polp struggled with a highwayman?" Lakesby frowned then shook his head. "No."

"No?"

Lakesby grinned. "What, and ruin his waistcoat?"

Despite herself, Georgiana smiled.

Lakesby grew serious again. "Polp was an amiable enough fellow, but can you imagine him challenging a highway robber?"

"No, I can't say that I can," said Georgiana slowly. "Although even if he did – " She stopped. Her brow furrowed and her eyes creased in concentration.

Lakesby watched her. He waited expectantly. "Miss Grey?"

Georgiana came out of her reverie. "I beg your pardon, Mr Lakesby." She considered how to voice her thoughts without indulging the speculation she knew to be in his mind. "It appears to me," she continued slowly, "a little strange that a highwayman would hold up a carriage, presumably with a pistol, and then use a different weapon to kill his victim."

Lakesby nodded. "To me also. In fact, it rather suggests the killing was planned in advance."

"Yes." A chill ran through Georgiana at the thought. She shook her head. "Poor Mr Polp."

"Yes." Lakesby glanced towards the clock. "It grows late. Your cousin will be anxious for your reputation. If I stay much longer I shall be obliged to marry you."

Georgiana's eyes widened. Where had that come from? Lakesby looked as startled to have said it as Georgiana was to have heard it. He drained his glass quickly and moved towards the door.

"Thank you for escorting us home, Mr Lakesby," said Georgiana, as he opened the door and held it for her to go out of the room.

"My pleasure, Miss Grey."

She looked towards him, concern in her expression. "I will try to call on Louisa tomorrow," she said. "I hope she does not have nightmares."

"No," said Lakesby, accepting his coat from James. "Nor you."

"I am well enough."

"Goodnight, Miss Grey."

"Goodnight, Mr Lakesby."

Georgiana turned towards the stairs as James closed the door after Lakesby.

"Emily's gone to your room, miss," said the footman. "She thought you'd be wanting her."

"Thank you, James. Go to bed yourself, do."

"Very good, miss. Goodnight."

Georgiana took a candle and walked slowly up the stairs. She was not surprised to see a glimmer of light under her cousin's door. While Selina's natural inclination was for early hours, Georgiana knew she would not be easy going to sleep in the knowledge that her charge was entertaining a gentleman unchaperoned. Georgiana hesitated briefly at Selina's door, but thought better of it and went to her own room.

There was a small welcoming fire, which gave a burnished glow to the light cast by the branch of candles on the dressing table. Her maid, Emily, stood ready to relieve her of her attire, but before she could step forward her eyes widened.

"Miss Georgiana! Your necklace!"

Georgiana put her hand to her bare neck, forgotten in the further events of the evening.

"Oh, yes." She gave a rueful smile. "On the way to Mrs Milton's, we were stopped by a highwayman."

Emily's jaw dropped.

"I know. Ironic, isn't it?" said Georgiana, handing her cloak to the stunned maid.

"But... but... miss, how? Who?" Emily shook her head swiftly, as if to clear her brain. "What exactly happened, miss?"

"It was Harry."

"Your Harry? I mean – I beg your pardon, Miss Georgiana,

I only meant…"

"It's all right, Emily, I know what you meant." Georgiana walked over to the bed and sat down, her expression thoughtful. As she spread out and smoothed her skirts, Emily gave a little cry.

"Miss Georgiana, is that…?"

Georgiana glanced down in the direction of her maid's horrified eyes. There was a red smear daubed in the folds of her skirt, unapparent until she had seated herself. Georgiana also realised there was a shadow across the base of her right thumb where the dagger had caught her, which the loan of Lakesby's handkerchief had failed to remove completely.

"Blood, yes," said Georgiana coolly. "There's no need to look so alarmed, Emily, it's not mine. At least, not much of it."

"What happened, miss?" Emily poured some water into the basin on the washstand. Turning back to her mistress, with an almost imperceptible gesture, she beckoned her to rise and turn around, so she could unhook the dress.

"Actually, it was quite dreadful, Emily," said Georgiana, her voice remaining steady although a clammy coldness coursed through her at having to repeat the tale. "There was a death."

"When you were held up?" asked Emily, taking the dress from her.

"No, at Mrs Milton's house. It was Boyce Polp. He'd been stabbed. He arrived with – with the dagger still in him."

"Oh, my goodness, how horrible."

"It was," said Georgiana. Her voice sounded far away. She shook off the uncharacteristic languor and continued briskly, "Mr Lakesby tried to help him but he died soon after arriving at Mrs Milton's. It was rather a miracle that he was able to get there at all."

"But what happened?" asked Emily.

Pausing only to splash herself with water from the basin, Georgiana briefly recounted the whole sorry episode. Emily's eyes widened when she heard that Mr Polp claimed he had been held up by a highwayman, and she gasped on learning how the knife had been withdrawn in such a dramatic manner. It took some moments for Georgiana to allay her concerns about the cut to her hand.

"Truly, Emily, it is nothing. A mere scratch. It stings a little but I promise you there is no need to worry."

Emily peered at the slightly reddened area on her mistress's hand. Since Georgiana had refused Mr Lakesby's offer to bandage it, there was nothing else to indicate she had been hurt. Emily was obliged to be satisfied with assurances that a little salve would settle it soon enough.

"What concerns me more," said Georgiana, "is this business of the highwayman."

"Do you think it was Harry?" asked Emily.

"Harry may have held him up," said Georgiana. "He was certainly working on the road – but I can't imagine he would have stabbed Mr Polp."

"Do you think he carries a knife?"

"I can't think why he would," said Georgiana. "It looked rather valuable, a gold handle, jewelled. More of an ornamental dagger than a weapon. I suppose it's possible he took it from someone."

"Seems a strange thing to be carrying around," commented Emily.

"Yes, it is." Georgiana was thoughtful. "I wonder…"

Emily looked at her through narrowed eyes. "What is it you wonder, Miss Georgiana?" Emily's tone was suspicious.

Georgiana did not answer immediately. She stood in the

middle of her bedroom, apparently deep in thought. Suddenly she turned, went to a wooden chest at the foot of her bed and opened it.

"It seems to me," said Georgiana, lifting out a three-cornered hat and dark, heavy cloak, "that there is only one thing to do. Ask him."

3

Georgiana paid no heed to the stern, despairing tones of her maid, but continued to pull out masculine attire from the chest. With a sigh, Emily came over to help her.

"What are you going to do, miss, just go to the Lucky Bell tavern and ask Harry if he stabbed Mr Polp?" Emily asked, shaking out a waistcoat.

"Oh, no, I trust I shall be more subtle than that," said Georgiana. Having divested herself of the remainder of her feminine garments, she pulled on a pair of black breeches, followed by a white shirt which she swiftly buttoned. Emily held out the dark waistcoat.

"Miss Georgiana, I wish you wouldn't."

"I don't intend to be out longer than necessary." She took a ribbon from her dressing table and handed it to Emily, who tied back Georgiana's thick auburn hair. The aristocratic young lady, who but a few minutes earlier had been dressed in a fashionable, if bloodstained, evening dress, was now a lithe, masculine looking figure. Seated on the bed, she held out her feet for Emily to assist with her boots.

"There was a light under my cousin's door when I came up," said Georgiana. "Would you mind checking if it's still there?"

Emily nodded silently, all protest gone. She rose from her knees to obey, and came back to report that the house was all in darkness. Georgiana looked up from the task of checking a pistol held in her lap. Emily's lips pursed, her eyes fixed on the weapon. Georgiana chose to ignore the disapproval and rose to her feet, securing the pistol in her belt and gesturing for the heavy, dark cloak which bore little resemblance to the one she had worn to travel to and from Mrs Milton's. Emily placed it around her shoulders and tied the cord securely. Georgiana thanked her and picked up from the bed a large black kerchief, which she folded into a triangle and proceeded to tie over the lower half of her face. Emily moved behind her to help carry out this awkward task. When it was completed, Georgiana picked up the tricorne, now adorned with an impudent red scarf, and placed it on her head.

"Lord, Miss Georgiana, if your cousin could see you now."

"We must take care that she never does," said Georgiana. "You're sure the house is quiet?"

Emily nodded. Georgiana picked up a candle and slipped into the hall; Emily closed the bedroom door quietly behind her. She moved with silent ease down the back stairs and through the kitchen, and placed the candle on the ledge of a small window near the door to the yard. She picked up a couple of carrots from a basket, hoping fervently that neither the cook nor the housekeeper, Mrs Daniels, had counted them.

Slipping out into the night, Georgiana moved nimbly towards the stable, finding her way easily through familiarity and the half light of the moon. The horses stirred at her approach, but with no more than some shuffling, low whinnying and an occasional snort, insufficient to disturb anyone. At the stall she wanted, Georgiana drew back the bolt and moved inside quickly, holding out a carrot and murmuring low endearments as the animal greeted her. The mare's soft nose nuzzled her gloved hand and Georgiana stroked the animal's head before moving across to the wall where bit and bridle hung. She saddled the animal with an ease which would have raised an eyebrow or two among her society acquaintances.

"Come along, Princess."

Georgiana kept her tone low but clear. The mare followed obediently as she led her out, eyes watchful for a potentially alert groom or stable boy. Her luck held, however, and within very few minutes she was trotting away from the elegant, newly developed residential square to a less well populated vicinity. A fresh breeze blew against her cheeks as they moved on, soon accompanied by the rustling of leaves as the road led towards the wood.

All was quiet. There was no sound of approaching carriages or horses, and Georgiana thought it likely that all but the most hardened partygoers and travellers would have arrived home and retired to bed by now. She slowed Princess down to a walk. The sound of hooves echoed along the road, and quiet as it was, she thought it best to minimise any possibility of attracting attention. The horse followed the road with ease and raised no objection when Georgiana steered her in a less well travelled direction, steadily picking her way over the uneven surface, through the increased shadow of trees.

Eventually they emerged into a small clearing, where stood a lively tavern with a row of horses tethered in front. As Georgiana dismounted a scrawny boy ran out from a side door and offered to look after Princess. Georgiana handed him the reins, tossed him a coin and strolled inside.

It was not an establishment one would expect to be frequented by a young lady of quality, but Georgiana stood calmly scanning the room, paying no heed to the boisterous spirits and rough talk which would have caused most females of her acquaintance to swoon.

Georgiana spotted her quarry quickly and began to make her way through the crowded room to the other side. Seated at a small table near the hearth was the highwayman who had a few hours earlier relieved her and Louisa of their jewels. There seemed to be some sort of dispute in progress, but this died away at her approach as Harry looked towards her.

"Well now, here's my friend the Crimson Cavalier. How goes it, lad?"

There was no trace of recognition of the young lady whose carriage he had earlier stopped.

"Well enough." Georgiana nodded towards the other two men seated at the table, trying to keep her gaze from Selina's brooch and her own gold necklace which lay on its surface. Of Louisa's pearls there was no sign. She looked towards Harry. "Can we talk?"

"Aye, lad." Harry scooped up his treasures into his pocket, tossed off the contents of his tankard in one draught then led the way from the taproom to a door leading to a small private parlour.

"Got some booty, lad?" said Harry, closing the door behind them.

"Not this time," said Georgiana. "There was a problem."

"Oh?" said Harry.

"A death," said Georgiana. "A man was stabbed."

"What?" said Harry. "You in trouble over a killing again, lad?"

"No," said Georgiana hastily, recalling her own experience of discovering a body on the road. "I thought you might be."

"Me? Where'd you get an idea like that, lad? Killing's not my game."

Harry seemed indignant. Genuinely surprised too,

Georgiana thought. She wanted to make clear that she was not accusing him.

"I know that, Harry, but I heard something had happened on the road where you were working."

"Where did you hear that, then?"

Georgiana shrugged. "Does it matter?" She had been considering how best to explain how she knew about Boyce Polp's death and had decided that she should simply brazen it out and not offer an explanation at all. Highwaymen did not ask questions of one another. Harry was unlikely to question her closely if he thought her knowledge was connected with some activity of her own which she did not wish to disclose.

"Suppose not." Harry shrugged himself.

The door suddenly opened and a cheerful, curly-haired girl bounced in, carrying a tray with a bottle and two glasses.

"Out!" Harry roared.

The girl looked startled. "But Cedric thought…"

"Never mind what Cedric thought. We don't want to be disturbed. On your way, wench."

Harry's tone was a growl. The girl accepted it and fled. Georgiana herself was taken by surprise; she had only ever seen the affable side of the gruff highwayman. But though in general he adopted a businesslike approach to his role, she had occasionally thought Harry could be a dangerous enemy if roused to anger.

Harry turned back to Georgiana. "Well, lad, what is all this?"

"I don't believe you killed anyone, Harry," said Georgiana, "but if you were on the road you will be suspected. Trust me."

"Someone killed on the road?" said Harry.

Georgiana nodded.

"I've not heard of anyone being found," said Harry.

"Not found on the road," said Georgiana. "I heard he managed to get himself to a house to ask for help. It was there he said he'd been stopped."

"He? Not one of the young ladies I stopped, then," said Harry. "Well, I'm glad 'tis not one of them."

Georgiana made no comment on his remark although a part of her was touched by this expression of concern. Her tone remained brisk. "Was there anyone else?"

"A couple of carriages going to a party," said Harry. "Did you see no one yourself?"

Georgiana shook her head. "When I heard of the stabbing, I thought it best not to linger."

"Can't say as I blame you," said Harry, "not after that trouble you had with that dead beak."

Georgiana nodded. Her discovery of a dead magistrate of her acquaintance on the highway several months earlier had caused her some difficulty; she had been seen near to his body, dressed in her highwayman's garb. The passers-by drew the obvious, though incorrect, conclusion, and a hue and cry was raised for the Crimson Cavalier, giving her no choice but to go in search of the real killer in order to prove her alter ego's innocence.

He paused and looked at her ruefully. "Aye, I'm grateful to you, lad. I know you've had a taste of this kind of thing yourself. Still, I saw no one dead or dying." He frowned. "Stabbed, you say? Strange, that. Never heard of anyone take to the High Toby with a knife."

"Yes, I thought it odd," said Georgiana. "Perhaps it was a valuable one, picked up as part of some booty."

"Could be," said Harry thoughtfully. "Odd thing for someone to carry though," he added, unconsciously echoing the thoughts Emily had voiced. "Are the Runners looking for me, do you know?" he continued.

"Not that I'm aware," said Georgiana. "I wanted to warn you before they started."

"Good of you, lad." Harry nodded. "Good of you," he said, almost to himself. His tone became businesslike. "Aye, 'twill only be a matter of time, I suppose. I'd best let Cedric know, in case anyone comes asking."

"Was anyone else working that stretch of road?" asked Georgiana.

"Not so far as I know," said Harry. "Bad form, to trespass on someone else's patch."

"Yes, I know, but still..." Georgiana knew highway robbers did not intrude on one another's preserves. However, it was always possible that someone new or less concerned with the etiquette of the road could have strayed into the area. "A newcomer, perhaps?" she ventured.

"Could be, though I didn't see anyone."

Georgiana let it go; her mind was moving on to another matter.

"Some nice pieces," she commented, gesturing towards his pocket.

"Aye, not a bad night's work," said Harry.

Georgiana considered how to make her approach.

"The ladies you stopped," she said, "was one of them the one who took in Tom?" Harry knew that young Tom, formerly the errand boy at this very hostelry, had been offered a post at Georgiana's home after he had been shot during his one futile attempt to hold up a carriage. Georgiana thought a reminder might prompt a spirit of generosity with regard to the jewels he had stolen this evening.

Harry's jaw dropped. "Lord, lad, what made you ask that?"

"I was riding past through the thicket. I thought I recognised the carriage."

Harry took out the pieces of jewellery and stared at them.

"Why the devil hasn't the boy given them the password?" he asked.

Georgiana shrugged.

"Well, I've no wish to cause trouble for the lady who gave Tom a home. Cleaned him up and fed him right well from what I saw."

Georgiana nodded. Harry was frowning. Suddenly he scooped up her simple gold necklace and Selina's brooch and held them out to her.

"Can you get to Tom?" he asked.

"Possibly," she said, hoping she sounded uncertain.

"I'd consider it a favour if you'd give him these, to pass on to his lady."

"All right." Georgiana accepted the two items. There was still no sign of Louisa's pearls. Either Harry wanted to salvage something for his night's work or he had already sold them. Either way, she could hardly ask. Harry was already doing her a tremendously good turn in offering what he did.

"I'm sure Tom will be grateful for you returning his mistress's belongings," Georgiana said, resisting an impulse to thank him on her own behalf.

"Aye, well, he's a good lad, and he seems to think a lot of the lady." Harry stood and put a hand on Georgiana's shoulder. "Thanks for the warning about the other business. I'll keep an eye out for the Runners. Watch yourself, though. If you were nearby, you don't want the law after you."

"No," said Georgiana with feeling. She pocketed the

jewels Harry had given her, nodded farewell and departed.

As she untethered Princess from the rail to which the boy had tied her, Georgiana's mind was on the best way to return the jewellery. Quite apart from the fact that Selina was likely to ask a lot of questions about how she had retrieved the brooch, Georgiana knew that her pageboy Tom was still in communication with his old friend Harry. If the two items found their way back to their original owners without going through an intermediary, there was a strong possibility that Tom could mention this to Harry. This might even put her at risk of identification as the notorious highwayman, the Crimson Cavalier. Even if Harry maintained his discretion, such knowledge would put Georgiana in a dangerous position. But using Tom as a go-between for the trinkets' return presented its own difficulty; she would have to find a way which would not suggest any connection between the Crimson Cavalier and Miss Georgiana Grey.

Georgiana pondered the matter as she rode towards the road. The quiet of the night suggested it was likely she would arrive home without further incident.

She was mistaken.

4

"What the devil did you mean, stabbing that bloke?"

The voice came from the open air as Georgiana began to approach the open road. She drew back into the cover of the trees.

"He asked for it," a sulky voice replied. "No-good, jumped-up –"

"All right, all right. So what are we supposed to do now?"

Georgiana peered through the trees. She saw two figures on horseback, both in dark cloaks and hats, faces hidden. She hadn't recognised either voice.

"Nothing."

"Nothing?"

"He's dead and it was well deserved. A very good thing if you ask me."

"I didn't. What happens when the law starts asking questions?"

"Why should the law ask us anything? He was robbed by a highwayman. I heard him say so myself, and so did everyone else. Why should anyone ask questions of us?"

There was no response. Georgiana looked through the thicket of trees and sensed, rather than saw, the other man's grimace.

"Here."

Georgiana heard a jingling of coins as the first man spoke again. His voice seemed slightly more cultured than that of his protesting companion.

"For your trouble."

"And keeping my mouth shut, I suppose?"

"Would it hurt? I notice you don't refuse my offering."

There was some grumbling, and the two men parted company, turning in opposite directions. Georgiana waited a moment or two until the road seemed quiet, then slowly moved from her cover. Princess picked her way through stones and broken branches which carpeted the ground, and Georgiana kept her as close to the edge of the road as she could. Against the backdrop of the woods, she would be a less conspicuous target than a lone rider sallying forth in the middle of the road.

Her senses were ever alert for the unexpected, but Georgiana was nevertheless surprised to see one of the horsemen who had participated in the discussion riding back along the road. She cursed her luck. While it was possible the individual would do no more than touch his hat and go on his way, the conversation had told Georgiana enough to put her on her guard. If they wanted a highway robber to blame for the stabbing of a gentleman, the Crimson Cavalier would do as well as Harry Smith. It seemed to Georgiana there was only one way to deal with the matter. She drew her pistol.

"What the – ? Well, I'll be… I've nothing left, you rascal."

"No?" Georgiana's tone was mild, but the pistol indicated that she meant business.

"No. Another of your kind has already stripped me of my valuables. Unless you want the clothes off my back, you might as well let me pass."

The sneering reference to 'another of your kind' made Georgiana's hackles rise. The individual in front of her looked haughtily down his nose, but most of his own face was camouflaged by the muffler he wore. As it was not a particularly cold night, this in itself was enough to arouse her suspicions. She was tempted to use the barrel of her pistol to loosen the scarf, but something told her this could result in a bullet to her own head. Instead, she inclined her head civilly, raised her pistol further and spoke as if suggesting they play a hand of cards.

"I beg you will spare me that. However, my good sir, surely all gentlemen have something secreted for an emergency."

"Not I."

"No? Please be good enough to check." The pistol was raised slightly.

Georgiana's victim stared at her for some seconds then shrugged, plunged his hand into a pocket of his voluminous cloak and drew out a handful of coins. He held them out briefly for Georgiana's inspection then flung them on the ground.

Georgiana's eyes followed the sparkle and jingle as they scattered, spun and settled on the ground. Her pistol remained steady as her thoughts raced; clearly the gesture was intended to put her at a disadvantage. Dismounting to collect the treasure would leave her open to a cosh on the head, or worse, from the mounted man, while refusing to submit to the indignity of scrabbling around on the ground would make her appear ineffective and lacking in credibility. That was the sort of information which would spread quickly, on both sides of the law.

"Dear me," was all she said. "What shall we do now?"

Georgiana's victim shrugged, then prepared to ride off.

"Not so fast, my friend," she said, stopping him with the point of her pistol against his chest. "Your task is incomplete."

"You asked for my valuables. There they are." He spread a hand out, gesturing towards the ground. "You are welcome to whatever you find."

"But so untidy," said Georgiana. "Please be good enough

to collect them."

"I?"

"Are we to endure the indignity of a dispute on the public highway? I assure you, sir, it will be much simpler if you co-operate."

The man sat glowering astride his horse. Rescue suddenly came from an unexpected source.

"I'll do it."

The voice was familiar to Georgiana but she was no less surprised than her opponent. Trudging up the road was a small figure, wearing a dark coat. He stopped in front of Georgiana, looked up at her and pushed the brown hair out of his eyes.

"I'll do it, sir. You keep him covered."

"Thank you." Georgiana's gaze went back to the horse-man, who looked anything but pleased at this turn of events. "You are fortunate. My young friend has saved you from spoiling what I'm sure is an excellent pair of breeches."

The horseman said nothing but waited until the boy stood, coins gathered in his hand. He was still looking about the ground.

"I think that's all of them, sir."

"Very well. Thank you." Georgiana turned to the horse-man. "You may go. I bid you good evening."

The gentleman rode off without a word. The two remaining figures did not speak until the sound of the horse's hooves had died away.

"What are you doing out here, Tom?" Georgiana asked.

Tom looked up at her. His expression and manner gave no indication that he thought he was addressing anyone other than a highwayman: certainly not his employer, Miss Grey. Georgiana had never shared her secret with him and she had no reason to suppose he had guessed it.

"Going to see Harry. Where you been?"

"Busy."

The boy nodded. He appeared to be about thirteen or fourteen years old; Georgiana knew he was not certain of his age himself, and the work he had done in the Lucky Bell before she took him in as her page had made him seem older in some ways and younger in others.

Georgiana untied a black velvet bag from her belt and held it for Tom to pour in the contents of his hand. She gave him two of the coins, and his eyes widened. "I have seen Harry myself," she said. "He asked me to give you these."

As Georgiana handed him her own necklace and her cousin's brooch, Tom's look of astonishment grew.

"I understand they belong to the lady you serve," said Georgiana, still watchful for any sign of recognition and grateful that it did not yet come.

"Harry wants me to give 'em back?"

Georgiana nodded. "He said the lady's been good to you and he doesn't want to cause trouble for her."

"She has." Tom nodded vigorously. "Still, it's right good of Harry."

"Yes, well, I suggest you go home and keep them safe until you can return them to her." Georgiana took care to keep her tone matter-of-fact, disguising the relief she felt at this piece of good fortune. Her problem had been solved with almost no trouble. Now she had only to find out what had become of Lady Winters's pearls.

"Aye, that I will, sir. Where are you going?"

Georgiana said nothing; she merely looked at him in disbelief. Tom hastily apologised; he knew it was not the done thing to ask questions of a highwayman. Georgiana bade him goodnight and waited until he began to walk in the direction of her house, then crossed the road to another thicket of trees. It appeared she would have to take a more circuitous route than she had intended. The last thing she needed was to be leading Princess into the stables as Tom was opening the back door to return to the servants' quarters. Neither could she rule out the possibility that he would disobey her and go to the Lucky Bell to see Harry anyway.

Georgiana arrived home without encountering anyone else. She kept an eye about her for Tom's return while stabling Princess, but there was no sign of him and all remained quiet as she let herself in through the back door.

Emily was waiting for Georgiana in her bedroom and seemed relieved at the sight of her, moving forward quickly to take her cloak. She rolled her eyes as Georgiana removed the black velvet pouch from her belt, but made no comment.

"The man who gave me these," said Georgiana, jingling the bag, "was right in my path. I could not avoid him."

"I see, miss." Emily folded the cloak.

Georgiana dropped the black velvet bag on her bed. "Take that to the village tomorrow, would you, Emily? I'll leave it to your discretion to decide how it should best be distributed. I'm sure you will know who needs it."

"Yes, miss." Emily glanced towards Georgiana. "Is something wrong, Miss Georgiana?"

"The gentleman I stopped," said Georgiana. "I don't know who he was, but before I stopped him I heard him talking to someone else on the road. About a stabbing."

"What?"

"I didn't recognise either of them," said Georgiana. "The gentleman I stopped wore a muffler over his face."

"He wasn't a highwayman himself, miss?"

"I suppose that is possible, but I don't think so. The way they were talking, it sounded as if they were intending to lay the blame for the stabbing on a highwayman." She paused and spoke solemnly. "I'm sure they were talking about Mr Polp. One of them spoke as though he believed Mr Polp deserved what he got."

"That's horrible."

"Yes," said Georgiana. "I can't believe someone would think that of Mr Polp. I did not know him well but he seemed perfectly amiable."

"What did your friend Harry say?"

"He didn't seem to know anything about the stabbing, though he did say he stopped a few people tonight."

"Do you believe him?" Emily asked.

"Yes, I do," said Georgiana. "In fact, when he heard that one of the carriages he held up was Tom's employer, he returned my necklace and Selina's brooch."

"Good grief. You told him you knew whose carriage he stopped?"

"I told him I'd been nearby and recognised it."

"That seems quite a risk," said Emily.

"Possibly. It's of no matter. He asked me to give the two pieces of jewellery to Tom to return to his lady."

Emily looked at her with dawning suspicion.

"Ironically," Georgiana continued, "I met Tom on the road after I stopped the gentleman."

Emily groaned, one hand rubbing her forehead as she sank down on to a chair.

"As a matter of fact, he was quite helpful," said Georgiana conversationally. "The – er – gentleman threw his coins on the ground, to make me dismount to collect them. Tom happened along and picked them up for me."

Emily raised her head. "Where was Tom going?"

"The Lucky Bell."

"After you told him not to?"

"Yes. I know it's not the first time. However, I was hardly in a position to take him to task over it." She handed Emily her waistcoat.

"No, I suppose not. Did you…?"

"Give him the jewellery I got from Harry? Yes."

"Miss Georgiana!"

"As he is still communicating with Harry it would have looked very odd if I did not. Harry would either think I couldn't be trusted – "

"Miss."

"Or," continued Georgiana, "he might suspect a connection between the Crimson Cavalier and Miss Georgiana Grey."

Emily accepted this. "Bad enough Mr Lakesby does. Do you think Tom can be trusted to return the two pieces?"

"I think so. He would have to answer to both Harry and the Crimson Cavalier if he did not." She paused. "There was one odd thing, though. Harry returned Selina's brooch and my bracelet, but I didn't see Louisa's pearls."

"Perhaps he had already sold them."

"Perhaps," said Georgiana thoughtfully. She knew this was a possibility, but it seemed to her there had been insufficient time for Harry to dispose of them. And if he had, why had he still been in possession of the other two items? She found herself wondering whether Harry had kept it back for some reason of his own.

Georgiana fell asleep with this thought running through her head, and woke with a burning curiosity as to what such a reason could be. When Emily brought her morning chocolate, she also delivered the news that Tom was anxious to see her.

"Is he indeed?" said Georgiana. She sipped the hot, aromatic drink. "Did he say what he wanted?"

"No, miss, but fair hopping up and down, he was. Mr Horton looked quite stern about it. James has taken him off to the kitchen for one of Mrs Daniels's biscuits."

"That should calm him down."

"I'm not sure, miss. It's a long time since we've seen him that excited."

"Well," said Georgiana, "send him in to the breakfast parlour, before the tea is served. I think we know what he wants to say, there's no need to delay it."

As Georgiana had predicted, a little while later Tom stood before her in the breakfast parlour holding the two pieces of jewellery in his hand. He offered little explanation, saying only that his friend Harry had come across them. Georgiana did not press him but thanked him gravely and asked if Harry would take a reward. Tom shook his head vigorously.

"Very well. Thank you, Tom, and pass my thanks on to your friend. Would you ask for the tea to be sent in, please?"

"Yes, miss."

Tom trotted off, almost colliding with Selina, who opened the door to the breakfast parlour just as he was about to leave the room. She stood still until he had gone. As soon as the door was closed behind him, she gave a shudder. "That boy. One of these days, Georgiana, your charitable impulse will cause trouble."

"Quite possibly," said Georgiana calmly. "Today is not that day, however." She held up Selina's brooch. "Well?"

Miss Knatchbull stepped forward openmouthed, seemingly unable to speak.

"What...? How? Georgiana, how on earth...?" she sputtered.

"Never mind how," said Georgiana, putting it down on the table beside her cousin's teacup. "Just take it and be grateful. It's probably best not to ask questions."

Selina seemed to accept this advice but cast curious glances at Georgiana as she consumed her breakfast. Georgiana kept the flow of conversation moving on a series of mundane subjects, into which her cousin entered willingly enough. They rose from the table each with separate plans for the day. Selina went off to apply herself to a few tasks of domestic interest.

Georgiana decided to visit Louisa, still concerned that her young friend had been shaken by Boyce Polp's death. She elected to walk the short distance to the Winters residence, and Emily accompanied her. They were admitted by the butler who showed her into the drawing room to wait for Louisa, while Emily was taken to the kitchen. Her friend joined her in a few minutes, looking pale and tired, her normally bright complexion dimmed by dark shadows encircling her china blue eyes. Behind her was a solidly built, respectable looking, dourly dressed female, whose facial expression matched the drab grey of her attire. Georgiana took her to be the governess who had been given the task of looking after Louisa in her mother's absence, an impression which was confirmed by Louisa's uncertainty over whether or not to introduce her companion. Georgiana noticed the woman looking towards her in a steady, appraising fashion. Smiling, she stepped forward and greeted her friend.

"How are you, Louisa?"

"Oh, I am very well. Shall we – shall we have some tea?"

"Allow me, Miss Winters," said the chaperone, in a tone less forbidding than her aspect.

"Oh. Thank you, Miss Trent," said Louisa, as the woman

went out through the door.

Georgiana looked closely at the girl. "How are you, really?"

"All right. Though – oh, Georgiana, I barely slept. I had the most ghastly dreams. I had not thought seeing a man killed could affect me so much. I seemed to see Mr Polp and that knife over and over. It was horrible."

"Yes, well, I would not have imagined you would ever expect to see a man killed."

"No," said Louisa in a small voice.

"Good heavens, Louisa, I meant no criticism. It is no wonder it has been a shock for you."

"Oh, I see. I'm sorry, Georgiana."

"There's no need to apologise." Georgiana paused and glanced at the door. "I assume that is your old governess?"

"Yes," said Louisa gloomily. "I don't know why Mama had to ask her to come. What does she imagine I'm going to do?"

"You are young, Louisa. It is only natural that your mother should be concerned for your well-being."

"She doesn't trust me," said Louisa in prosaic tones. "She insists on treating me as a child."

"It isn't just a question of protecting you," said Georgiana. "There is also the issue of propriety. For a young, unmarried lady to be left alone – "

"But you are unmarried and no one thinks – Oh." Louisa stared straight ahead as enlightenment dawned. "That is why your cousin lives with you?"

"Well – "

"Oh, I see. I thought it was because she was poor and… Oh, I'm sorry, this is none of my business."

"Never mind that. Did you tell your… chaperone what happened last night?"

"Mr Polp's death or the highwayman?" asked Louisa. "It doesn't matter though. No, I have not said anything. She would go into hysterics and lock me in my room, and very likely send for Mama."

Georgiana was inclined to think this an exaggeration but considered Louisa was probably right to keep the events of the evening to herself. While Miss Trent might not react in quite the manner Louisa described she would certainly be concerned, and it was not beyond possibility that she would see it as her duty to lay the matter before Lady Winters.

Louisa was looking gloomy. "Georgiana, what about Mama's pearls?"

Georgiana had been giving thought to this very matter herself. "How long do you expect your mama to be away?" she asked.

"A few more days. Max said he would tell her but…"

Georgiana sat thinking. If Selina happened to encounter Louisa, or for that matter Lady Winters on her return, she was quite capable of pouring forth the tale of the recovery of her own brooch. Admittedly, neither of the Winters ladies would expect Georgiana to be able to account for the where-abouts of the pearl necklace, but it made the recovery of the other two items look very odd.

"May I make a suggestion?" asked Georgiana.

Louisa nodded vigorously.

Georgiana lowered her voice to escape the ears of Miss Trent, who had just reappeared in the doorway bearing a laden tea tray.

"We should ask Tom."

5

Louisa's jaw dropped. A reproof delivered in stern, clipped fashion from Miss Trent pulled her back to her surroundings. She meekly begged pardon and nodded in childlike fashion as the governess asked whether she should pour the tea. Georgiana could have cursed the woman's ill-timed entrance. She wondered whether there was any way of getting rid of her but suspected there was not. Miss Trent was clearly someone who took her duties seriously and Georgiana had no doubt that any pretext to send her out of the room would rouse her suspicions.

Georgiana accepted the tea which the governess handed her and watched as Louisa took hers, thanking the older woman almost deferentially. She had clearly been schooled well. Miss Trent took her own tea and returned to her chair by the wall, taking sips and turning the pages of the book in which she was apparently immersed.

Louisa looked towards Georgiana, her own cup tightly held. Curiosity goggled in her eyes, though it was clear she dared not ask the question on her mind.

"How – how is your cousin?" she got out.

"Well enough," said Georgiana. "She is not much accustomed to late nights so I think she was glad to be home early, despite the circumstances."

"Oh, I see." Louisa glanced towards her governess.

"You must come for a visit. Perhaps you would like to dine with us. Bring your own cousin, if you would like his escort."

"Oh, yes. Thank you. I should like that."

"What about tomorrow?" Georgiana continued. "Or this

evening, perhaps? Selina is very good at preparing menus and I daresay you will be glad of some company with your mother away."

"Oh. Yes. Of course. Thank you. I must ask Max but…"

Georgiana noticed Miss Trent glance furtively towards them. Her eyes returned as quickly to her book, but her lips remained pursed in apparent disapproval. Georgiana wondered whether she dared make another suggestion.

"Perhaps you would like a walk? I'm sure the fresh air and exercise would be beneficial. My maid is with me. We could have a closer look at that bonnet you were admiring a few days ago."

Louisa cast a look towards the governess. Georgiana wondered whether the girl had been instructed to seek Miss Trent's approval for any activity she wanted to undertake.

"Miss Winters, I am not sure your mother – "

"Why don't you join us, Miss Trent?" said Georgiana, averting her eyes from Louisa's horrified expression.

"Well, I – " Miss Trent seemed taken aback.

Louisa was chewing her bottom lip, nervously watching the older woman. Miss Trent lifted her chin and met Georgiana's friendly gaze. Georgiana had the feeling she was being challenged.

"Where had you in mind to walk?" asked Miss Trent. "A young lady must be careful."

"Oh, of course," said Georgiana, in warm agreement. "But if you were to accompany us you could be easy in your mind, knowing we were not venturing into any unsuitable areas."

Louisa looked bilious. Miss Trent's expression grew even more disapproving, as if she sensed she was being mocked.

"Miss Winters is prone to chills."

Georgiana stared in astonishment.

"I'm not," Louisa said indignantly.

"Your mother trusted me to look after your welfare. She would be sorely disappointed in me if I were to fail in my duty."

Louisa looked disgusted. Georgiana looked from one to the other, feeling she was in a world that was not quite real. Suddenly the younger girl changed from nervous and uncertain to decisive and rebellious.

"Have you finished your tea, Georgiana? We can ring for your maid and perhaps walk down to Conduit Street. I saw another bonnet there which I quite liked. I think I have just enough left of my allowance."

"Very well," said Georgiana, casting an eye towards Miss Trent.

The governess rose, laid down her book and moved to look at the clock on the mantelpiece. She stood with hands clasped in front of her, watching it for a moment, then turned slowly to face Louisa.

"Would you not be more comfortable in the carriage? Please allow me to ring for it."

"No, there's no need," said Louisa, her breezy tone covering what Georgiana suspected was a hint of petulance.

Miss Trent pursed her lips again. Georgiana thought it prudent to interfere. "I think a walk would be very beneficial exercise," she said. "I'm sure you need not fear for Miss Winters's health. She is unlikely to contract a chill on such a day as today."

Miss Trent did not speak for a moment. Then, to the surprise of both young ladies, she smiled suddenly. It was incongruous, even disturbing.

"Very well. I will fetch our cloaks, Miss Winters."

Louisa had no time to school her appalled expression when the door opened to reveal her cousin standing on the threshold, one hand on the door handle. He raised an eyebrow. "Pleased to see me, Louisa?"

"Max. The very thing. There is no need for you to come with us, Miss Trent. Max can escort us, can't you, Max."

"Yes, certainly," said Lakesby, looking from Louisa to Georgiana. "Escort you where?"

"Now, Miss Winters, a gentleman like your cousin will not wish to go and look at bonnets with you."

There was a patronising edge to her voice which Georgiana found irritating. She could only imagine how much it irked Louisa, to whom it was directed and with whom she was sharing a roof, albeit temporarily. Georgiana caught Lakesby's glance. While Georgiana was sure little would bore him more than choosing millinery with his cousin, he seemed to sense something of their predicament.

"I see," said Lakesby. "Please don't concern yourself, Miss Trent. I shall be happy to accompany my cousin and Miss Grey. I'm sure you must have other things to do."

"Very well." Miss Trent's tone was dignified. It was clear the matter was at an end now that Mr Lakesby had made his views known. She picked up her book from the chair and left the room inclining her head slightly as she walked past them.

Lakesby stared.

"Good grief," said Louisa. "Thank you, Max."

"What was all that about?" Lakesby demanded.

"Georgiana and I said we were going for a walk and she was going to come with us. Though Georgiana did invite her." Louisa looked at her friend accusingly.

"I'm sorry, Louisa, I did not expect her to accept. In truth, if anything, I thought it would discourage her."

Lakesby laughed. "A good notion, Miss Grey. But, Louisa, if you think I'm going to spend the morning at your mantua-maker's establishment, waiting for you to choose some bonnet – "

"Oh, never mind the bonnet," said Louisa impatiently. "That was just an excuse. It's shockingly ugly anyway. We just wanted to get out of the house. Miss Trent was so – so… Wasn't she, Georgiana?"

"Quite."

Lakesby grinned. "Am I not at least to be offered a cup of tea before we set out?"

"Oh. I am not sure there is any left," said Louisa, lifting the lid and peering into the teapot. "I suppose I can ring for some more if you really want it."

"Never mind, you foolish girl. I'm only teasing you. Fetch your pelisse so we can be off before your watchdog returns."

Louisa went off obediently, leaving Georgiana shaking her head in resignation. She looked up at Lakesby from her chair. "You should not tease her."

"Nonsense. She is well enough. What brought you here?"

"Good heavens, Louisa is a friend of mine. Do I need to justify paying a call on her?"

"Not at all. I just wondered."

"I was a little concerned about her, after last night," Georgiana admitted.

"Yes, so was I," said Lakesby, "though she seems well enough. What about you?"

"I'm perfectly all right," said Georgiana, surprised.

Lakesby studied her. "Have you slept? You look tired."

"How flattering."

Lakesby ruefully begged her pardon.

"Of course I've slept," said Georgiana. "Thank you for your concern, Mr Lakesby, but I am quite well, I assure you."

Louisa returned at that moment, pelisse around her shoulders, reticule and bonnet in her hands.

"Are you ready?" she asked her companions.

"Anxious to be away?" queried her cousin. "Do you fear Miss Trent will be here in a moment with her cloak and gloves?"

Louisa glowered at him and he opened the door, holding it for the two ladies to pass through before he followed them out. The outing began along conventional lines; conversation proceeded in an ordinary fashion, with no reference to the events of the previous evening. The day was fine, and as they came upon Berkeley Square Lakesby suggested they pay a visit to a nearby confectioner's shop to enjoy an ice. This prospect cheered Louisa and her expression had brightened considerably by the time Lakesby found them a seat under a maple tree while he went to the confectioner's. She was watching the activity nearby. It appeared a number of people had chosen to take advantage of the fine weather; several open carriages had drawn up in the shade, and gentlemen stood beside them to converse with the ladies who occupied them. As they waited for their refreshment, Louisa observed that it was a pity they had chosen to walk, as it looked so pleasant.

"I think it would have been difficult for your cousin to fit both of us in his curricle," said Georgiana. "He would have found it rather hard to drive. Perhaps you should have come with him on your own."

"Oh no," Louisa exclaimed. "Max is far more agreeable when you are here."

Georgiana suppressed a smile at her young friend's

naivety. Fortunately she was spared the need to reply, as Lakesby returned at that moment, carrying three ices.

Louisa immediately put her hand up to take the orange one, thanking him with the eagerness of a child brought out for a treat. Lakesby smiled, and handed a burnt filbert ice to Georgiana, brushing a leaf from his shoulder before starting to consume his own. Louisa continued to look around the square, chatting amiably and exclaiming when she caught sight of someone she recognised or noticed some curiosity of wardrobe. Eventually Lakesby went to the confectioner for a second ice for her, expressing the hope that it would stop her incessant prattle.

"What a beast you are, Max," Louisa called as he walked away. But moments later when he returned with the confection she was all smiles; she thanked him graciously and informed him she could not wish for a better cousin, bringing a suspicious look into his eyes.

Happily occupied with her second ice, Louisa continued to be cheerful for some minutes, laughing at Lakesby's continued efforts to brush away the leaves which continued to attach themselves to his elegantly tailored coat. However, she grew gradually more subdued, and her increasing quietness prompted a reaction from her cousin.

"What is it, Louisa?" Lakesby's voice was gentle.

The girl looked up. "Nothing."

"I see." Lakesby glanced towards Georgiana. "Do you believe her?"

"I do not think you should accuse your cousin of lying, Mr Lakesby."

"Not lying, perhaps, but shall we say, some bending of the truth?" Eyeing her closely, he continued, "Is it because I suggested you were talking too much?"

"Oh, you are horrid," said Louisa angrily. "Why must

you always talk to me as if I were a child?"

"I beg your pardon."

Louisa's mutinous eyes suggested she did not think him serious.

"I don't think your cousin was trying to treat you like a child, Louisa," Georgiana interposed. "However, Mr Polp's death was a shocking thing for anyone to see; it would be a matter for wonder if you were not shaken by it."

"Yes, it was quite horrible," admitted Louisa. "Poor Mr Polp. He was a pleasant enough man, I believe, but I didn't know him very well."

"Did anyone?" asked Georgiana suddenly.

"What?" Lakesby looked startled.

"Know him very well," said Georgiana.

"I've no idea." Lakesby sounded all at sea.

Louisa's eyes focused on her friend. "What is it, Georgiana?" she asked.

"Well, none of us knew Mr Polp very well. It just made me wonder whether anyone did."

Her two companions exchanged a look, then glanced at Georgiana in puzzled fashion.

"Miss Grey, the fact that we did not know Mr Polp very well does not mean – "

"Does not mean someone else was not well acquainted with him," Georgiana finished. "Thank you, Mr Lakesby, I am well aware of that. However, do you know of anyone who was close to him?"

"No, but – "

"No. Perhaps I am mistaken but from the little I saw of Mr Polp, he appeared to be something of a social butterfly, flitting from one person or event to another."

"Not landing anywhere?" said Lakesby in an amused tone.

"You could put it that way. I meant rather than being particularly close to anyone. He appeared at most functions, didn't he? He always talked to a number of people, but I don't think he spent longer with any one person than another."

"Distributing his favours evenly," commented Lakesby.

"Possibly."

"Does it matter?" asked Louisa.

"I don't know. Perhaps not," said Georgiana. "I just wondered."

Lakesby watched her closely, his expression thoughtful. Louisa went back to her ice.

"What am I going to do about Mama's pearls?" she said.

"I'll try to make some inquiries," said Lakesby.

"But where?" Louisa looked directly at him. "It's hardly the sort of thing one's acquaintance can tell you, even at your gentlemen's clubs."

"Don't worry about that. You can leave it in my hands."

Louisa's expression grew more worried. "But if we need to offer a reward…"

"Don't worry, Louisa," Lakesby repeated. "I don't think we will need to plunder your allowance. Even if it were to come to your mother's ears, I don't think she would consider a reward unreasonable for their recovery."

"I hope you're right," said Louisa devoutly.

"I am."

Louisa continued to look doubtful and Georgiana herself wondered about Lakesby's confidence. Was it based on the knowledge that Lady Winters would be anxious for the return of her pearls? Could he have some idea of where to begin making inquiries? Georgiana suspected this would not be all she heard of the matter; indeed, she fully expected Lakesby to initiate a conversation on the subject with her if a tête-à-tête gave him the opportunity.

As they walked back to the Winters residence Lakesby continued to reassure his cousin, and by the time they arrived Louisa seemed to have recovered much of her equanimity and was in a more cheerful frame of mind. All three went into the house. Louisa did not wish to face the company of Miss Trent on her own just yet, and Lakesby had offered to escort Georgiana home; Emily had been sent back when they set out for their walk.

As the footman admitted them to the house, Louisa turned to offer Georgiana and Lakesby refreshment, but was startled by a peremptory voice from the staircase before she could utter the words.

"Louisa."

The girl turned her head and looked up. Her china blue eyes widened. "Mama."

Lady Winters gave a fleeting glance towards her daughter's companions but there was little indication of interest in anyone but Louisa.

"Perhaps you can explain the meaning of this?"

Dangling from Lady Winters's forefinger were the pearls which Louisa had surrendered to Harry Smith.

6

Louisa's eyes widened. "Mama!"

"Louisa, please do not stand gawping in that fashion. For a young lady to stand with her mouth hanging open is most unseemly." Miss Trent's voice came from the end of the downstairs corridor.

Louisa looked towards her, blinked and begged pardon.

"Thank you, Miss Trent," said Lady Winters, descending the stairs. "You may leave us for the moment. I do not wish to detain you."

"Very well, your ladyship." Miss Trent withdrew and began to walk slowly up the stairs, casting a quick surreptitious glance back at Lady Winters, who was now on the ground floor.

"Good day to you, Maxwell. Miss Grey."

"Hello, Aunt Beatrice."

"Good day, Lady Winters. Pray excuse me, I should be on my way," said Georgiana.

Louisa looked pleadingly at her friend but it was Lakesby who spoke. "Please wait, Miss Grey. You cannot walk home alone. I shall escort you as we discussed."

Georgiana looked warily towards Lady Winters, who nodded abruptly. She led the way to the drawing room. Lakesby closed the door behind him when all four were inside. Lady Winters turned to face them, her daughter looking anxious.

"Am I to understand, Louisa," began her ladyship, "that when I lent you my pearls for Mrs Milton's party, they were lost?"

"Well, you see, Mama…"

"They were stolen by a highwayman," interposed Lakesby.

"What?" Her ladyship looked startled.

"Louisa, Miss Grey and Miss Knatchbull were held up by a highwayman," Lakesby said. "Miss Grey and her cousin also lost some items, is that not correct, Miss Grey?"

"Yes," said Georgiana.

Lady Winters looked towards Georgiana. "I see." She turned back to her daughter. "And you were wearing the pearls, Louisa?"

"Yes, Mama. You had said I could borrow them. I'm sorry. I did not mean to lose them but…"

"You didn't lose them, Louisa. They were stolen," said Lakesby. "The fellow had a pistol pointed at them, Aunt Beatrice; there was little they could do."

"No, of course there wasn't." Her ladyship's tone softened briefly, then regained its acerbity as she addressed her nephew. "This is your fault, Maxwell."

"I thought it might be," he murmured.

"You should have escorted your cousin and her friend."

"I assure you, Lady Winters…" Georgiana began.

"For young ladies to be riding about the country unescorted is quite unacceptable."

"Yes, Aunt Beatrice. Had they no coachman?"

"That is not the issue."

"I thought it might not be," Lakesby responded cheerfully.

"Mama, how did you come to get the pearls back?" asked Louisa before her mother could deliver a lecture to her cousin. "And why are you home so soon? I did not expect you for a few days yet."

Lady Winters's attention went to her daughter. "Under the circumstances, I believe an early return was warranted."

"Circumstances?" Louisa continued to look puzzled.

"I, too, was held up by a highwayman. However, in my case, the *gentleman*..." Lady Winters shuddered over the word, her voice quivering with abhorrence. "The gentleman tossed my own pearls through the carriage window."

"I beg your pardon?" said Georgiana.

"Yes, well might you stare, Miss Grey." Her ladyship inclined her head as her visitors did just that.

"He threw them in?" asked Georgiana, stunned.

"Perhaps 'threw' is too strong a word," said Lady Winters. "However, he certainly tossed them to me. He even had the effrontery to bow and offer me his compliments. His compliments, indeed! My own pearls. Can you imagine how I felt?"

"I cannot," said Georgiana.

"Most peculiar," said Lakesby dryly. "It seems unusual for a highway robber to return property, wouldn't you agree, Miss Grey?"

Georgiana ignored him and addressed Lady Winters. "What did he look like?"

"What did he look like? He looked like a highwayman, Miss Grey."

"It wasn't the Crimson Cavalier?" asked Louisa.

"No, it was not," said her mother.

"I thought you said it wasn't the Crimson Cavalier who had held you up, Louisa," said Lakesby.

"Well, I don't know how these things are done," said Louisa. "He might have passed Mama's pearls on to someone else."

Lakesby rolled his eyes. "That does not sound very profitable," he commented.

"Or sold them. I don't know," said Louisa crossly. "I'm not in the confidence of highwaymen."

Georgiana felt Lakesby's glance flicker towards her. "No," he said.

Georgiana made no comment; her own thoughts were travelling in an entirely different direction. She assumed Harry had been the highwayman in question, but could not rule out the possibility that he had quickly disposed of the pearls, and another gentleman of the road had returned them to Lady Winters. Either way, it was a bizarre situation.

Louisa voiced the next question in Georgiana's mind. "Mama, how could he have known they were yours?"

"Perhaps he recognised the family crest on the carriage," said Lakesby.

"But I was in Georgiana's carriage when we were held up," objected Louisa. "She and her cousin called to take me to Mrs Milton's."

"So they did," said Lakesby.

Georgiana thought it best not to be drawn into the discussion. Lakesby had begun to suspect her connection with the Crimson Cavalier not long after they had met. So far, he had shown no sign of wishing to share his suspicions with anyone else, but it seemed to amuse him to taunt her.

Georgiana was reassured that Lady Winters showed no inclination to blame Louisa for the loss of the pearls. She supposed it was possible that their safe return had mellowed her ladyship. Had they still been lost, she might have looked at the matter very differently.

"Mama, did you – did you hear about Mr Polp?" inquired Louisa.

Lady Winters's face softened unexpectedly. "Yes, a dreadful shock. I have always found Mr Polp extremely agreeable."

"Did you know him well, Lady Winters?" asked Georgiana.

"I met him a few times," said her ladyship. "He always

seemed very pleasant and civil. It was a shocking thing to happen. These highwaymen are the scourge of the roads." Her expression changed suddenly, as a thought occurred to her. "Why, I wonder whether that was the reason *that person* threw my pearls into my carriage."

"I beg your pardon?" asked Georgiana, unclear as to the logic of this.

"If there was a hue and cry out for Mr Polp's murderer, a highwayman, very likely he did not wish to be caught in possession of anything which he'd stolen."

"I see," said Georgiana.

"So he tossed the pearls into your carriage to dispose of them, and it was a coincidence that they happened to be yours," said Lakesby.

His tone was sceptical. Georgiana, for her part, thought it best not to respond. Lady Winters shrugged.

Louisa's eyes widened. "You don't think that's what happened, Max?" asked Louisa.

"Anything is possible, Louisa," he replied, "but if the man's aim was to get rid of evidence, how likely it is that of all the carriages on the road, he should choose the owner of the pearls?"

Louisa digested this, nodding slowly.

"Besides," Lakesby continued, "even if he were caught with stolen property, it doesn't mean he killed Boyce Polp. The pearls did not belong to him."

"No."

It was clear Louisa had not previously considered this aspect of the matter. Lady Winters seemed uninterested. Georgiana judged it time to depart and made her farewells. She accepted Lakesby's offer of escort, and the two took their leave. The last thing they heard as the drawing room door closed behind them was Louisa asking her mother whether Miss Trent would soon be leaving.

Lakesby shook his head. "Poor Louisa. She will be glad to be free of Miss Trent. I have not brought my curricle, Miss Grey. Are you content to walk?"

"Yes, certainly. It is a fine day and it is not very far."

They were silent for a few minutes, occupied with their own thoughts. Georgiana spoke first.

"Was Miss Trent with Louisa for many years? It cannot be so very long since Louisa was released from her charge."

"She has been out of the schoolroom a little under a year," said Lakesby. "I believe Miss Trent was Louisa's governess for about two years. Louisa was never much interested in her lessons, and she was reaching an age at which her mother was starting to consider her ready for marriage."

"I see." Georgiana stole a glance at his profile. "You don't agree?"

Lakesby shrugged. "Another year or so, I daresay. I see no need to rush the matter. I have no wish to see the girl tied to some coxcomb or fortune hunter, or worse, to some elderly roué."

"No, indeed," said Georgiana, thinking of the attentions Louisa had received from Sir Robert Foster when they had first become acquainted.

There was a pause, then, "Miss Grey, I must thank you for your concern for Louisa. I know you feared last night's experience may have upset her."

"It was a shock to everyone."

"Yes. Nonetheless, you have been a good friend to her."

"She has been a good friend to me," said Georgiana. "I am very fond of her."

Lakesby nodded absently, but did not immediately respond to this.

"That was an odd business about my Aunt Beatrice's pearls," he said at last.

"Yes."

"I do recall something similar happening to me on one occasion, though my experience was not quite so dramatic."

"Oh?"

"Surely I told you, Miss Grey. I was held up by the Crimson Cavalier, and shortly afterwards my property was returned to me."

"Thrown through a carriage window by a highwayman?"

"No," he acknowledged. "It was wrapped in a piece of paper and delivered to me by a small boy."

"I daresay the Crimson Cavalier sold it. Perhaps some wellwisher saw it and recognised it."

"Anonymous wellwisher."

Georgiana shrugged. "Not letting the right hand know what the left hand is doing."

"Perhaps. You could be right."

Lakesby's tone told her he didn't think so, but she did not pursue the matter.

"This incident my Aunt Beatrice recounted is far more curious."

Georgiana had to admit he was right.

As they arrived at Georgiana's front door, Lakesby took his leave, asking her to pay his compliments to her cousin. As he walked down the street, idly swinging his cane, Georgiana walked up the stone steps, totally mystified by the experience Lady Winters had recounted. While she was glad for Louisa's sake that the pearls had been returned to their owner, she could not imagine what would prompt Harry to behave in such a manner.

It was a few minutes before the front door was opened and an inquiry as to the cause of the delay died on Georgiana's lips as she became aware of the furore indoors. The normally calm and stately Horton looked harassed, James's patience appeared to be exhausted and she could hear Tom's far from dulcet tones raised in something like strong indignation.

"What is going on?" asked Georgiana.

"I beg your pardon, miss," said Horton, in a tone very unlike his usual calm and measured delivery. "I'm afraid Tom has reacted in a rather – er – unfortunate manner to something which was said to him, and things have rather, um, taken an unpleasant turn."

"Oh, dear," Georgiana sighed.

"I'm sorry you should have to witness such a thing, miss," said the butler. "We had hoped to have it resolved before your return."

"Never mind, Horton," said Georgiana. "Tell me what there is to resolve."

Horton and James exchanged a look. There had clearly been some discussion between them as to whose place it was to tell Georgiana.

It was James who spoke. "The fact is, miss, I believe Miss Knatchbull said something to which Tom took exception."

Horror dawned in Georgiana's mind. "Oh, no. Did she accuse him of something?"

James hesitated. "In a manner of speaking, miss. I believe it was something to do with the highwayman who robbed you last night. We are not sure exactly what happened, but it's possible Miss Knatchbull gave Tom the impression that…"

"That she thought he had something to do with the robbery," finished Georgiana. "Good grief."

"I am sure Miss Knatchbull would not have made such an accusation without being certain," said Horton. "I daresay

Tom misunderstood her. Had he simply held his tongue, I'm sure the confusion would have been sorted out quite easily."

"Possibly," said Georgiana. "I assume they are now engaged in an argument?"

"Yes, miss," said James.

"I am sorry for this upset, miss," said Horton. "The boy should not have responded as he did to Miss Knatchbull. He needs to learn the correct way to speak to his betters."

"Yes, well, he is young yet and still quite new to the household," said Georgiana. "I'm sure he will learn in time. He has not the advantage of your long years of experience."

"No, miss," said Horton woodenly, as if deliberately stopping himself from asking what advantage Tom did possess.

"I am more concerned with the present situation," said Georgiana. "I shall see what I can do. It sounds as if they both need to be calmed down before we can get to the bottom of what has happened."

Georgiana began to walk towards the drawing room; James stepping ahead of her to open the door, but they were both just a moment too late. As James's hand reached for the handle, the door was flung open. Tom stalked out, looking at neither of them as he walked past. Georgiana looked at him, then exchanged glances with James before turning her attention to her cousin, who was still inside the room.

Miss Knatchbull stood trembling before the fireplace, face white and angry, arms crossed.

"Selina, what has happened?" asked Georgiana.

"That boy," said Selina with feeling. "He has – he has – " She paused and took a breath. "He will give us no more trouble, Georgiana. I have discharged him."

7

"You discharged him." Georgiana controlled her voice with difficulty.

"Yes," said Selina. "I am sorry, Georgiana. I know you were trying to be charitable by offering him a place, but he is clearly beyond redemption."

"Is he?"

The deliberate steadiness of Georgiana's voice would have alarmed both her brother Edward and Emily, who had been her maid since she left the schoolroom. Miss Knatchbull, however, seemed oblivious to it. As she spoke, her face grew flushed and she became more and more pleased with herself. "I'm sure when you have thought about it, you will agree it was the right thing to do."

Georgiana did not speak immediately. She took a deep breath and kept her eyes fixed steadily on her cousin. For the first time in the course of the conversation, Miss Knatchbull began to look uneasy.

"Georgiana?"

"No, Selina. I do not agree that discharging Tom was the right thing to do."

Selina looked startled. "But… you don't… you don't know what happened, what he did, how he spoke to me."

"I am sure you will tell me," said Georgiana tersely, "and I shall also speak to Tom and find out what he has to say on the matter. However – "

"But, Georgiana – "

"However," Georgiana continued, a little more loudly, "you do not have the right to discharge my servants."

Selina's mouth fell open in stunned silence. Georgiana

raised an eyebrow. Selina swallowed. Her voice, when finally managed to speak, sounded less confident.

"I – I have not the right?" she faltered. "What – what do you mean? I thought… Is this not my home, too?"

Georgiana continued to look at her, trying to determine the best way to express her thoughts. While it was true Selina had been foisted on her by her brother's insistence that she needed a chaperone, she had never wanted her cousin to feel she was living on charity. She was not comfortable reminding Selina whose house it was and who was responsible for paying the servants. However, Selina had exceeded her place by dismissing Tom.

"Selina," Georgiana said in a controlled voice, "it was I who engaged Tom and therefore I am responsible for dismissing him if such action is warranted. Until I have heard the full story, I do not know that it is."

"I see." Miss Knatchbull's tone now grew dignified. Her bosom swelled. "So he may talk to me as he wishes, this… this *protégé* of yours."

"I did not say that," said Georgiana patiently. "However, I would like to know what happened that made you deem such a course of action necessary."

"The way he spoke to me, the language he used…"

"Selina…" Georgiana's patience was wearing thin.

Selina sat down. She looked up at her cousin, her mouth set in mutinous lines that reminded Georgiana of a rebellious child.

"Very well," said Georgiana, her patience exhausted. "I shall speak to Tom."

"You would take that ragamuffin boy's word over mine?"

"I don't know whose word to take," said Georgiana matter-of-factly, "unless you tell me what happened. So far you have given me no actual information."

Selina glowered at her, then took a deep breath. "Very well," she said in a tone of great dignity. "I asked the boy how he came to get our jewels back and he said… well, he said they were given to him."

Georgiana's heart sank. Why could Selina not have left the matter alone?

"I see," was all she said.

"Well, it seemed to me that it must be someone he knew when he was a highwayman. In fact, he probably told him how to find us."

Tom had made one failed attempt at highway robbery. In Georgiana's eyes this did not make him a highwayman, and certainly did not support Selina's assumption that he would pass on information about their social engagements and travelling plans. It was clear this had not occurred to Selina, who chewed her bottom lip, looking uncertain.

"Go on," said Georgiana.

"I asked him if it was one of his highwayman friends and – "

"Selina," said Georgiana, pronouncing each syllable with deliberation, "did you accuse him of arranging for some highwayman friend to rob us?"

"I am not sure that I would say 'accuse' precisely – "

"Oh, for heaven's sake, Selina, what is the matter with you? I told you to accept the return of your brooch and not ask any questions," said Georgiana.

"How could I not ask?" said Selina, stung, "when under my own roof – I beg your pardon, *your* own roof…"

"What happened then?" Georgiana asked before a tirade could burst forth.

"As I said, the boy turned on me, and used the most abominable language."

"Disregard the language for a moment and please keep

to the point."

Selina stiffened. "He lost his temper, and denied it, of course."

"It didn't occur to you that he might be telling the truth?"

"Well, he would deny it, wouldn't he?"

Georgiana closed her eyes and took a deep breath. "How can – ? Oh, never mind. Go on."

"As I said, he became angry, and began shouting at me. For a servant to speak so – " Selina caught the look in her cousin's eye and went quickly back to her recital of the facts. Her tone, when she spoke, was heavy with dignity. "So I discharged him. It did not occur to me you would object. I know you have a partiality for the boy but I would never have expected you to condone such impertinent behaviour."

Georgiana kept her eyes fixed steadily on her cousin for a moment. Selina looked increasingly uneasy.

"Tell me, Selina, if you were accused of some criminal act and you weren't guilty, wouldn't you be angry with the person who had accused you?"

Selina looked horrified. "Yes, of course, but – but why – why on earth would anyone accuse *me* of something criminal?"

"I'm sure they wouldn't," said Georgiana. "That is not the point. I simply wanted you to consider how Tom must have felt at being so accused."

Selina's eyes widened. "But the boy is – was…" She faltered under her cousin's gaze.

"I see," said Georgiana. "Because he has attempted highway robbery in the past, he must be guilty of involvement in a theft now."

Selina opened her mouth to speak.

"Oh, really, Selina," Georgiana continued. "Why could you not let the matter go as I asked? You have your brooch back. There was no need for all this upset. Now I am going to talk to Tom."

Georgiana turned on her heel and left the room before her cousin could make any further attempt at self-justification. She heard what sounded like a small whimper from Selina, but ignored it.

James was in the hall. She asked him to send Tom to her, then returned to the drawing room, where she quietly suggested that Selina might prefer to wait in her own room while she interviewed the boy. When her cousin seemed hesitant, Georgiana pointed out that, in fairness, she should speak to him privately, and she would rather do so in the drawing room than in the boy's quarters. This was sufficient to prompt Selina to gather her skirts and excuse herself, rising sedately. She had the misfortune to be going out through the door as Tom arrived. He glowered at her but walked quickly past as Georgiana summoned him.

"Close the door, would you, please, Tom?"

"Yes, miss."

Georgiana sat with hands folded in her lap and waited until Tom was standing before her.

"I understand my cousin has discharged you."

"Yes, miss," he responded morosely.

"Perhaps you would like to tell me what happened."

There was a sulky set about Tom's mouth. He glanced at Georgiana and gave a shrug. "She said I'd told Harry to hold you up."

"Did she say you had or ask you if you had?"

Tom looked puzzled. "Do it matter, miss?"

"Perhaps not," Georgiana said with a sigh, knowing his grasp of grammar to be limited. "Go on."

"Well, she'd no reason to say it, miss. It weren't true. Right out of the blue, it come."

"You got angry?"

"Well, wouldn't you, miss?"

"Yes, I imagine I would." Georgiana recalled that anger was not paramount among her feelings when she found herself, in the guise of the Crimson Cavalier, under suspicion for a murder she had not committed. However, she could understand Tom's indignation. He came from a background where people said what was on their minds.

"My cousin was rather shocked about the way you spoke to her," she continued. "She is not accustomed to such direct speech."

"Oh. Well, I beg your pardon, miss."

"Very well. Tell me what else happened."

"She didn't believe me when I said I didn't do it," Tom went on. "I know I shouldn't have shouted at her, miss. I know it wasn't proper. I'm sorry. But it wasn't fair, miss. I got your bits back, didn't I? At least," he amended, "a friend of mine did and I gave them back to you. I didn't run off with them."

"That is true," said Georgiana.

"Then she gives me the sack," said the boy, aggrieved.

"Well, don't worry about that," said Georgiana. "However, as you said, it is not proper to speak to my cousin, or anyone else, for that matter, with a lack of respect. I trust you will learn to curb your tongue so it will not happen again."

Tom was looking at the floor. His manner was surly. He shuffled his feet and slouched in a manner reminiscent of his first interview with Georgiana. Her impromptu rescue of him after he had been shot holding up the carriage in which she was travelling had left her with the problem of what to do with him when he recovered. His initial suspicion and defensive sulkiness had only abated when he realised her offer of a post was genuine.

"Tom!"

He looked up.

"I know how it is," he said. "I'm to take only what I brought. Except there was only the clothes on my back and they was got rid of."

"What?"

"When I go. I won't take no silver, nor any of your gewgaws."

"I assume you are doing me some sort of favour. If I knew what you were you talking about, I might be better placed to appreciate it."

Tom sighed, looking at Georgiana as though she was slow. "I won't take any of your precious bits and pieces when I go. I know what your cousin thinks but I don't steal from them who's fed and housed me."

"Go?"

"Well, you don't want me here, do you? You nor your cousin."

Georgiana realised Tom had made the assumption that his dismissal remained in effect.

"Do I get any wages before I go?" he demanded.

"Certainly, if you choose to go," said Georgiana coolly.

"If I choose…?"

"You imagine my cousin has made the decision for me?" Georgiana said.

"Well, no – that is…"

"Believe it, or not, Tom, I make my own decisions. As I said when you first came here, you are not a prisoner. If you choose to go, you are free to do so. If not, you still have a post here."

"I ain't sacked?"

"No, you are not sacked."

Tom's mouth fell open in astonishment, another feature

reminiscent of their first interview.

"Are you a fish?" Georgiana inquired.

Tom shook his head quickly. "No, miss. Sorry, miss."

"Do you plan to go back to work?"

"Oh. Yes, miss. Thank you, miss."

Tom's face brightened.

As Tom turned to go, Georgiana recalled something and called him back. "There is another matter on which I wished to speak to you, Tom. I am hoping you can help me with something."

Tom looked surprised but willing. "I'll try, miss."

Georgiana considered for a moment how best to phrase what she had to say.

"When our carriage was stopped," she began carefully, "my friend Miss Winters was with my cousin and me. She lost a pearl necklace belonging to her mother."

Tom grew defensive. "And you think I took it, miss? That I kept it when I gave back the other gewgaws?"

"No, Tom, calm down. I don't think anything of the sort. It is simply that there has been a rather strange occurrence."

Tom looked at her expectantly. "Miss?"

"I have learned the pearls were also returned, separately and in a rather different way." Georgiana paused and took a breath. "They were tossed through the window of a carriage by a highwayman."

Tom's eyes widened.

"Lor'"

"Quite."

"I never heard of such a thing, miss."

"No. I imagine few people have, " said Georgiana calmly. She looked closely at the boy. "Can you think of anyone who might have done that?"

Tom looked at her uncertainly.

"Tom," said Georgiana, "I am not seeking to set the law on your friends. However, it seemed a very strange thing to happen – "

"Yes, miss."

"Perhaps I am being overly curious," said Georgiana, "but I could not help wondering who would do such a thing and why."

"'Tis a rare strange thing, miss."

Georgiana looked searchingly at him. She was satisfied that Tom was telling the truth. He seemed as baffled as she that any highwayman would do such a thing. Nevertheless, Georgiana also knew he would not wish to betray his friends. While a part of her was grateful for such discretion and loyalty, it made her next question more difficult.

"Very well. There is one other thing I would like to ask you, Tom. At the dinner party I attended last night, a man died."

"I'm sorry, miss," Tom said, looking puzzled as to why Georgiana was sharing this information. "Was he a friend of yours?"

"No, I hardly knew him."

Tom's expression grew wary.

"He said he'd been held up by a highwayman," Georgiana continued, "and the suggestion was that the highwayman killed him."

Tom shook his head. "What for, miss, if he got the booty?"

"Yes, that was my own thought," said Georgiana. "The gentleman was stabbed."

"Sounds nasty, miss."

"It was. Do highwaymen normally carry daggers?"

"No, miss."

It was every bit as much of a waste of time as Georgiana had expected. She was about to dismiss Tom with a recommendation that he stay out of her cousin's way for the foreseeable future when there was a knock at the door. It opened and James stood on the threshold, looking at Georgiana apologetically.

"I beg your pardon, miss. There is a Bow Street Runner here to see you."

8

Tom looked at Georgiana accusingly, a sense of betrayal in his eyes.

"Here?" asked Georgiana. "Did he say what he wanted?"

"Only that he wished to speak with you."

"I see."

Tom was still glaring at her. She felt what seemed an excessive need to reassure him. A suspicion began to dawn in her mind.

"He didn't mention anyone from the house sending for him?" Georgiana gave a brief glance towards Tom.

James looked at her in as puzzled a fashion as his position would allow. "No, miss."

Georgiana sighed, "Very well. You had better show him in."

"Yes, miss," said James.

Georgiana turned towards her page. "You may go, Tom."

"Yes, miss."

The boy left the room as the visitor entered. The Runner gave the boy barely a glance. The newcomer came forward holding his cap, his manner respectful though with the confidence of one carrying out his duty. Georgiana sensed determination in his demeanour.

"Mr Rogers, miss."

"Thank you, James."

"I must beg your pardon for intruding on you, Miss Grey." The Runner was unexpectedly well-spoken.

"That's quite all right, Mr Rogers. Please come in. Won't you sit down?"

"Thank you, no. I hope I won't have to detain you for

long." He paused briefly. "It is about the death of Mr Polp."

"I see. What can I do to help?"

"I believe you were present when Mr Polp died. I would like to ask you about the events of the evening."

"Certainly."

Mr Rogers gave her a smile of thanks.

"I understand you and a Mr Lakesby tried to help Mr Polp as he was dying?"

Georgiana nodded. "Yes. Mr Lakesby tried to staunch the wound but I'm afraid Mr Polp could not be saved."

The Runner was watching her attentively. "I was told Mr Polp had said something before he died, mentioned something about a highwayman?"

"That's how it sounded," Georgiana said cautiously.

"I was told your party was held up by a highwayman on the way to Mrs Milton's gathering?"

"Yes, but he offered us no violence."

Rogers raised his eyebrows questioningly. "Oh? Didn't he have a pistol?"

"Well, yes, he did," admitted Georgiana. "I know that sounds odd. It is quite true that he held a pistol on us when he stopped the carriage. However, once we handed over our valuables, he let us go on our way. He made no attempt to attack us. In fact, he was rather polite; he went so far as to thank us."

Rogers gave a small smile. "Yes, I have heard of highwaymen acting rather gallantly. There was no one waiting on the road on your way home?"

"No," said Georgiana. "Surely there would have been no point? We had already lost all we had of value."

"A different highwayman would not have known that."

"No, I suppose not," said Georgiana slowly. "I had not thought of that." She saw no need to mention that most highwaymen had their own areas of work and did not generally encroach on another's preserve.

"Miss Grey, it is possible that Mr Polp was not killed by a highwayman."

This statement came as a surprise to Georgiana. She had taken it for granted that general opinion wanted to lay the killing at a highwayman's door.

"Not a highwayman?"

Mr Rogers spoke carefully, as if trying to spare Georgiana's sensibilities. "I understand you may have seen the dagger which killed Mr Polp. It was an ornamental piece, rather valuable." He paused. "I know it is popular to blame high-waymen and footpads for all the crime which takes place, and it is quite true that a great many of them are active. However, I am not altogether sure that is the case here. A dagger is not usually the sort of weapon a highwayman carries."

"I see. Do you have any idea as to who might have had the weapon?"

"Not as yet."

To Georgiana's surprise, Mr Rogers reached into a pocket of his greatcoat and retrieved an object swathed in a hand-kerchief, which he unwrapped with care. He held it out before her. It was the dagger.

"Good heavens."

Georgiana raised her eyes to the Runner. His were solemn.

"I understand this must be difficult for you, Miss Grey," said Rogers apologetically. "I know you may not have seen the dagger properly at the time of Mr Polp's death, but I must ask if you recognise it."

Georgiana studied it. "May I?" she asked, holding out a hand.

The Runner nodded, allowing her to take the dagger.

Its blade was clean and its gold hilt shone. It was a tasteful design, clearly costly, with small jewels of different colours embedded at regular intervals. On another occasion she might have admired it. Knowing it had taken a man's life, it filled her with distaste.

"You found it at Mrs Milton's?"

The Runner nodded. "Yes. She was kind enough to hand it over it to me. A servant had found it and Mrs Milton kept it safe, thinking it might be needed. I think she was glad to get it out of her house."

"That is understandable."

"Had you ever seen it prior to the killing?"

"I don't think so," said Georgiana.

"Did you notice anything particular last night?"

Georgiana hesitated. "In what respect?"

"Well," he said, "anything unusual, anyone behaving oddly."

Georgiana did not feel able to mention the conversation she had overheard on the road.

"No, nothing, apart from poor Mr Polp staggering into Mrs Milton's home, having been attacked." She paused, her nose crinkling. "There was something. I don't know whether it means anything, but when Mr Lakesby was tending to Mr Polp, someone pulled out the dagger, quite quickly. I think it must have been very painful for him; he gasped quite horribly. He died almost immediately."

Rogers was watching Georgiana intently as she spoke, his manner respectful, almost sympathetic.

"I understand your cousin was with you?" he said.

Georgiana nodded.

"Yes, Miss Knatchbull."

"Would it be possible for me to speak to her?" Rogers inquired.

"Certainly. I believe she is at home."

Georgiana went to the bell pull, and James appeared at the door almost immediately.

"James, will you ask my cousin to join us, please?"

"Yes, miss."

James was away for a few minutes, during which neither Georgiana nor Rogers spoke. Miss Knatchbull came tripping into the room, hands clasped in front of her, a nervous expression in her eyes.

"Selina, this is Mr Rogers. He is a Bow Street Runner and needs to speak to you about what happened at Mrs Milton's last night. Mr Rogers, my cousin, Miss Knatchbull."

Rogers gave a respectful bow.

"Oh, I see," said Selina, sitting in an armchair with a look like a scared rabbit on her face. "How do you do, Mr Rogers? I'm not sure I can help you. I really didn't see very much, though of course I'm sorry for poor Mr Polp."

"I understand, Miss Knatchbull. I am sorry to disturb you. I know this must be very distressing."

Rogers produced the dagger and held it out to Selina, resting flat on the palm of his hand. Unlike her cousin, she made no move to take it; instead she shuddered and shrank into herself. Rogers seemed suddenly less composed; he straightened and stammered an apology.

"It is all right, Mr Rogers. I understand you have your duty to do," said Miss Knatchbull. Suddenly she gave a metallic little laugh. "It is quite dreadful to think such a pretty thing could kill a man."

Georgiana's eyes widened. Was her cousin trying to flirt with the Runner? For his part, Rogers flushed. For the first time since his arrival, he seemed at a loss for what to say. He cleared his throat.

"Yes, ma'am, it certainly is. It – it is an ornamental dagger.

I have not yet discovered to whom it belongs. You do not recognise it?"

"I? Oh, no. Good heavens, no. How should I have seen such a thing?" Selina looked horrified.

Mr Rogers seemed uncomfortable at her reaction. "I beg your pardon, Miss Knatchbull. I intended no slight. It is simply a matter of duty. I need to gather information."

"Oh, yes, of course," Miss Knatchbull gave a prim little smile. She looked at him at an odd angle, her eyelids flickering.

Georgiana thought Mr Rogers looked as if he wanted to flee, but he stood his ground, schooling his face into an expression of interest.

Miss Knatchbull spoke again. "I can think of someone who may know something about it," she said.

Georgiana detected a sly note in her cousin's voice, which raised her suspicions. "Selina," she cut in, "I don't think you should trouble Mr Rogers with mere conjecture."

"Miss Grey, I think I should hear what Miss Knatchbull has to say," said Rogers, to Georgiana's chagrin. "I assure you no one will he accused without good reason, but at this stage I would be glad of any information."

Selina cast a triumphant glance towards her cousin then edged forward more comfortably on her chair.

"There is a boy employed here who used to be a high-wayman. He might well know something about it."

Georgiana turned towards the mantelpiece, leaning her head on her hand. She could have struck Selina. This was no more than malice.

"A highwayman? In service here?" Rogers seemed puzzled.

Georgiana interposed. "The boy my cousin speaks of is my page. His background is… unfortunate, and I'm afraid he did make one quite unsuccessful attempt at highway robbery some time ago. He was injured. I brought him here and offered him the post of page when he had recovered. He has worked hard and behaved well since that time."

Selina made a small noise which might have been something between a cough and a laugh. Rogers looked towards her. Georgiana tried to hide her irritation.

"I have never slept easily since he has been in the house," Selina told the Runner earnestly, leaning forward in her chair.

"And yet you have not been murdered in your bed," Georgiana murmured.

Rogers looked from one to the other. "I'm not sure your cousin's page could help, Miss Knatchbull," he said. "This is an ornamental dagger. It may have been on display in someone's house, and it is likely it was stolen from there. Have you ever seen it before the night Mr Polp was killed?"

"No, I don't think so," said Selina.

"I really don't think that Tom would have had the opportunity to steal from the house of one our acquaintance," said Georgiana.

"He could have – " began Selina.

"Thank you, Miss Knatchbull, I will bear it in mind," said Rogers. "I don't think I need to talk to your cousin's page at the moment but I am glad of the information." Rogers's tone was tactful.

"There is something else," said Selina. "We were stopped by a highwayman on the way to Mrs Milton's."

"Yes, Mrs Milton did mention that to me," said Rogers. "I have spoken to your cousin about it but I would be grateful if you would tell me what you think."

Selina looked pleased to have her opinion sought. She straightened up in her chair. "It was quite terrifying," she said primly. "He pointed his pistol at us, right through the window of the carriage, and demanded our jewellery."

"That must have been dreadful for you," said Rogers. "Did you notice anything particular about him?"

"He had a mask, so we couldn't see his face," said Selina.

"Yes, that is quite a regular practice," said Rogers. "I know that makes it difficult, but there may have been something else about him which was noticeable."

Georgiana could not help but admire the way the Runner handled her cousin.

"You think the same highwayman killed Mr Polp?" said Selina eagerly.

Mr Rogers looked at her. Selina's eyes fell. She folded her hands in her lap.

"Well, he was an older man, quite rough, a very common voice." Selina shuddered as she recalled it. "He had rough clothes as well."

"I'm afraid it's not usually an occupation for gentlemen," said Rogers.

"No, course not." Selina looked earnest.

Georgiana suppressed a smile.

"He didn't look as if he had shaved," said Selina, "and his mask was over his eyes. A frightening looking fellow."

"I'm sure."

"However, Mr Rogers, we got our belongings back."

"That was fortunate. Sometimes, Miss Knatchbull, if a reward is offered, items can be recovered."

"Oh. Did you offer a reward, Georgiana?" Selina asked, looking at her cousin. She continued, not waiting for an answer, "It did occur to me that the boy could have had something to do with it."

"I beg your pardon?" Rogers's puzzled expression returned.

"I think he knew where to find our belongings," said Selina.

"Miss Knatchbull, it is not against the law to return property."

"But if he had something to do with the robbery?" said Selina.

"Selina, you don't know that Tom had anything to do with either the robbery or retrieving our jewellery." Georgiana kept her voice level to mask her growing anger at her cousin's determination to implicate Tom.

The Runner was looking thoughtful. "I think," he said slowly, "I should speak to your page, if you don't mind, Miss Grey."

"Certainly." Georgiana went to the bell pull. When James answered, she addressed him calmly. "James, would you please ask Tom to attend us?"

James looked hesitantly at the company. "I beg your pardon, Miss Georgiana, but Tom is not in the house."

9

"You see." Selina's expression was triumphant. "I knew he had something to hide. Now he has run away."

"We don't know that he has run away," said Georgiana in exasperation. "James, are you saying he has been sent on an errand?"

"No, miss. He came into the servants' hall a few minutes ago and left through the back door without speaking to anyone."

Georgiana sighed; this was too bad of Tom. She turned to the Runner. "I beg your pardon, Mr Rogers. It is true that my page has occasionally wandered off without permission, to visit friends. However, he has always returned."

"So far," said Selina in a doom-laden tone.

Georgiana ignored her. "He has a healthy appetite and my cook is inclined to spoil him. I have no doubt he will return."

Rogers nodded. "I understand, Miss Grey. Boys are like that. I'll call back if I may."

"Of course." Georgiana nodded to James who still stood on the threshold. "Goodbye, Mr Rogers."

"Goodbye, Miss Grey. Thank you for your time. Goodbye, Miss Knatchbull."

James stood aside to allow Rogers to pass then closed the door quietly after him. Selina looked warily at her cousin.

"Why did you do that?" Georgiana finally asked in a quiet voice.

"What? What did I do?"

"You know very well what you did," said Georgiana.

"Blaming Tom in that fashion without any evidence to suggest he is guilty. Really, Selina."

"That is not fair, Georgiana. He used to be a highwayman."

"He made one foolish, unsuccessful attempt at highway robbery and, as I recall, you weren't there. If Mr Lakesby had no wish to take the matter further, I cannot imagine why you are so eager to see him blamed for something."

"Mr Lakesby does not have to live under the same roof as that boy," Selina got out.

Georgiana took a deep breath. "I see. You have always had a grudge against Tom, haven't you, Selina?"

"What? No, of course not. But after all…"

"After all," said Georgiana, "in the time he has been here, you have not lost any jewellery and you have not been attacked."

"Well, no, but – "

"That being the case, perhaps you will cease making these unfounded accusations. Now, if you will excuse me, there are a few things in need of my attention."

Georgiana left the drawing room quickly and went to her own room, still furious with her cousin. She sent for Emily and was seated at her dressing table, staring into the mirror, an uncharacteristically hard expression on her face, when the maid arrived.

Emily looked guardedly at her mistress. "Is everything all right, Miss Georgiana?"

Georgiana sighed. "Not really, Emily. Have you any idea where Tom has disappeared to?"

"No, miss. But you know what he is like. Very likely he's gone to the Lucky Bell to see his friend Harry."

"Yes." Georgiana shook her head and looked towards the maid. "Did you hear of this upset with my cousin?"

"I heard something had happened." Emily's tone was cautious.

"My cousin discharged him."

"What? Beg pardon, Miss Georgiana, but does she – er – "

"Have the right to discharge him? No, she does not."

Emily was silent, watching her mistress. Georgiana sighed.

"I'm afraid I made my views on the subject very plain to her. She took offence, of course."

"Oh dear."

"Yes, well, I have told Tom he need not consider himself discharged. What concerns me more is that my cousin suggested to the Bow Street Runner that Tom might know something about the dagger which killed Mr Polp."

"What? How could he?"

"Oh, I don't know. Because of where he came from, my cousin is convinced he had something to do with Harry holding up our carriage."

"And so with Mr Polp's murder?" Emily asked in puzzlement.

"I know. A strange logic. It may just be spite. However, Tom's disappearance doesn't reflect well on him. The Bow Street Runner now wants to talk to him. I don't think he would have done so otherwise."

"What do you wish to do, miss?"

"I'll wait until he comes back and speak to him then. If he has gone to see Harry he may well mention the Runner being here. He was just leaving the room as Mr Rogers arrived. He may also come back from the Lucky Bell with something useful."

Emily raised her eyebrows. Georgiana told her about the strange return of Lady Winters's pearls. Her reaction was similar to Tom's. "Does that sound like something your friend Harry would do, miss?"

"I don't know. It is possible he had already sold the necklace."

"To some friend of her ladyship?"

Georgiana shrugged. "Who then made the dramatic gesture of tossing it through the carriage window. I don't know, Emily. It does sound odd." She bit her bottom lip.

"Did you ask Tom to speak to Harry?" said Emily.

"No, it would have looked too much like prying. I hope he will think to do so himself."

"You think he'll be back?" asked Emily. "I mean with the Runner being here...?"

"I know. I hope so," said Georgiana. "Harry has certainly given me the impression he thinks Tom is better off here than in the Lucky Bell."

"Well, of course he is."

"It is certainly less adventurous for him. However, I believe Harry has some influence over him, so he may send him back." Georgiana frowned. "I have to confess, I'm curious about the business with the dagger. It does rather concern me."

"Oh?"

"It was a bejewelled ornamental item. I didn't look at it very closely when Mr Lakesby was attending Mr Polp."

"It doesn't belong to Mrs Milton?"

"Presumably not. I didn't see Mr Polp arrive but I rather had the impression he had already been stabbed."

"Someone could have slipped outside, miss."

"Yes, that's true. Perhaps I should talk to Mrs Milton. Fetch my bonnet, will you?"

"Would you like me to come with you, Miss Georgiana?"

Georgiana heard the slam of her cousin's door.

"Yes, please, Emily. We had better take the carriage."

"Yes, miss. I'll ask James to send for it."

While Emily went to speak to her brother, Georgiana drew on her gloves, thinking about the visit of the Runner. She could cheerfully have wrung Tom's neck for disappearing like this. It was clear he had no idea how suspicious it looked.

Georgiana joined Emily downstairs in the hall, where James was also waiting to help her on with her pelisse. The drive to Mrs Milton's was less eventful than the previous evening's. Georgiana did not often visit acquaintances such a distance away during the day. It was unusual to see the sun coming through the trees in an area the Crimson Cavalier was accustomed to visit in darkness.

Georgiana and Emily spent the time talking about the Bow Street Runner's visit and his conversation with Selina.

"I am so angry with her, " said Georgiana. "It seems nothing but the meanest spite. I cannot believe how determined she was to blame him for something."

Emily was frowning. "You didn't tell Miss Knatchbull Tom had returned your jewellery?"

"No, of course not." Georgiana grew thoughtful. "I suppose there is an element of logic in her reaction, in view of Tom's attempts to be a highway robber."

"He's never really cut off his connection with the Lucky Bell as you asked, has he, miss?"

"No, but in some ways I must admire his loyalty. He clearly did not want to implicate Harry. He is also a great deal more discreet than I would have expected. He has never given away the Crimson Cavalier."

"Well, that is a mercy," said Emily.

They were drawing up outside Mrs Milton's elegant abode and were fortunate to see the lady of the house in conversation with a servant just outside the front door. She caught sight of them and waved, dismissing the servant before coming forward.

"Miss Grey, how good of you to call. Won't you come inside?"

"Thank you, Mrs Milton."

" I hope you arrived home safely without any further incident from highwaymen?"

"Yes, indeed, thank you."

"You'll take tea with me, I hope?" Mrs Milton glanced towards Emily. "I will arrange for your maid to have some refreshment. Please go with my footman and he will take care of you."

"Thank you, ma'am." Emily's tone was demure, and her hands were folded in front of her.

Mrs Milton turned back to Georgiana and smiled. Georgiana thought she detected a hint of unease in her expression. For the first time it occurred to her that Mrs Milton might be embarrassed to receive a visitor on the day following a violent death in her home. However, it was too late to draw back now.

Georgiana followed her hostess into a small saloon. It had a cosy, homelike appearance, a world away from the scene of the previous night. Georgiana suddenly felt sorry for Mrs Milton; though the ruin of a party was a relatively small matter in comparison with a man's life, it must have been extremely distressing for her to have such a thing happen in her home, and it would certainly colour any future hospitality which she might want to offer. Even at present, it was clear Mrs Milton did not know what to say.

"How are you, Mrs Milton? I hope you managed to get some sleep after everyone left."

"What? Oh, yes, thank you, Miss Grey. A little." She fell silent for a moment. "It was such a dreadful thing to happen," she said at last. "Poor Mr Polp. I shall never forget how he looked."

"No."

"Such a kind man, so amiable. I am sure he must have

89

come to every one of my little gatherings, and was always such good company."

"So he was a good friend of yours?" asked Georgiana.

"Not a friend exactly, but I had been acquainted with him for some time. My late husband knew him rather better than I did. Indeed, at one point I rather hoped he and my daughter would make a match of it."

"Really?"

"Oh, yes. He is – I mean, he was of such good family, you see, and comfortably established. However, my daughter wanted to marry Mr Saxon, who was also a good match, and it seemed that matrimony was never a part of Mr Polp's plans. My daughter is happy enough, however."

"You must be glad of that"

"Oh, yes and as things transpired, she would have been a widow now, so it is for the best."

"Yes." Georgiana paused as a maid entered, carrying the tea which Mrs Milton had requested. She continued when the girl had departed. "Did Mr Polp leave many family members?"

"I'm afraid I don't know," said Mrs Milton." I believe his parents are dead, but I am sure I heard him mention a sister. I believe she lives a long way off." Mrs Milton waved her hand vaguely. "Somewhere in the north."

"I see." Georgiana looked intently at her hostess over the rim of her cup. "Then it is his friends who will feel his loss."

"Oh, yes, they will. He was such joyful company, he livened up any gathering. Why, even last night…" Mrs Milton took out a lace handkerchief and dabbed at the corner of her eye. "He was making jokes, funning about his waistcoat even when he was dying."

"Yes."

"And that dagger," said Mrs Milton. "Poor Mr Polp. To be

killed with such an elegant little piece…"

"There is certainly something incongruous about it," agreed Georgiana.

"You know it belongs to Sir Charles Ross?"

"I beg your pardon? No, I had not heard that. Are you certain?"

"Oh, yes," said Mrs Milton. "In fact, I recall his telling me a few weeks ago that it had disappeared. He liked to keep it on display on a wall in his house, so he would know very quickly that it had gone missing."

"Indeed," said Georgiana slowly. "You are certain it is the same one?"

"Certainly I am. The stones were arranged in a distinctive pattern."

Georgiana had not noticed anything especially distinctive, but clearly Mrs Milton was better acquainted with Sir Charles Ross. "It is odd that it should have disappeared from his home," she said. "When did he first notice that it was gone?"

"Oh!" Mrs Milton fluttered nervously. "I am not sure," she said "I think he said it was after a weekend house party some time ago."

"Well then, perhaps – "

"I know what you are going to say, my dear," said Mrs Milton. "It is a shocking thing to consider that it might have been a guest. I believe Sir Charles thought of that himself. However, apparently there was a firework display which everyone went out to watch. So you see, the house was empty for a good half-hour, at least. Plenty of time for a footpad to sneak inside and steal it."

"What about the servants? " asked Georgiana.

"Busy with their duties, I expect."

"I suppose so," said Georgiana, "but it seems such a risk. Anyone might have come back indoors at any time."

She smiled wryly at her hostess. "It will be very distressing for Sir Charles to learn that his piece was used to kill someone."

"Yes, indeed," said Mrs Milton.

"I fear he will take it badly."

"Well of course, that's to be expected."

"Oh, it is much more than that. Sir Charles is a very sensitive soul, very sensitive indeed. His mother was widowed when he was very young, he has a young sister who needs much of his attention, and, well, his fiancée died last year."

"Good heavens. The poor man," said Georgiana.

"Yes, he has had a difficult time." Mrs Milton looked solemn.

A thought occurred to Georgiana. "Was Mr Polp a friend of his?"

"What? No, I don't think so, no more than anyone else. In fact, I suspect they were no more than acquaintances."

"I see."

"Sir Charles had hoped to come last night, but his mother was unwell and he had to send his apologies. As things turned out it was probably for the best." Mrs Milton sounded disconsolate and Georgiana hardly knew how to comfort her.

"Please, Mrs Milton, there is nothing to gain by continuing to think about it. It was not your fault. There was no way such an incident could have been foreseen."

"These highwaymen," said Mrs Milton vehemently, sniffing into a handkerchief.

Georgiana said nothing, allowing her hostess a few tears to relieve her feelings. She had often taken up the argument that a highwayman was not necessarily a killer, but recognised that this was not the moment to engage in it.

As she waited for Mrs Milton to calm down, something else occurred to her.

"How did Sir Charles's fiancée die?" she asked when the other woman had put away her handkerchief.

"Some illness. I don't know what it was. She was always quite pale and frail, poor girl."

"That is quite sad," Georgiana gave a brief smile and stood up. "I must go. I have taken up enough of your time. Thank you for the tea."

Mrs Milton escorted her visitor to the door after ringing for the carriage. "Thank you for your visit, Miss Grey, and for your kind words. You have been such a comfort."

This surprised Georgiana. Bidding her hostess farewell, she climbed into her carriage, where Emily was already seated. Her head was filled with questions, not the least of which was how had Sir Charles Ross's dagger come to be the murder weapon of Mr Boyce Polp? The fact that Sir Charles had not been at Mrs Milton's dinner party aroused Georgiana's suspicions. However, she had no way of knowing whether he had reason to want Polp dead.

Recalling the two men she had overheard on the road, Georgiana found she had a great desire to meet Sir Charles.

10

"Really, Georgiana, what were you thinking?"

Georgiana took a deep breath before answering her cousin. She realised she had left little time to prepare for a dinner party since issuing her invitation to Louisa the previous day – but it was still her right to invite whomever she chose to her home.

"Louisa's mother had not returned when I invited her, Selina. I thought she might be glad of some company, rather than being shut away with her governess."

"Well, yes, I daresay but..." Selina's mouth tightened. "But did you have to invite her cousin as well?"

"He was included in the invitation as her escort."

"Oh." Selina could find nothing to fault in this concession to propriety. "But her ladyship!"

"What was I do, Selina, withdraw the invitation when Lady Winters returned unexpectedly? If I had done so, you would now be berating me for gross incivility! I am afraid it was to be expected that Louisa's mother would wish to accompany her. We shall have to make the best of it."

"I suppose so." Miss Knatchbull sighed.

"I must say, you have done an excellent job in preparing the menu," said Georgiana, aiming to soothe her cousin's ruffled feathers after their earlier disagreement. "You should be proud. I am sure our guests will be impressed."

"Why, thank you, Georgiana," said Selina, mollified. "If I say so myself, I am sure you need not be ashamed of your table."

"No, indeed. I have no doubt it will go well."

"There is one thing which concerns me," said Selina.

"Mr Lakesby is the only gentleman. Will he sit by himself with the port if the ladies withdraw?"

"That will be his decision. I suspect he will not linger."

The three dinner guests arrived promptly. Mr Lakesby ushered in his ladies; Louisa smiled shyly and Lady Winters nodded benignly at the company. Georgiana was actually surprised her ladyship had consented to the expedition, but accepted it was probably a sign of Lady Winters's approval of her daughter's friendship, something of which Georgiana had never been certain. She knew Louisa would probably not feel able to express herself as freely with her mother present, but Lakesby's presence would lighten the atmosphere.

The first course went smoothly; conversation was confined to ordinary small talk and appreciative murmurs about the duck soup. Georgiana was surprised at how at ease Lady Winters seemed, and even more so at the sight of her ladyship's pearls around Louisa's neck. The girl did appear nervous, and confided in a quiet moment to Georgiana that it was only the presence of her cousin which has given her courage to yield to her mother's persuasions to wear them.

"Your mother wanted you to wear them?" Georgiana asked, handing Louisa a cup of tea from the tray served after dinner.

Louisa nodded. "I own I was surprised, especially after what happened, but Mama seems very anxious that I should wear them."

"Well, they become you very well."

Louisa blushed and thanked Georgiana, whose attention was then caught by a remark Lady Winters made to Miss Knatchbull.

"Yes, of course, it is quite sad about Mr Polp, and I am

sorry Louisa was subjected to such a distressing scene. However, I must confess I did not know him well and never felt able to warm to him."

Lakesby joined the ladies from his solitary port just in time to hear this. "Really, Aunt Beatrice?" he said. "I was under the impression that he was rather an amiable fellow."

"I daresay," said Lady Winters. "Please don't mistake me, Maxwell, I have nothing against the gentleman, I am sure he was pleasant enough though it seemed he tried a little too hard to be pleasant."

"Yes, I see," said Lakesby. "Interesting."

"You think there was something false about him, Lady Winters?" asked Georgiana.

"Perhaps 'false' is too strong a word, Miss Grey, but certainly not quite – quite genuine."

The others looked at her in some surprise. Louisa in particular seemed puzzled by her mother's words.

"It sometimes seems to me," continued her ladyship, "that if someone is excessively charming, the charm is intended to hide something."

"An… unusual thought," said Lakesby.

"Yes," said Georgiana, her eyes on Lady Winters, "but not, I think, one which should be ruled out."

Louisa stared at her mother, wide-eyed. Selina looked appalled.

"Why, what a dreadful idea," said Selina. "That's quite shocking, to think one must be suspicious of someone who is charming, of one's own acquaintance!"

"I don't think that is quite what her ladyship is saying, Selina," said Georgiana.

"No?" Selina looked around the assembled company.

"Not at all," said Lady Winters. "You exaggerate my meaning, Miss Knatchbull."

Cowed, Selina said nothing. Georgiana considered a change of subject suitable.

"I called upon Mrs Milton yesterday, to see how she was."

"Oh yes, poor Mrs Milton," said Selina, casting an uneasy glance towards Lady Winters, as if she were uncertain whether she should be speaking. "What a shocking thing to happen in her house."

"How was she?" asked Lakesby.

"She was quite shaken," said Georgiana. "However, she seemed well enough otherwise. She did happen to mention that the dagger which killed Mr Polp belonged to Sir Charles Ross."

"Oh, Charlie lost that dagger ages ago," said Louisa.

Eight eyes fixed on the girl.

"*Charlie?*" said Lady Winters with awful solemnity.

"Oh, I…" Louisa coloured and stared at the floor. "I beg your pardon, Mama. I meant to say Sir Charles, of course."

"You know Sir Charles, Louisa?" asked Lakesby casually.

"I used to be acquainted with him, quite some time ago. I haven't seen him in a long while. He was engaged to a friend of mine."

Georgiana looked at Louisa in surprise.

"Did the young lady break it off?" asked Selina sympathetically.

Louisa shook her head. "No, she died."

The room fell silent. Georgiana looked down on her hands folded in her lap. Miss Knatchbull looked mortified with embarrassment, and struggled to compose a sentence which would smooth over her *faux pas*. Even Lady Winters looked stunned.

"You have never mentioned this, Louisa," said Lakesby.

Louisa shrugged. "Why should I?"

Her companions' continued silence proved effective in breaking down her reluctance to speak.

"Well, is it anyone else's business when one of my friends dies?" she asked in hostile tones.

"No, of course not," said Georgiana gently. "It must be upsetting for you, and if you would rather not talk about it there is no need to do so."

Louisa looked at her hostess from under her lashes in an uncharacteristically sombre manner. Selina, recovering from her discomfort, appeared to be about to speak, but the girl did so first.

"Barbara and I came out at about the same time. She was always rather pale and delicate. I think she met Charlie at one of the first parties she attended. He made her an offer not very long after that. Don't you remember, Mama?"

"Yes," said Lady Winters, looking thoughtful. "You could have had him yourself, Louisa. Still could, for that matter."

"Mama!"

Lady Winters raised her eyebrow. This time the silence grew uncomfortable for everyone.

Eventually Louisa continued, "Barbara's parents were very pleased, and so was Charlie's mother. I don't think his sister was terribly happy, but she was always a little odd. They had just started planning the wedding when Barbara became unwell, some sort of consumptive thing. She was coughing a lot. She even started coughing up blood."

"My dear," said Lady Winters in distaste.

"I went to see her just once," said Louisa softly. "Within a week of becoming ill, Barbara was dead."

"I am so sorry, Louisa," said Lakesby gently.

Louisa gave a small smile. "Poor Charlie was devastated. Actually, I haven't seen him since." She looked at Georgiana. "Was he supposed to come to Mrs Milton's?"

Georgiana nodded. "I believe so. Mrs Milton said he had been unable to attend as his mother was not well."

"Oh." Louisa digested this.

Lakesby was frowning. "That dagger. Surely he would have recognised it if he had seen it?"

"Oh, I am sure he would have," said Louisa. "A family heirloom, I think he said, from the Crusades or something. It was on a wall at his family home."

Georgiana thought this was probably the extent of Louisa's knowledge of the Crusades. However, she was more interested in the girl's knowledge of Sir Charles and his late fiancée. It had come as a surprise that Louisa had known the couple. She noticed that Lady Winters was watching her daughter closely.

"When did Sir Charles lose the dagger?" asked Lakesby.

Louisa crinkled her nose. "A few months ago, I think. He held a weekend house party and it disappeared. He noticed after everyone had left."

"He told you this?" Lakesby asked.

Louisa nodded. "He didn't like to think that one of his guests might have had something to do with it. He thought perhaps the house had been robbed by footpads before the party and he hadn't noticed. Either that or it had been sent away to be cleaned."

"Such an optimist," murmured Lakesby.

Louisa continued, "Charlie hadn't noticed the dagger was missing while he was attending to his guests. He didn't like to ask any of them about its disappearance, for fear it would look as if he was accusing them."

"Was anything else taken?" asked Georgiana.

"I don't think so," said Louisa. "I think he only noticed the dagger was gone because it was up on a wall, but in a study, not a room the guests were using."

Georgiana stored away this information in her mind, impressed with the extent of Louisa's knowledge of the matter.

"It seems unlikely," said Lakesby, "that a footpad would force entry into Sir Charles Ross's home for the sole purpose of taking an ornamental dagger."

"I suppose so," said Louisa. She shook her head slowly. "Now I think of it, I'm sure Mr Polp was at Charlie's weekend party." She crinkled her nose again. "Poor Charlie will be upset when he hears his dagger was used to kill Mr Polp."

"Really, Louisa, it hardly seems proper for you to refer to Sir Charles Ross as Charlie, even if he was betrothed to your friend."

Louisa hung her head. "I beg your pardon, Mama. I'll try to remember."

"Were you at this weekend party?" Lakesby asked.

"Me? No, I ran into Char – Sir Charles somewhere else a while afterwards."

Selina had taken no part in the conversation and sat fidgeting with her hands, looking uncertain what to say. "Would anyone like more tea?" she finally got out.

Lakesby accepted and came forward with his cup.

"These highwaymen are a scourge," said Lady Winters after a brief silence.

"Including the one who returned your pearls?" asked Georgiana quizzically.

"I daresay that was some sort of joke," said Lady Winters, "Not very amusing, I grant you, but some of these young men can become rather wild. I believe some of them also indulge in a sport known as 'boxing the Watch.'"

"I assure your ladyship, being held up was no joke," said Selina with an earnestness which made her look even more mousy than usual. "It was quite frightening, was it not,

100

Miss Winters? Georgiana?"

Louisa, to whom an encounter with a highwayman was always something of an adventure, did not answer.

"It certainly seemed genuine," said Georgiana.

"If we may return to the subject of this party at Sir Charles Ross's home," said Lakesby. "Do you know who attended, Louisa?"

"Lord, I don't know," answered his cousin. "It was for gentlemen, I think, shooting and cards, I suppose. You didn't go, Max?"

"I don't know Sir Charles that well. We don't move in the same circles."

"It is unthinkable to imagine any of Sir Charles's guests would steal an heirloom," said Selina. "Surely no gentleman would so abuse the hospitality they had been offered. It must have been a housebreaker."

"Quite," said Lady Winters. "Miss Grey, I believe it is time we took our leave. Thank you for a pleasant evening."

Georgiana moved towards the bell to ring for James, but was superseded by his arrival in the doorway. She looked at him in some surprise.

"I beg your pardon, miss, but you have another visitor," he said apologetically.

"Oh?"

"Yes, miss. It is the Bow Street Runner, Mr Rogers."

11

This created something of a sensation. Louisa's jaw dropped, and snapped closed again as her name shot from her mother's lips in instant reproof. Lakesby's brows lifted, while Selina looked mortified, clearly deeming such a visit at this time a source of embarrassment which would never be lived down. Georgiana remained composed.

"Mr Rogers?" she said. "Here, now? Well, I suppose I had better see him. Perhaps you would show him into the library, please, James?" She rose, addressing her guests. "I beg your pardon. Will you excuse me for a few minutes?"

"Surely there's no need to disturb yourself, Miss Grey," said Lakesby coolly. "The man can be shown in here, unless, that is, he specifically needs to speak to you privately?" He looked inquiringly at James.

James hesitated, and glanced towards Georgiana. "Well, no, sir, he didn't say so."

Georgiana gave him a bright smile. "Certainly, then, if no one objects. Show Mr Rogers in here, James."

Lady Winters shuddered, clearly horrified at being obliged to be in the same room as such a person at a social function. Selina looked acutely uneasy and threw Georgiana a look which said she had expected disaster all along.

Mr Rogers entered, holding his hat in front of him in a respectful manner. He immediately apologised for his intrusion, and his pale, intelligent eyes took in the company, lingering for a fraction of a second longer on Louisa.

"Your brother asked me to call, Miss Grey."

"Edward? Really? Please go on, Mr Rogers."

"Thank you. It was simply to alert you to the fact that a

trap is being laid tonight for the highwayman who is believed to have killed Mr Polp."

"I am glad to hear that!" said Lady Winters.

Rogers glanced towards her ladyship. "There could be danger," he said. "It would be better if innocent parties were safely indoors."

"I see," said Georgiana.

"In that case, we must leave immediately," said her ladyship. "Miss Grey, would you be good enough to send for our wraps?"

"Of course, Lady Winters."

As Georgiana rose and went to the bell, she glimpsed Louisa looking at the Runner through lowered lashes. Just as she reached out her hand to pull the cord, the door opened to admit James again. Close behind him was another visitor.

"Mr Grey, miss."

"Good evening, Georgiana." Edward Grey walked across the room to greet his sister, who was still standing by the bell pull. "I must apologise for interrupting." He turned towards Georgiana's guests, his voice trailing off as he caught sight of Lakesby.

"Mr Rogers said you asked him to call," said Georgiana, "to let us know there was a plan to trap a highwayman."

"Yes," said Edward. "Rogers suggested using the dagger as bait, as it might tempt the ruffian."

"I see," said Georgiana.

James was about to close the door; Georgiana forestalled him. "James, would you fetch my guests' cloaks and have their carriage brought around?"

"Yes, miss."

As the door closed behind James, Georgiana turned back to face her brother. "Would you like some tea, Edward?

Or perhaps some wine?"

"No, thank you, Georgiana."

Georgiana looked at the Runner. "Mr Rogers, would you care for some refreshment?"

Rogers looked surprised. Lady Winters barely suppressed a gasp; her nephew failed to conceal a grin.

"No, thank you, Miss Grey," said Rogers.

"Suppose this bait of yours doesn't work?" said Lakesby.

"Why wouldn't it?" asked Edward before Rogers could speak.

"Oh, I don't know. What is the plan? Presumably you have arranged for someone to ride about with the dagger until a highwayman stops him?"

"It seems quite straightforward," said Rogers. "A few volunteers have offered to help with the villain's apprehension."

"Very public spirited," said Lakesby. "However, what if you were to attract the wrong prey?"

"There would still be one highwayman fewer on the roads," said Lady Winters sternly. "And a very good thing, too."

Georgiana hoped she was the only one to notice the fleeting glance she exchanged with Lakesby.

"You could come with us, Lakesby," said Edward.

Knowing her brother's opinion of that gentleman, Georgiana was surprised at this, even allowing for the fact that the situation was hardly a social one.

"I suppose I could," Lakesby mused. "I must, of course, escort my aunt and cousin home first."

"Please don't trouble yourself, sir," said Rogers. "We will do well enough, and your first duty is to your family."

"Very well."

"Though if I might make so bold, sir, it would be helpful

if you did not mention our little plan to anyone. It would not do if our quarry were to get wind of it."

"Certainly you may depend on my discretion," said Lakesby. "Do you imagine I number many highwaymen among my friends?"

Edward rolled his eyes. Georgiana schooled her expression carefully.

"We aim to apprehend the culprit with as little trouble and danger to innocent parties as possible," said Rogers. He glanced towards Louisa again.

Georgiana suddenly realised that the Runner might not have spoken to Louisa about Boyce Polp's killing and would certainly need to do so. However, he was clearly finding it difficult to address her in the presence of her mother, since he had not been introduced to either of them. She immediately took steps to remedy this.

"Lady Winters, Louisa, forgive me; I have neglected to introduce Mr Rogers to you. He is the Bow Street Runner who is investigating Mr Polp's death?"

Lady Winters inclined her head in a stately manner, and showed no other interest in pursuing the acquaintance of Mr Rogers. Louisa gave a shy smile and a soft, "How do you do?" in response to Mr Rogers's bow.

"Louisa, I think Mr Rogers may need to speak to you about Mr Polp's death," said Georgiana.

"Oh." Louisa looked alert and turned to face the Runner.

Rogers threw Georgiana a grateful glance.

"Now?" demanded Lady Winters.

"I could call at your home if it would be more convenient," said Rogers.

"Very well." Her ladyship sat down again, folded her hands, gave a sigh of resignation and looked expectantly at the Runner.

Mr Rogers gave Lady Winters a brief glance which could have been interpreted as nervousness, then turned his attention to Louisa. As when he questioned Georgiana, he produced the dagger. Lady Winters gasped, while Selina looked mortified at such a breach of etiquette during a dinner party. Lakesby's eyes were on his young cousin, whose lips were pressed together anxiously.

"I am sure you realise this is the dagger which killed Mr Polp," said Rogers.

Louisa nodded.

"Have you ever seen it before, miss?"

"Well, yes, as a matter of fact, I have."

In response to Rogers's enquiring look, and Edward Grey's rather stunned one, Louisa told him what she knew about the dagger and her acquaintance with Sir Charles Ross. As she mentioned its disappearance from Sir Charles's home, Rogers and Edward exchanged a look.

"Beg pardon, miss, but do you know whether your acquaintance took any steps to recover his property?" asked Rogers.

Louisa shook her head. "No, I don't. I am sorry. He only mentioned it in passing. You see, I have not been much in his company since his engagement to my friend Barbara ended. She died, you know."

"I see. I'm sorry to hear that, miss." Rogers frowned in thought. "You don't know who the guests were at his week-end gathering?"

"Well, really!" said Lady Winters.

Rogers kept his eyes on Louisa. She shook her head. "No. I am sorry, I don't. I believe it was a gentlemen's shooting party."

Rogers nodded. Lakesby spoke as if in anticipation of the Runner's next question. "I am afraid I was not one of the party, Mr Rogers," he said.

"Thank you, sir," said the Runner. He glanced towards Edward, who had been standing silent.

"Sir Charles didn't like to accuse his guests," said Louisa anxiously. "He didn't believe any of his friends would have taken it. Perhaps it was taken down for cleaning or something, and lost."

"Perhaps," said Rogers.

"I still think it was a housebreaker," said Lady Winters, rising from her chair. "May we go now?"

"Yes, of course, your ladyship. I am so sorry to delay you." Rogers turned back to Louisa, giving her a reassuring smile. "Thank you for your help, Miss Winters. I am very grateful."

Louisa blushed but looked pleased with herself. "You're v-very welcome," she stammered.

Once again, James was summoned. This time the outdoor garments of the visitors were brought, and Lady Winters and Louisa departed, escorted by Mr Lakesby. Before he left, he offered his card to the Runner, telling him he was welcome to call. Rogers thanked him and put the card away. Lady Winters's expression was a combination of disbelief and disapproval.

As the door closed behind the dinner guests, there was silence for a few moments. Georgiana sat down. "Shall I ring for some more tea?" she said. "Mr Rogers, please sit down. I assume you have some more questions for us, and that my brother is helping you."

Selina looked surprised and glanced from Georgiana to Edward and back. Edward sighed.

"No, thank you, Miss Grey, though it's very kind of you," said Rogers. "I must be on my way. There is a trap to be set." He looked at Edward. "I will see you later, Mr Grey?"

"Yes, of course."

When Rogers had departed, Selina let out a breath she appeared to have been holding a long time. "Well!"

"Do you want some tea, Edward?" Georgiana asked calmly.

"No, thank you, Georgiana. As Rogers said, I have agreed to help in the laying of this trap for the highwayman."

"Oh yes, of course."

"I was never more mortified, Georgiana," said Selina. "A Bow Street Runner questioning our guests." Her lips pursed a little. "I beg your pardon, *your* guests. Whatever will Lady Winters think?"

"I shouldn't allow it to concern you," said Georgiana.

Edward glanced towards Miss Knatchbull in some puzzlement. "Lady Winters seems extremely eager for the highwayman to be caught," he said. "I understand you were held up on the way to Mrs Milton's party?"

"Yes," said Georgiana.

"We got our property back," said Selina.

"Did you?" Edward looked from one to the other in surprise.

"Yes, as a matter of fact we did," said Georgiana. "We were fortunate."

"Fortunate!" snorted Selina.

Edward's expression grew more puzzled. "Is something wrong, Selina?"

Georgiana rolled her eyes as Miss Knatchbull's chin lifted.

"Of course I am pleased to have my mother's brooch returned," she said. "However, it seemed odd that it was found so quickly."

"There are ways of retrieving things if the right reward is offered," said Edward.

"Was a reward offered, Georgiana?" demanded Selina,

repeating a question she had earlier asked. As then, she did not wait for an answer, turning instead to address Edward. "I don't see how it can have been so. We retrieved our property very quickly."

"Then we should count our blessings," said Georgiana.

"Selina, I don't understand the problem," said Edward.

"It's that boy," Miss Knatchbull hissed.

"What boy?" asked Edward.

"That young highwayman whom Georgiana took on as a page."

"Was it he who held you up?" asked Edward.

"Certainly not," said Georgiana.

"Then why…?" Edward looked perplexed.

"Well, he is clearly accustomed to consorting with criminals," said Selina. "How can he be trusted?"

Edward looked towards his sister, who was shaking her head.

"Perhaps Georgiana is right," said Edward, to his sister's surprise. "You were fortunate to get your property back at all."

"But don't you think it was too much of a coincidence that we got it back so quickly?" said Selina insistently.

"I am hardly in a position to say," said Edward, beginning to look uncomfortable.

Georgiana was watching her brother closely. He seemed different of late, as if changed by his own recent difficulties with the law. Being falsely accused of murder and undergoing the indignity of a stay in Newgate prison had clearly shaken his confidence, not to mention his faith in the law. It was not long ago that he was confidently putting forth his own opinions on his sister's household arrangements.

"In fact," Selina continued, looking at Edward as if she expected his support, "I wanted to discharge him, but your sister thought otherwise."

"Selina, pray, do not start all that again," said Georgiana impatiently. "I'm sure Edward has more important things to do than hear about our domestic disagreements."

"It is true I should be going to assist Rogers and the other men," said Edward, beginning to rise from his chair.

"Yes, of course," said Selina. "A very worthwhile endeavour. I do hope you catch the culprit."

"We shall do our best," said Edward.

"Although," Selina continued, "I do think you should speak to that boy. He might know something."

"I suppose it is possible," said Edward.

"Oh, really, this is such nonsense," said Georgiana.

"Is it?" asked Selina shrilly. "Is it? How do you know he didn't steal that dagger, Georgiana? If one opens one's home to criminals, one must be on one's guard." She glanced towards her other cousin with a prim, slightly smug little smile. "I'm sure Edward and Amanda do not have a highwayman among their servants."

"In that case," said Georgiana, "perhaps you would prefer to live with Edward and Amanda."

12

There was silence. Selina looked stunned. Georgiana caught a look of horror on her brother's face before he recollected himself. A desire to laugh dispelled her anger.

"Are – are you asking me to leave, Georgiana?" Selina asked in a small voice.

"Well, you don't seem very happy here."

Selina looked at Edward. He had schooled his features to polite blandness, but he remained pale.

"I see." She rose. "Very well. I shall start to pack."

Miss Knatchbull left the room with frosty dignity. Edward stared after her.

"Georgiana, you can't be serious."

Georgiana gave him her most innocent look. "Is something wrong, Edward? I thought you were fond of Selina."

"That is hardly the point."

"No? You had no trouble in suggesting she come to live with me."

"That is different," he said. "You can't live alone. It isn't proper."

"I'm sure I can find another solution."

Edward seemed incapable of speech for a moment. Georgiana waited in some amusement as he desperately cast about in his mind for some further argument.

"She could help with the children," Georgiana said.

Edward looked more horror-stricken than ever. "Georgiana, no! Besides, the way things are with Amanda…"

Georgiana had to acknowledge the truth of this. She knew things had been difficult between Edward and his wife since she had discovered his liaison with the beautiful

Lady Wickerston. Edward had only recently returned to the marital home after some weeks' sojourn at his club. There was still some tension and, Georgiana suspected, awkwardness, between husband and wife. She sighed.

"Oh, very well. I'll speak to her."

"Thank you." Edward looked genuinely grateful. He glanced towards the clock. "I must go. Rogers will be needing my help."

"So what are you going to do to trap this so-called highwayman? I can't imagine anyone would be taken in by someone parading a valuable item along the road, waiting for it to be stolen."

"No, of course not," said Edward. "But there will be men concealed on the road, watching."

Georgiana was frowning. "It still seems rather… haphazard. Even assuming a highwayman did kill Mr Polp, which is far from certain, how do you know you will get the one you want? Or do you agree with Lady Winters that any highwayman should be removed from the road?"

"They certainly cause problems. For goodness sake, Georgiana, you've been held up a couple of times yourself."

"Yes, but I've survived the experience."

"In any case, I believe the highwayman community is rather close-knit. Even if another is captured, he may well know something useful."

"There is no reason to suppose he will share it."

"He will not wish to hang for murder," said Edward.

"Is that worse than being hanged for highway robbery?" demanded Georgiana.

Edward closed his eyes in exasperation.

"Oh, never mind," she said. "You had better go and catch your highwayman before Selina comes down with her valise."

This sent Edward on his way briskly. Georgiana went upstairs to find her cousin had retired to bed, no doubt having put off her plans to move in with Edward and Amanda until the morrow.

A large part of Georgiana was tempted to let Selina go. Her presence was suffocating, and of late she had grown more petulant and demanding. However, she knew it would not do. If she chose to live unchaperoned there would certainly be gossip. Worse, there was a very real risk that society would ostracise her.

She determined to speak to Selina in the morning. In the meantime, her mind turned to the trap which was being set, ostensibly for Boyce Polp's killer, though in reality for any highwayman unlucky enough to happen along. She knew Harry worked the road on a regular basis; there was a very good chance he would be taken. While she did not imagine him guilty of Mr Polp's murder, she knew him well enough to be certain that he would decline to share any information; such blatant refusal to co-operate would result in his being hanged for his own activities, even though the authorities could not prove him guilty of murder. In any case, neither Edward nor Rogers had mentioned the possibility of a pardon for anyone who did provide useful information.

Georgiana was deep in thought as she entered her bedroom. Her instinct was to ride out and warn Harry, but under the circumstances it was likely that the Crimson Cavalier would be taken before reaching the Lucky Bell. Emily, waiting for Georgiana in her bedroom, noticed her abstraction and stood silently watching her. As Georgiana met her gaze, suspicion crept across the face of the maid.

"Miss Georgiana…"

"Emily, if you're about to suggest the Crimson Cavalier should not venture out tonight, I am in full agreement with you."

"You are?" Emily looked even more suspicious.

"Indeed I am. The Bow Street Runner, Rogers, and my brother, in view of his experience as a magistrate, are laying a trap for Boyce Polp's killer, whom they believe to be a highwayman."

"Well then – "

"I am concerned about Harry. He should be warned."

"But, Miss Georgiana, if there's a trap laid – "

"The Crimson Cavalier is likely to be taken, I know."

"Well, you can't seriously mean to go – "

"I don't," said Georgiana. "I'm going to send Tom."

"What?" Emily blinked, her disbelief evident.

"I thought it might be safer to send Tom," said Georgiana in measured tones.

Emily looked doubtful. "What if he gets picked up?"

"Why should he?" said Georgiana. "He made only one attempt at highway robbery – quite unsuccessful, I might add – and has been legally employed ever since. Edward may even recognise him as my page, though I'm afraid he does not often pay close attention to servants."

"He may also recall where the boy came from," pointed out Emily. "They might follow him."

"That is true," admitted Georgiana. "However, Tom knows the area well and he visits Harry frequently. I'm sure he can find a route which will avoid the Runner and his associates."

"How are you going to explain it to him?" asked Emily. "You're not supposed to know Harry, remember?"

"I know that," said Georgiana, "but Tom has mentioned Harry to me occasionally. I am simply doing him a good turn by warning him of the danger to his friend."

"Won't he think that odd?"

"Odd, perhaps, but not unthinkable."

Emily looked doubtful. "I suppose it might work," she said, but her voice lacked conviction.

"Besides," Georgiana continued, "I can ask him about Lady Winters's pearls. The Crimson Cavalier does not know what became of them."

"No," said Emily. "So help me, Miss Georgiana, one of these days you're going to forget which of you knows what, and then you'll be in the soup."

"Not a day any time soon, I trust," said Georgiana. "Would you mind speaking to James to find out whether Tom has gone to bed? I suspect his... unauthorised absence yesterday may have left him somewhat exhausted, so he may already have retired. If he hasn't, I'll come down and have a word with him."

Emily nodded, picking up a candle as she went. She was no more than a few minutes about her errand, returning to report that Tom was still awake.

"I asked James to send him to the small saloon," said Emily. "I said you would be down to speak to him in a few minutes."

"Thank you, Emily." Georgiana took the candle her maid had put down and retraced her steps, along the landing and down the stairs of the near-dark, silent house.

Tom was waiting for her. From his sudden jolt upright, she assumed he had been sitting on the edge of a chair. Judging by the odd angle at which his shirt sat on his shoulders, Georgiana suspected he had been about to go to bed. She smiled and apologised for summoning him at such a late hour. Tom's eyes widened in surprise.

"I'm sure you are thinking of your bed," said Georgiana.

"However, I thought you might like to know of something I had heard which could affect your friend. Harry, isn't it?"

Tom nodded, his eyes creasing together in puzzlement. "Yes, miss."

Georgiana considered how to phrase her information, in order to sound convincing.

"You may have been told that I had a visit this evening from a Bow Street Runner. He is looking for Mr Boyce Polp's killer."

"Did he think he'd find him here, miss?" Tom's tone was truculent, but a look from Georgiana subdued him. "Beg pardon, miss."

"It doesn't matter why he came," said Georgiana. "However, he mentioned that he and a party of men will be out on the road tonight with the aim of trapping the highwayman they believe responsible."

"Harry ain't no killer, miss. Nor's the Crimson Cavalier."

"Possibly not," said Georgiana, grateful for his loyalty. "Nevertheless, these men intend to take into custody any highwayman they catch on the road." She paused. "It occurred to me you might want to warn some of your friends."

Tom looked up, his eyes growing even wider as they met hers. "Really, miss?"

Georgiana nodded. "Yes, if you wish. But slip out quietly, please, Tom, and not a word to anyone."

"No, of course not. Thank you, miss."

"Very well."

As the boy was leaving the room, a thought came into Georgiana's mind. "Tom…"

He turned on the threshold. "Yes, miss?"

"It would be as well if you were not mistaken for a high-wayman yourself. You wouldn't want to caught in the trap."

"No, miss."

The boy went on his way, and Georgiana retired to bed. She slept little, and found herself listening out for his return. It would look odd to demonstrate her concern for Harry by quizzing Tom as soon as he arrived home, but as well as care for the older man's safety, she felt a certain anxiety for Tom himself.

Eventually, she heard his approaching footsteps outside in the square, receding as he went round to the back of the house. Relief at the knowledge that he was safe allowed her to doze, though her curiosity about how he had fared kept her from sleeping soundly. A very short time seemed to have passed before Emily stood in the doorway, asking if she was ready for her chocolate.

Georgiana was pensive when her maid returned, her mind divided between the outcome of Tom's mission and the need to speak to her cousin. It was the latter concern which gave her greater unease. She would gladly have dispensed with it and allowed her cousin to sweep out of the door in a dudgeon to take up residence with Edward and Amanda. Indeed, were it not for the current fragile state of her brother's marriage, she might have given way to this impulse, even though Edward would never have forgiven her! As it was, she determined to speak to her cousin over breakfast.

Emily's voice intruded on her reverie. "Miss? Are you all right?"

Georgiana looked up and found the maid gazing at her with some concern. She blinked and roused herself. "What? Oh, yes, I'm quite well, Emily. I beg your pardon. My mind was elsewhere."

Emily poured chocolate into a china cup from the long-spouted pot. "So I see, miss. Can I help at all?"

"I don't think so, thank you. Unless you wish to speak to

my cousin and persuade her not to go live with my brother and his wife?"

Emily's expression spoke more eloquently than any words.

"I thought not," said Georgiana. She groaned. "Breakfast will be a long affair."

In fact, Georgiana partook of a solitary meal. There was no sign of Selina. As far as the parlourmaid was aware her cousin had not left the house; she was therefore either sulking in her room, or making preparations to depart for Edward's home. Georgiana thought savagely that it was probably both. In any case, it was clear that any move towards reconciliation would have to come from her; she would have to take the initiative and approach Selina in her room. Georgiana found this irritating, but nonetheless realised she had little option. However, she was disinclined to treat the matter as urgent; first she wanted to know the outcome of Tom's nocturnal expedition. She summoned James and asked him to send the boy to her.

"Yes, miss," said James. "Er… There is one other thing, miss."

"Oh? What's that?" asked Georgiana, peering into the teapot.

"Miss Winters has called, miss."

Georgiana looked up. "What? On her own? Show her in at once."

Louisa entered a couple of minutes later, looking charming but gloomy, her pretty features almost funereal in contrast to the jaunty pale blue bonnet which framed them.

"Good morning, Louisa," said Georgiana. "Would you like some tea? Or perhaps you'd prefer coffee?"

"No, thank you," said Louisa dolefully.

"Whatever is the matter?" Georgiana looked at her friend

in some concern.

Louisa gave a sigh and sat down in the chair Georgiana indicated. "It's Miss Trent," she said in a woeful voice. "She's not leaving."

"I beg your pardon?"

"She's not leaving." Louisa's gloom seemed to increase with every word. "I thought she was only to be there while Mama was away, but it seems she is to stay for a while." Louisa gazed dismally at her lap for a moment or two. "It's just as if I was a child again," she said petulantly at last.

"I daresay it will only be for a few days. Your mother will hardly want to re-engage Miss Trent as a governess at this stage in your life. I imagine she is just being hospitable, especially since she arrived home unexpectedly early. It might seem uncharitable to send her away sooner than she had anticipated."

"Mama is not given to an excess of hospitality," said Louisa.

The door opened suddenly and Selina stood on the threshold, her expression fixed and mutinous, a dark cloak around her shoulders.

"Good morning, Miss Knatchbull," said Louisa.

"Good morning." Miss Knatchbull looked stonily towards her cousin. "I am ready to go, Georgiana."

Georgiana glanced towards Louisa. Selina could not have chosen a worse time.

"Selina, this is not necessary. Why don't you sit down and have a cup of tea?"

"No, thank you. I trust you will not object that I have ordered the carriage."

"No, of course not, but – "

"Thank you." Miss Knatchbull turned towards Louisa. "Good day to you, Miss Winters."

"Good day," said Louisa, her voice as bemused as her face.

Miss Knatchbull turned and left without another word. It was Georgiana's turn to sigh. Louisa glanced towards her, curiosity in her eyes. "Is something wrong, Georgiana?"

Georgiana leaned her elbows on the table, her hand covering her eyes. She knew she should not discuss the previous evening's altercation with Louisa, but it was difficult to avoid doing so.

"I'm afraid my cousin and I had a disagreement after you left last night," said Georgiana. "She has decided to... spend some time at my brother's home."

Louisa looked startled and a touch embarrassed. "Oh. I'm very sorry, Georgiana." The implications of this suddenly dawned on her. "So you will not have a chaperone?"

"No."

A mischievous light came into Louisa's eyes. "Perhaps you could take Miss Trent in."

"Very amusing," said Georgiana. "I'm sure that won't be necessary. I expect it to be a temporary situation. I don't imagine it will be convenient for my brother and sister-in-law to accommodate my cousin for more than a few days."

Louisa said nothing, but watched her friend closely. It was a few moments before she spoke and then on a different subject. "Actually, Georgiana, I was wondering whether you'd like to meet Charlie."

13

Georgiana stared. "By Charlie, I assume you mean Sir Charles Ross?"

Louisa nodded.

"I thought you had not been in contact with him since your friend's death."

"I sent him a note this morning," said Louisa. She suddenly looked anxious. "You won't tell Mama, will you?"

"No, of course not," said Georgiana. "But Louisa, I think you had better tell me what you said in this note? You didn't mention the dagger?"

Louisa shook her head vigorously. "No, I thought it might upset him. I thought it would be better to tell him face to face. I just said there was a matter of particular importance about which I wished to speak to him."

"But, Louisa, we can hardly call at his house. How would it look, two unmarried ladies calling at a gentleman's residence? I dread to think what your mother would say."

"I have already thought of that," said Louisa. "If we go for a drive or a walk, we may encounter him by accident."

"I see."

"My maid is outside." Louisa seemed anxious to reassure Georgiana. "And we can bring yours if you are concerned."

Georgiana heard her cousin's voice in the hall, followed by the sound of the front door closing. She sighed. It seemed best to let Selina go her own way for the moment. Smiling, she turned her attention back to her friend. "Very well. Let us go for a walk."

Within a few minutes, the two young ladies were setting off down the road with their maids walking sedately behind them. It was not until they were clear of the square that Georgiana thought to inquire what excuse Louisa had given to her mother for this visit.

"I told her I was coming to see you, and that we might go shopping."

"She didn't suggest you bring Miss Trent?"

"Well," said Louisa, a guilty flush tingeing her cheeks. "I had the feeling she was about to suggest it but I told her my maid would accompany me."

"Well, as long as she was satisfied with that."

"Why wouldn't she be?" said Louisa. "I am doing nothing improper." Her brows knitted together studiously. "It seems as if Miss Trent is there to spy on me. Even with Mama at home, she is still very inquisitive about what I am doing. It's quite unbearable."

"Yes, I can imagine," said Georgiana. "I can't tell you how grateful I am to have such a treasure offered to me." She smiled, to lighten the mood.

Louisa returned her smile.

"Was Sir Charles surprised to get your note?" asked Georgiana.

"I'm not sure. I think he may have been. He did send a reply." Louisa hesitated before continuing. "I wondered if he would feel uneasy seeing me after Barbara died. Whether it would remind him too much of her. That was why I didn't get in touch with him."

"That's understandable. And very thoughtful of you, to consider his feelings."

"Do you think so? Thank you." Louisa fell silent for a few moments, then stole a sideways glance at Georgiana. "Do you know whether your brother and that Bow Street Runner managed to catch their highwayman?"

"No, I haven't seen Edward this morning," said Georgiana,

recalling that she hadn't seen Tom either. "I daresay we shall hear more soon enough."

Louisa did not respond immediately. There was still a reflective expression on her face. "You'd met the Bow Street Runner before, hadn't you?" she asked.

Georgiana looked surprised. "Yes, when he came to speak to me about Mr Polp's death."

"Oh. I thought he was an acquaintance of your brother."

"Well, yes, that's quite true," acknowledged Georgiana. "My brother mentioned that they were acquainted when he became a magistrate. However, I had not met Mr Rogers before."

"He's not how I thought a Runner would look," said Louisa.

"Oh?"

"No. He seems quite – quite gentleman-like, doesn't he? I thought he might be rather vulgar."

Georgiana looked at her friend curiously, surprised at this speculation over the Bow Street Runner. She wondered how Lady Winters would view it. "He seems a man of sound good sense, certainly," she said. "He would need to be, of course, to investigate criminal activity."

"True," said Louisa, in a faraway voice. "Do you think he will need to talk to me again?"

Georgiana glanced at Louisa in some amusement. When they had first met, the girl had demonstrated a fascination for highwaymen, the Crimson Cavalier in particular. Georgiana would have been more than a little relieved to see this attraction transferred to someone else, but could not imagine Lady Winters looking with approbation on an interest her daughter might show in a Bow Street Runner.

Her friend had slowed down. A young man was walking towards them.

"Hello, Charlie, I mean, Sir Charles," said Louisa, a shy smile appearing on her face.

The young man removed his hat at their approach. He had dark hair and eyes, and a pleasant, round face which suggested an open temperament. He took hold of Louisa's hand and bowed over it, smiling at her in an affable manner.

"Charlie is quite good enough," he said. "We are old friends, after all, though I have been rather remiss about it of late."

"My mother doesn't approve of me calling you Charlie," said Louisa matter-of-factly. She turned towards Georgiana. "May I introduce my friend, Miss Grey? Georgiana, this is Sir Charles Ross."

Sir Charles extended his hand to Georgiana, expressing himself pleased to meet her. Turning, he fell into step between the two young ladies, their maids still walking behind.

"Why did you need to speak with me, Loui – Miss Winters?" Sir Charles asked, after the usual civil inquiries after her own and her mother's health.

Louisa cast a glance towards Georgiana, as if seeking help. It occurred to Georgiana that she should have realised Louisa would find this conversation more difficult than she had expected.

The girl tried again. "You see, the fact is, you may get a visit from a Bow Street Runner."

Sir Charles looked surprised. "Oh?"

Louisa nodded. "It's about Mr Polp. Did you hear that he died at Mrs Milton's party a few days ago?"

Sir Charles stopped swinging the cane he was carrying. "Yes. I understand he had been attacked before he arrived. It sounds a very tragic business."

"It was," said Louisa, clearly uncomfortable. "But the

dagger which killed him – I recognised it, Charlie. It was that ornamental one you lost ages ago."

"*What?*"

Sir Charles stopped walking, forcing the two ladies to stop beside him. Louisa tugged his arm. He began to walk again, slowly, almost absently. "I thought I had simply mislaid it."

"How can you mislay something which was on display on a wall?" Louisa pointed out reasonably.

"If it was taken down for cleaning…"

Louisa looked at him as if questioning his sanity.

"The prevailing thought seems to be that it was taken by a footpad or housebreaker, Sir Charles," said Georgiana. "Is that your own view?"

"I suppose so," he said in a voice which lacked conviction. "Though it seems very odd that none of my servants mentioned that any of the doors or windows had been disturbed."

"I see." Georgiana guessed from his manner that he did not wish to admit the possibility that a house guest had taken it.

"I daresay it was taken down for cleaning, and went astray." Sir Charles's manner grew more solemn. "Now it has been used to kill Mr Polp. How horrible."

"You're not to blame, Charlie," said Louisa.

"No, but still…" He gave a tragic little smile. "Poor Mr Polp. Such a friendly, outgoing man. It was a shocking thing to happen."

"Was he a friend of yours, Sir Charles?" asked Georgiana.

"No, I wouldn't say that. An acquaintance, merely. Good company, certainly. I met him at a few functions, card parties, that sort of thing."

"I didn't know you were fond of cards, Charlie," said Louisa.

"I'm not, particularly. But it's a way of passing the time, meeting with friends, you know, since…"

"Yes, I know." Louisa's voice was gentle.

Georgiana looked at her friend in surprised admiration. Fond as she was of Louisa, she usually thought of her as somewhat capricious. Now she was demonstrating a level of sympathy and sensitivity beyond her years.

"I believe Mr Polp was rather fond of card parties," said Sir Charles. "He found them amusing. If you're looking for his friends, that fellow Lewis something was occasionally with him. What was his name? Lewis… Lewis Brook – Brookwood? No, Brookstone, Lewis Brookstone."

"That vulgar banker fellow?" said Louisa. "Isn't he quite old?"

Sir Charles laughed.

"He might be near forty but he's hardly a relic. A little older than your cousin. By the way, how is Mr Lakesby?"

"Oh, Max is very well," said Louisa cheerfully. "We dined at Miss Grey's last night, with Mama, of course."

"I hope you had a pleasant evening," said Sir Charles.

"Oh, yes," said Louisa. "Though the Bow Street Runner came while we were there. That's when he showed me the dagger and I told him it was yours. I hope that's all right, Charlie."

"Yes, of course."

"I don't want to get you into trouble," said Louisa.

Sir Charles shrugged. "Why should you? No, please don't worry, it's perfectly fine."

"Sir Charles, I understand you were unable to attend Mr Milton's party as your mother was unwell," said Georgiana. "I hope she is improved."

"Yes, thank you, Miss Grey. Nothing serious, I am glad to say, but it was a matter for concern."

"Yes, of course," said Georgiana.

"I beg your pardon," he said. "I should have asked where you ladies are going? I should be pleased to escort you."

"Oh. Thank you," said Louisa. "We hadn't really thought, just some air. I wanted to get out of the house, away from – oh."

Louisa stopped dead suddenly. Her two companions followed the direction of her eyes. Georgiana's own widened. Some distance away was Miss Trent, dressed in an unremarkable tan cloak and matching cap. She seemed unaware that she was under observation, and was engaged in earnest conversation with a young man. Holding his own cap in his hands, he looked to be in his twenties, fresh faced, with dark hair falling over his forehead.

"Well, imagine that," said Louisa. "Miss Trent is having a secret assignation. Do you think he is her lover?"

"Good grief," Georgiana laughed. "Very likely he is a relative or some acquaintance from her home."

"Yes, I'm sure you are right," said Louisa, a twinge of disappointment in her voice. "It does seem shockingly dull, though."

"Poor Miss Trent," said Georgiana. "Really, Louisa, you should not say such things."

"I should dearly like to know who that young man is," said Louisa. "Shall we go and bid her good day?"

"Good heavens, no," said Georgiana, taking hold of Louisa's arm as she began to step forward, surprised that she seemed inclined to carry through her suggestion.

Louisa looked ready to resist.

"Think how odd Miss Trent would find it," said Georgiana.

Sir Charles looked puzzled. Louisa hesitated, then shrugged. "Oh, I suppose that's true. Miss Trent would probably not tell us anything, anyway." The gleam of mischief reappeared in her eye. "Perhaps I shall ask her later."

Georgiana shared her friend's curiosity, but nonetheless took hold of Louisa's elbow and propelled her forward. Miss Trent did not notice them as they passed, but they caught the sound of the young man's voice. This time it was Georgiana who turned her head.

Louisa looked at her. "Georgiana?"

"It's nothing," said Georgiana, slowly resuming her step beside her companions. "I just thought for a moment – oh, never mind, it's nothing." How could she possibly explain to Louisa and Sir Charles Ross that the young gentleman with Miss Trent sounded exactly like one of those she had overheard on the highway discussing Boyce Polp's death?

"Louisa, if you have no specific destination in mind, perhaps we should return to my house and have some tea. Sir Charles, would you care to join us?"

Sir Charles accepted rather diffidently, with a fleeting glance at Louisa. She cheerfully agreed this would be a good idea, and they began to retrace their steps. Conversation revolved around fairly ordinary matters as they walked, with references to mutual acquaintances whom they had seen of late, and who had attended what party. Boyce Polp was not mentioned. Georgiana's own mind was turning over the scene they had just witnessed, considering ways in which she might learn more about the acquaintance of her friend's former governess.

James showed the party into the drawing room on their arrival at Georgiana's home, and instructed the parlour-maid to serve tea. However, as he helped Georgiana out of her wrap, he advised her that Tom begged the favour of a word with her.

"Oh?" Georgiana raised a quizzical eyebrow. "Tom said that?"

James suppressed a grin. "Perhaps those were not quite the words he used," he acknowledged. "Nevertheless, he is very anxious to speak to you."

Georgiana glanced towards Louisa and Sir Charles. "You would recommend that I do so now, James?"

"That's not for me to say, miss. However," James continued in a cautious tone, "he has been very excitable all morning."

"Very well. Send him to the small saloon, would you?"

"Yes, miss."

Georgiana moved just inside the doorway of the drawing room to speak to her guests.

"I beg your pardon, will you excuse me for a few minutes? There is a household matter in need of my attention."

"Oh, yes, of course," said Louisa.

"Tea is on the way. I shall join you presently."

Tom did not keep Georgiana waiting long. Although he stood still before her, in the way he had been taught was proper for a page, Georgiana sensed nervous energy about him. She wondered whether he would ever grow into the typical impassive servant, able to mask his emotions and maintain a bland exterior at all times. A part of her hoped he would retain his liveliness and originality. She looked at him now, his eyes shining with eagerness and she reflected that she was no less anxious to hear what he had to say than he was to say it.

"I understand you wanted to speak with me, Tom," said Georgiana. "What can I do for you?"

Now that the moment was upon him, Tom seemed oddly hesitant. He began shuffling his feet. "Well, you see, miss," he said at last, "I thought you'd like to know, my friend Harry…"

"Yes?"

"Well, he's safe, miss. At least, he were last night. Kept

out of the Runner's way, said he'd go to ground."

"That's probably wise of him," said Georgiana.

"There is one other thing, though, miss. Your friend's gewgaw, the necklace you mentioned – Harry said he'd seen it before."

"Really?"

Tom nodded.

"That's right, miss. He said he'd seen the clasp before, said it was one of a kind."

"Good heavens." Georgiana had no recollection of either Louisa or her mother mentioning any previous occasion when the pearls had been stolen. "Did he say when he'd seen them?"

"No, not that, miss. He said it belonged to some old sweetheart, so he thought he'd give it back to her."

14

Georgiana stared at the boy.

"Something wrong, miss?"

"No. No, nothing, thank you," said Georgiana. "Are you sure that's what your friend said?"

"Yes, miss. I'm sure 'cos I remember thinking it was a rum go. Never knew Harry had a sweetheart."

Georgiana reflected there was probably a great deal about Harry that neither Tom nor the Crimson Cavalier knew. She dismissed Tom and returned to her guests in the drawing room. She could not help but wonder whether Tom, or Harry for that matter, had made a mistake. Another possibility was that Harry had found it amusing to lead the boy on. The notion that Harry could ever have been romantically involved with Lady Winters seemed preposterous. No, he must have been joking. At most, he could have seen her and admired her from afar, but even that seemed to stretch the bounds of possibility. How much attention could he have paid to someone he met briefly on the road, and at the point of a pistol? This was even supposing that, at the age Louisa was now, her ladyship was in possession of beauty and warmth to equal her daughter's.

"Georgiana?" Louisa was looking at her in concern.

"Miss Grey, are you quite well?" Sir Charles inquired.

Georgiana gave herself a mental shake, and smiled at her guests. "Yes. Yes, thank you. A small domestic crisis… I'm afraid it has rather stolen my attention. Oh, dear," she added, as Louisa approached her holding out a cup of tea. "I really must beg your pardon. It's quite remiss of me to leave you to fend for yourselves in this way."

Both her visitors protested, and Georgiana turned the conversation to more mundane topics than the one in her head. But her mind could not let go of the image Tom had placed there. The seed he had planted began to develop, and one question turned over and over in her head: what if it were true?

Georgiana's eyes rested on Louisa, and she thought of the girl's infatuation for the Crimson Cavalier and Lady Winters's great antagonism towards highwaymen. She had always found it rather strange that her ladyship had such a keen, albeit hostile, interest in gentlemen of the road. However, if she had endured unwelcome attention from one in her youth, or, heaven forfend, had suffered a disappointed love affair, it was not beyond belief that she would turn against them. Georgiana wanted to shake her head to clear away what seemed such a far-fetched thought. Despite their friendship – or possibly because of it – she would find it difficult to question Louisa about the matter. Quite apart from the impropriety, it was unlikely Louisa would know anything about it. Georgiana had no doubt the girl would laugh away the notion of her mother having any personal interest in highwaymen, even in her youth.

Sir Charles rose to take his leave, thanking Georgiana for her hospitality. He turned to Louisa and offered to escort her home. As she nodded acceptance and stood up, James entered the room. He apologised for the interruption and informed Georgiana that her brother had called. Before her visitors had time to say farewell, Edward himself pushed past the footman and came into the room. The tightness around his mouth was sufficient to speed his sister's guests on their way with more haste than convention decreed.

Georgiana had no doubt about the cause of his anxiety.

"Hello, Edward," she said cheerfully when they were alone. "Would you like some tea?"

"I don't want any confounded tea," he said. "What the devil do you mean by sending Selina to us?"

"I didn't," said Georgiana.

"No? What about that business last night? That suggestion of yours that she might be happier with Amanda and me? What was that if not sending her to us?"

"I'm sorry, Edward. Come, you heard that conversation. It was a momentary anger."

"Well, she's taken it literally enough. She certainly wasted no time before packing her bags. I thought you were going to put a stop to it."

"I tried."

"Not very hard, I suspect."

Georgiana could not argue with this. "I barely saw her this morning," she said, "and by the time I did, she was ready to leave and Louisa had called. I'm sorry, Edward, but do try not to worry about it. She will calm down sooner or later."

"That's easy for you to say. She hasn't taken up residence in your home."

Georgiana suppressed a laugh at the irony of his statement, trying and failing to give him a look of sympathy. As she caught his eye, he shook his head and gave a rueful smile, rubbing his hand over his forehead.

"Oh, Georgiana, she is impossible."

"Now you know how I have felt all this time."

Edward made no answer to this.

"Who was that gentleman with Miss Winters?" he asked after a brief pause.

"Sir Charles Ross. He is an acquaintance of Louisa's."

Edward nodded absently.

"More importantly, how did your expedition go last night? Did you catch any highwaymen?"

Edward shook his head. "No. The fellow must have gone to ground."

"What do you and Mr Rogers plan to do now?"

"I don't know. We could try again but I suspect the same thing will happen. I believe there is a tavern which is something of a thieves' haunt, but it's no use going there; no one is likely to volunteer information." Edward paused, looking thoughtful. "I think Rogers is going to speak to Mr Polp's acquaintances. I can't interfere but I find it difficult to believe he was killed by someone he knew. He was such a pleasant fellow, very well liked."

"Yes. But Edward, one never knows what lies behind the civility."

Edward looked at her oddly. "What are you going to do about Selina?" he asked after another pause.

Georgiana considered the matter for a few moments. "Louisa suggested her former governess could come here to act as chaperone, but I'm not sure it would be the best arrangement," she said blandly.

Edward glared, and Georgiana laughed. "I'm sorry about Selina, Edward, truly I am. I know she must already be driving you and Amanda distracted."

"It is not that ..."

"Oh yes it is," said Georgiana. "I will speak to her, but I think it had better wait until tomorrow. Can you bear her for one night?"

"Very well." Edward rose and kissed his sister's cheek. "Thank you, Georgiana."

As soon as he had departed, Georgiana went to her room and sent for Emily. The maid began to inquire what she proposed to wear for dinner that evening, but she interrupted. "You'd better sit down, Emily. I have news, and it may take a while."

She proceeded to pass on the information Tom had brought, and went on to recount what had taken place during her walk with Louisa – including their encounter with Miss Trent, and the familiar voice of that lady's young male acquaintance. By the time her recital was finished, Emily was staring at her open-mouthed.

"I think the Crimson Cavalier should pay a visit to the Lucky Bell this evening," said Georgiana. "I'd like to know a bit more about Harry's activities."

"But if he's gone into hiding, it's likely he won't be there," said Emily.

"Possibly," said Georgiana. "However, the Crimson Cavalier is known to be a friend of Harry's. If Cedric and his patrons trust him, they will let him know where Harry is to be found."

Emily looked dubious. "How can you ask him about these pearls, Miss Grey? It wasn't the Crimson Cavalier that Tom told about them."

"I know. Since Harry apparently had no qualms about telling Tom, I'm hoping he will prove willing to share the story with me as well." Georgiana gave her head a little shake. "Of course, he may not be willing to answer questions about Lady Winters, assuming what Tom said is true."

"Hard to believe that her ladyship could be an old sweetheart of a highwayman. Begging your pardon, miss, I know it's not my place to say so."

"I agree with you, Emily. It is hard to believe. Lady Winters's past is none of my business, though it could explain her vigorous antagonism towards highwaymen," said Georgiana, almost to herself.

"What do you mean, miss?" asked Emily.

"Well, I think there are two possibilities. Lady Winters had the attentions of a highwayman, let us say Harry, and did not return his regard, possibly considered him forward, or – "

"Or?"

"Or she did have some affection for him and was let down."

"That could make her bitter," observed Emily.

"Yes, it could. I can imagine Lady Winters carrying a grudge."

"So all highwaymen are villains. You're not going to blackmail her, are you, miss?" asked Emily with a grin.

"No, of course not. However, being able to remind her ladyship of – er – more tender feelings towards a highwayman could be useful. Remembering how she felt herself could give her another viewpoint."

Emily nodded. "Yes, I suppose so." Looking towards Georgiana, she changed the subject. "You really think visiting the Lucky Bell is a good idea?"

"Of course," Georgiana said positively. "Harry is no killer. I would like to know if he saw anything: those two men for instance. In fact," she continued, going to the bedside drawer and rummaging around, "I'll bring him these trinkets which the Crimson Cavalier took from one of the men." She put the items she retrieved into the black velvet bag which Emily had already laid on the bed.

"I won't bother changing for dinner, Emily," she said. "I shall be alone this evening, and I don't plan to linger. I shall retire early."

"Yes, miss. I'll ensure everything is ready."

Georgiana went back downstairs, leaving Emily preparing the Crimson Cavalier's attire for the evening. She occupied herself with domestic matters for the rest of the afternoon, and did not linger over her evening meal. She retired to her room as soon as she had finished eating, and the household appeared to follow her example. The house fell quiet earlier than usual, and it was not late when the Crimson Cavalier slipped down the stairs and out through the back door en route for the Lucky Bell.

The tavern was crowded but Georgiana could see no sign of Harry. As she cast her eyes around the taproom, she spotted Cedric, the proprietor, standing behind the bar. With a slight movement of his head, he beckoned her over.

"You looking for Harry, lad?"

Georgiana nodded, looking at him intently through the small gap between her tricorne hat and the dark mask covering most of her face.

"Come through here," Cedric said, gesturing to a door which led to a private parlour. "Harry's gone to ground," he said, closing the door behind her.

Georgiana kept her eyes on her host, watching him closely as he walked across the room. Her own world would be scandalised if it became known that she was in a room alone with a man.

"Young Tom came to see him last night," Cedric continued, "told him there was a Runner after him, some sort of trap, I think."

"You heard them?" Georgiana asked, surprised that either Harry or Tom would let themselves be overheard.

"No. It was Harry told me – said he'd have to disappear for a while."

"I see." She was not surprised to hear this, but it was vexing that she had missed him.

"You know about the Runner's trap, lad?"

"I heard something about it," said Georgiana. "Looking for the killer of that gentleman who was stabbed, I believe. But I think they'd pick up anyone they found on the road."

"Aye, they'd do that," said Cedric grimly.

"I heard a couple of fellows talking on the road a few nights ago, as if they knew something about the killing."

"Did you now? Well, that's interesting. Still, you'd best keep out of it," Cedric said, unconsciously echoing Emily's cautious sentiment.

"I wouldn't want to see Harry taken," said Georgiana.

"No, nor would anyone else. He's well liked, a good bloke. Still, you don't want to be taken yourself," he said.

Georgiana agreed, and thanked Cedric for his concern.

"Another odd thing," she said. "Harry gave me some trinkets he'd taken from the lady Tom works for. He asked me to give them to Tom to return them."

"That is odd," said Cedric. "Mind, Harry has a heart of gold and he's glad Tom's had a bit of luck. We all are. Don't think the lad would do well on the High Toby."

"Probably not," said Georgiana. "Anyway, the odd thing is, I heard there was another piece as well – he gave that to someone else. Said he'd recognised it as belonging to an old sweetheart."

Cedric began to chuckle silently. "He's always had an eye for a pretty woman – but a nob? Well, well. The old devil."

Georgiana had difficulty in picturing the redoubtable Lady Winters as a pretty woman, and wondered what she had been like in her young days, before age and mother-hood intervened.

"You think it was true?" asked Georgiana.

"Who's to say?" replied Cedric.

"Well, of course it's nobody's business but his," said Georgiana. She shook her black velvet bag. "I had a few pieces I wanted him to look at but they'll keep."

"I'll let him know if he comes in."

"I got them from one of the men I heard talking on the road."

Cedric laughed again.

"You're a brave lad, I'll say that."

Georgiana bade him farewell and went on her way. She cast another quick glance across the taproom as she went through, looking for signs of the two men she had overheard on the road, or anyone who could have been connected to Edward and the Runner. As far as she could see, the tavern was occupied by patrons she had seen there on previous visits. Georgiana knew that excessive curiosity would raise suspicion. Nevertheless, she felt dissatisfied to be leaving with so little information.

Someone waved at her: a man she had seen occasionally playing cards with Harry. She could not resist the opportunity to further her knowledge, and found herself walking across the taproom towards him.

"Hello, lad," the man said at her approach. "Leaving already?"

Georgiana nodded. "Yes. I had some business, but I can't take care of it tonight."

"Yes. Harry's away."

"Is he all right?" asked Georgiana. She lowered her voice. "I heard a Runner was looking for him, for that killing."

"Aye. Young Tom came in to warn him. He'd heard something." The man rubbed the stubble on his chin. "Good that Harry has such good friends. Have a drink, lad?"

"No, thank you," said Georgiana, nevertheless seating herself at the small wooden table. It rocked to one side as she leant her arm on it. "I heard some fellows talking about the killing," she remarked casually, "on the road."

"People will always talk."

"This didn't sound like gossip," said Georgiana. "More like a personal interest."

"Really?" the man said with a lift to his eyebrows. "Careless, that."

"I thought so."

The man did not answer immediately. His face was screwed into a frown of concentration.

"I wouldn't want to see Harry hang," said Georgiana at last.

"No." The man continued to sit in silent thought for a moment or two. "Did hear something interesting from old Ben," he said eventually.

"Oh?" Georgiana knew old Ben was the 'dealer' who purchased many of the items appropriated on the road.

"He gets a tip now and again from some of the nobs," explained Harry's friend. "They offer a reward sometimes, if they've lost something."

Georgiana nodded.

"Well, Harry had stopped this cove and relieved him of a few baubles. Said he didn't stab him, though," he added hastily.

"No."

"He did manage to take some of his booty to old Ben. Well, the old man told me he recognised one of the trinkets. Some nob had asked him about it a week or two earlier."

"A week or two?"

The man nodded.

"Aye. Not the cove who was stabbed, though. It was some other cove as was asking."

15

Georgiana rode home slowly, more confused than ever. She knew she had done well to obtain any information at all from a patron of the Lucky Bell, but the information she had been given made little sense. How did Boyce Polp come to be in possession of a trinket which someone else had been inquiring after some time earlier? Could it have been a gift? If that were the case, the giver must have secured its return remarkably quickly before presenting it to Mr Polp. Unless Mr Polp had purchased it himself from some source of dubious legality. Either way, it was ironic that he should have lost the item to a highwayman. Georgiana wondered who had been the original owner. She was not sure whether or not it was important, and clearly Harry's friend would not have been able to tell her.

Shaking her head to clear her thoughts, Georgiana urged Princess forward. The mare increased her speed to a canter, and Georgiana looked about her, ensuring the quiet of the night was not deceptive. She saw no sign of pursuit or travellers but remained alert for sounds as she guided Princess towards the road and home.

Her mind remained fully occupied as she tried to make sense of the volume of information which had assailed it in a short time. This evening's developments aside, she was concerned about Harry, and wanted to help him if she could; and her conscience was niggling about Selina. Despite the words she had spoken in anger, Georgiana had not meant to drive her cousin from the house. It was too late to call at Edward's house this evening, but she knew she should do so first thing in the morning.

Georgiana slowed Princess so she could look up and down the length of the road. The night was clear and still seemed quiet, but after a few moments Georgiana's alert ears caught a faint thrumming. Reining Princess back, she turned her head and strained to hear. Gradually the sound grew louder, sending a pronounced, steady vibration through the road. Georgiana turned Princess's head and guided her slowly into the cover of the trees. She ensured her mask was secure and sat watching the road, holding her breath and keeping her eyes steadily focused. Within a few minutes, the hum built up to the unmistakeable sound of carriage wheels. Georgiana slowly drew her pistol.

Her patience was soon rewarded as a travelling carriage pulled into view. It was substantial and well-built, the sort of vehicle that was capable of covering long distances. Being held up by a highwayman would not be a welcome end to a long journey, but Georgiana suppressed this twinge of conscience and moved forward with her pistol levelled. The coach pulled up.

The coachman raised his hands and swore, holding his whip upright in his right hand. "What the devil is going on?" demanded an angry voice from inside the coach. A man's head appeared through the window, eyes narrowed, peering through the darkness. As it disappeared back into the carriage, Georgiana caught a repetition of the coachman's oath.

Something familiar about the man's voice, muffled though it was, caught Georgiana's attention. She walked Princess forward to the door of the coach, the pistol steady in her black-gloved hand.

"Good evening," she said in a low drawl unlike her own voice. Through the window of the coach she saw an angry-looking man seated next to a young lady. The hood of her cloak was over her head and her eyes were wide with alarm. The lady's face, too, was vaguely familiar, but Georgiana could not immediately recollect where she might have seen it. She shrugged off the thought for the moment; it was possible the couple had been at one of the society squeezes at which she herself had also been present.

"Your valuables, please?" Georgiana requested politely.

"Now look here," the man began, in the manner of the indignant traveller which Georgiana heard all too frequently.

"Please, Adam." The young lady's voice was a plea. She was removing her bracelet with some alacrity, an air of panic about her.

The man continued to glare at Georgiana, then glanced towards his companion. With a shrug and a grunt, he removed a ring, then pulled off his cravat pin, handing both to Georgiana with as ill a grace as she had ever seen. The young lady, for her part, offered her bracelet almost timidly, then put her hands to her neck where she fumbled with the clasp of her necklace. Georgiana took pity on her.

"Pray do not trouble yourself, ma'am," she said. She held up the bracelet. "This will be sufficient."

"Oh. Oh, very well. Thank you." The young lady slid her hands down from her neck and folded them in her lap. She gave a shy smile. "Thank you so much."

The man snorted, muttering something which his companion did not seem to notice and Georgiana ignored.

Georgiana pulled Princess back from the road and waved the coachman forward. She waited until the carriage was out of sight before moving Princess towards home.

Emily was waiting when she arrived. The maid looked disapproving when she produced the items given to the Crimson Cavalier. Georgiana simply shrugged, offering no justification. As she undressed, she told Emily what she

143

had learned. The maid grimaced as she heard about the prior claimant to what Harry had stolen from Mr Polp. "That's an odd thing," she said.

"Yes." Georgiana nodded. "It all seems very odd." She fell silent, deep in thought.

"I shall have to go to Edward's first thing in the morning," she said at last.

"You need me to do something for you, miss?" Emily said.

"Well, yes, you or James. I am not sure which of you would be the better placed."

"Is it to do with the man you saw with Miss Winters's governess?"

Georgiana nodded. "The trouble is, one can hardly approach Miss Trent and ask her about a man we saw speaking to her on a public road."

"No, miss, and I can't imagine James would have much luck trying to turn Miss Trent up sweet. She looked very solemn, besides being so much older. She'd be bound to suspect something."

"Yes, that it true," said Georgiana.

"I could talk to Miss Winters's maid," offered Emily, "see if she knows anything. She might be able to introduce me to the governess."

Georgiana looked doubtful.

"I'm not sure Miss Trent would welcome an introduction, or be eager to discuss her personal business…"

"With a servant," finished Emily bluntly. "Probably not, but someone in the household may be able to tell me who the man is."

Georgiana was obliged to be satisfied with this; she suspected Emily did not want to be questioned too closely about the methods she planned to employ. She lay awake for a while, her own mind occupied by her impending visit to Edward's house, and the best way to present an olive branch to Selina.

Georgiana set out for her brother's home at about ten o'clock the next morning, sitting in her carriage dressed sedately in a pale morning dress, hands folded demurely in her lap.

When the butler admitted her, Georgiana was shown to the drawing room, where she was joined almost immediately by Edward's wife.

"Georgiana, I'm very pleased to see you," Amanda said, coming forward with hands outstretched.

Her sister-in-law kissed her cheek, and Georgiana returned the embrace. "Amanda, I'm so sorry about all of this. Has it been a dreadful inconvenience?"

"Well, no, I would not say that," replied Amanda.

"No, I don't imagine you would," laughed Georgiana. "You are far too polite. Where is Edward?"

"He went out quite early," said Amanda.

"Of course he did," said Georgiana with a shake of her head. "What about Selina?"

"In the nursery. She mentioned taking the children for a walk in the park." Amanda paused. Her tone, when she spoke again, was cautious, almost apologetic. "She wants to help with the children but I'm afraid Nanny…"

"Does not want her interference," said Georgiana. "I understand. Selina does like to be useful, but I'm afraid it doesn't always occur to her that it can be overdone."

Amanda sighed. "I don't wish to seem ungrateful, but –"

"No, it is my fault," said Georgiana. "When she took it upon herself to discharge Tom I lost patience with her, and she took offence."

"I see."

Georgiana could tell Amanda was curious, but concealing it as befitted a lady of polite society; she took pity on her sister-in-law. "We were stopped by a highwayman a few evenings ago, and Selina accused Tom of some involvement."

Amanda looked surprised. "That seems rather unlikely."

"Yes, well, Selina has never liked Tom."

"Never approved of him, perhaps," said Amanda, "but that isn't necessarily the same thing."

"It is in this case," said Georgiana. "Anyway, it all became rather unpleasant. I'm sorry to have involved you and Edward. I'll do my best to relieve you of her."

Amanda smiled and rang for some tea, asking the maid to send to the nursery and ask that Miss Knatchbull join them.

Selina appeared in the doorway a few minutes later. Her face froze into a mask when she saw Georgiana.

"Good morning," Miss Knatchbull said in a colourless voice.

"Good morning, Selina," said Georgiana.

"Selina, would you care for some tea?" said Amanda, quickly setting out the cups and saucers as soon as the maid put down the tray. She gave the girl a nod of dismissal and indicated that she should close the door behind her.

Her escape route cut off, Selina stood looking about her uncertainly, trying to maintain her dignity.

"I was going to take the children to the park," she said.

"Nanny will do that. Come and sit down," said Amanda.

Selina glanced towards her, then moved slowly to a chair, her back straight, her expression wary. "So you don't have need of me either, Amanda?" she said in a brittle voice.

Amanda sighed. "It is not a question of need, Selina. We are very glad to have your company. Now, please make yourself comfortable. Georgiana has come expressly to see you."

"Has she?" Selina looked at Georgiana, her face still frozen.

Georgiana gazed at her cousin thoughtfully. It was clear Selina had no intention of making this easy for her. She did her best to inject warmth into her smile. "Selina, I realise things became rather heated between us yesterday, but I hope we can put it behind us."

"I'm sure I don't know what you mean."

"Perhaps I should check on the children." Amanda, ever the diplomat, began to rise from her chair.

"No, please stay, Amanda," said Georgiana. She turned back to her cousin. "Selina, I'm sorry I upset you. Please come home so that everything can return to normal."

"I am no longer sure it is my home." Selina's voice was prim.

"Of course it is," said Georgiana. "There is no question about that."

"Well, after the way you reacted over *that boy*…"

Georgiana sighed. "Engaging and discharging servants is my responsibility, Selina. It will only confuse matters to have both of us doing so."

"It was the way you immediately took his side," complained Selina.

"There were no grounds for discharging him," Georgiana said. "Come, Selina, confess, you merely wanted an excuse to be rid of Tom because you don't like him."

Selina said nothing, but glowered at her cousin. After a moment or two, she sniffed.

"It is true I became impatient and spoke in anger," said Georgiana, "but you must know I had no wish to drive you away."

"I see just how it is," said Selina. "You want to make it clear to me that I am dependent on your charity."

"Nonsense. You know that is not true."

"It is not nonsense," insisted Selina. "Never did I think to find myself in the same position as poor Delia Trent."

Georgiana and Amanda exchanged puzzled looks. "Who is Delia Trent?" asked Georgiana.

Selina stared at her in astonishment. "Why, your young friend's former governess, of course."

16

Georgiana blinked, looking at her cousin in confusion. "I am not sufficiently well acquainted with Miss Trent to be party to her Christian name," she said. "I gather you are, Selina?"

"I know her well enough," said Selina, apparently disposed to be enigmatic.

"Who is Miss Trent?" asked Amanda, also looking confused.

"Louisa Winters's former governess," said Georgiana. "She was staying with Louisa when Lady Winters went away for a few days."

"I see."

"Poor Delia has to stay wherever she can when she gets the opportunity," said Miss Knatchbull sorrowfully. "Things are quite difficult for her." She suddenly seemed to realise Georgiana was looking at her with some interest, and her mood changed. "But I have said too much."

"Oh, yes, of course," said Amanda. "You must respect your friend's privacy, and we have no wish to pry, have we, Georgiana?"

"No, indeed," said Georgiana, who at this moment had exactly such a wish. She smiled at Selina. "In any case, there is no need for you to imagine yourself in a similar situation. You have a home with me and I should be very pleased if you would come back to it."

Selina hesitated, her attitude still wary. Finally she relented. "Very well, I shall return tomorrow morning, that is, if it's convenient for you, Amanda?"

"Yes, of course, Selina."

"Oh, but what about Edward?" Selina asked anxiously. "I fear he will think it shockingly rude of me to go off like this."

"Please don't give it another thought," said Amanda. "Edward will understand."

The object of this conversation was heard in the hall at that moment and entered the drawing room almost immediately. He greeted the assembled company with tense civility.

"Edward, Selina is leaving us. She will return to Georgiana's tomorrow," said Amanda.

"Is she?" As Edward looked towards his cousin, Georgiana saw him visibly relax.

"I hope you don't mind, Edward," said Selina in a tone Georgiana found rather cloying. "I can't help feeling it is dreadfully uncivil of me to run away so soon."

"Not at all, Selina," said Edward, his manner giving no indication that he wished her gone. "We have been very pleased to welcome you, of course, but if you need to go home, we would not dream of holding you here."

Georgiana eyed her brother. His use of the word 'home' had not escaped her, though she felt a grudging admiration for the way in which he conveyed to Selina that he was happy with her decision to leave without implying she had been unwelcome. Selina excused herself, expressing her intention to start her packing. Georgiana's gaze remained steadily fixed on Edward, and as the door closed behind Selina, he had the grace to blush.

"Do you want some tea, Edward?" Amanda asked before brother or sister could speak.

"No, thank you," he said, sitting down. "Rogers will be calling shortly. I shall have to offer him some wine. Don't trouble yourself, my dear," he said, as his wife's hand moved towards the bell. "I have already asked for it to be served in the library."

"Very well."

While things seemed outwardly normal between Amanda and Edward, Georgiana sensed a certain guard-edness on each side. She knew Amanda had been badly hurt when she had learned of her husband's liaison with the beautiful Lady Wickerston, but she had stood by him. Nevertheless, things were bound to be awkward for a while. Regardless of the personal irritations Selina had brought with her, Georgiana was sure the last thing they needed was a third party in residence while they were trying to rebuild their marriage.

"Why is Rogers coming to see you?" she asked her brother.

"The killing of Boyce Polp. He thinks there's something odd about it."

"Odd? In what way?" asked Georgiana.

"I'm not sure, but he doesn't seem convinced Mr Polp was killed by the highwayman who robbed him."

"It is possible he wasn't," said Georgiana.

"But how likely?" asked Edward. "He was very well liked, had scores of friends."

"How did he spend his time?"

Edward's look made clear he found the question peculiar. "I don't know. I've seen him occasionally at some function or other, but we haven't exchanged more than a passing word." He turned to his wife. "What about you, Amanda?"

"I have always found him agreeable enough, but generally we have exchanged no more than the usual pleasantries. However, on one occasion when I met him while I was out shopping he escorted me home and carried some of my packages for me."

"Did he?" asked Edward, bristling.

"Yes, I thought it was extremely kind of him." Amanda gave no indication that she had noticed anything amiss with Edward's tone. "I recall admiring a cravat pin he was wearing. He said it had been a bequest from some relative. In fact, he mentioned he had been left a comfortable legacy."

"Had he?" asked Georgiana.

Edward looked at her curiously.

"You are not normally interested in gossip, Georgiana. In fact, I was not aware you were particularly well acquainted with Mr Polp either."

"No, but I did see him die, Edward."

Edward immediately begged pardon.

"I wonder who this relative was," mused Georgiana. "Someone told me he had a sister, somewhere in the north."

"Half-sister, actually," said Amanda. "I believe his father died and his mother married again."

"How do you know that?" demanded Edward.

"He told me, the day he helped me with my shopping."

"He seems to have been very communicative," said Edward stiffly.

Amanda did not respond to this, and Georgiana tried to turn the conversation in another direction. "Mr Polp seemed to me the type of person who would be interested in art and music."

"What, museums and concerts and the like?" asked Edward.

"Yes, why not?" said Georgiana. "From what I saw of him, he had a rather cultured air."

"That was probably due to the time spent with his tailor," said Edward. "He was always well turned out – almost a dandy, in fact. Very likely he had little leisure for anything else."

Georgiana sensed the bitter edge of sarcasm in Edward's tone. He seemed to have taken Amanda's mention of casual conversation with Boyce Polp more to heart than she would have expected.

"Though if the company Polp kept is anything to judge by," continued Edward, "he was no stranger to the inside of gaming hells."

"Really?" said Georgiana.

Edward looked at his sister in disapproval. "A crony of his, Frederick Barclay, is well known in the more disreputable clubs. He certainly wouldn't hesitate to introduce any of his friends to such establishments. I wouldn't be surprised if the house gave Barclay a share of what they lost."

"That is hardly the action of a friend," said Amanda quietly.

"No," said Edward.

The door opened to admit the footman who announced the arrival of Mr Rogers. Edward rose, paused only to thank his sister for taking care of the matter of Selina, and left the room. Georgiana picked up her gloves and smiled at Amanda.

"I should be going myself," said Georgiana. "Would you mind telling Selina I said goodbye and I will see her tomorrow? I don't wish to disturb her if she is busy."

"Of course. Thank you, Georgiana."

Georgiana smiled. "Not at all. I am only sorry you were dragged into all this nonsense."

With one part of her life on its way back to normality, Georgiana turned her mind back to Boyce Polp. She had not set out for Edward and Amanda's home with any expectation of learning more about him, and had been surprised by the information Edward had disclosed. She had heard of Frederick Barclay of course, and had even seen him at one or two parties. His family background permitted his inclusion in polite social circles, but he was known to be a disreputable character. Wealthy though he was, even the most desperate of matchmaking mamas warned their daughters against him. For her part, Georgiana felt safer amongst the clientele of the Lucky Bell. Yet the notion of Boyce Polp in an illegal gaming hell seemed slightly incongruous. He had always had an elegant, refined air about him, yet did not appear possessed of the sort of naivety which made him a pigeon ripe for plucking.

Georgiana wondered about the possibility of obtaining more information about this side of Mr Polp's life. She knew it would not be easy. Both Edward and Lakesby would unhesitatingly block any attempt she made to inquire about these establishments. She suspected that even Harry, were he to reappear, would be shocked to find his friend the Crimson Cavalier showing an interest in such a place. Tom might be willing to try, but having plucked him away from a career as a highwayman and forbidden him to consort with his former associates, she felt it was not a wise avenue to explore.

Two possibilities raised themselves to her. One was to don her Crimson Cavalier garb and make inquiries herself among the patrons of the Lucky Bell. She was not sure how much this would achieve. Cedric might shield highwaymen and footpads, but Georgiana was not certain how likely it was he would welcome the sort of people who were employed in a gaming hell. While she was certain they would not be the elegant, well-trained servants in the establishments frequented by the *haut ton*, Georgiana also suspected they lacked the rough code of honour found among Cedric's usual patrons.

The other option was for the Crimson Cavalier to stop

Frederick Barclay on the road. If she could get hold of his purse, she might find it contained some information about places which enjoyed his patronage. Yet even as she considered this, another idea came into Georgiana's head. As it occurred to her, she wondered at the audacity of it. She would need an introduction to Mr Barclay, of course, something which she was certain both her brother and Mr Lakesby would refuse to give.

However, before facing that obstacle, she would need to find out if any of the customers of the Lucky Bell had a talent for pickpocketing.

17

The more Georgiana thought about it, the more she marvelled at her own daring. Even for someone who rode out at night as a highwayman, was this a step too far? Lifting Frederick Barclay's purse would be hard enough; returning it to him presented enormous difficulties. If she was caught, Georgiana had no doubt Barclay would expose her, or worse. If this occurred at some social function, it would be an affront to her hostess and great embarrassment for her family. Without even the mask of the Crimson Cavalier to hide behind, her own social position would be destroyed. As she stood waiting for her front door to open, Georgiana wondered whether she had run mad.

She had little time to ponder this point; James answered the door promptly. He spoke as she took off her bonnet and pelisse and handed them to him.

"I'm sorry to trouble you as soon as you arrive home, Miss Georgiana, but you have some visitors. A Mr and Mrs Adam Mortimer have called."

Georgiana looked at the card James presented to her from the tray on the hall table. "Mr and Mrs Adam Mortimer? I've never heard of them. What do they want?"

"I would have denied them, miss," said James apologetically, "but the lady claimed acquaintance with you from when you were away at school. She said you might know her as Sarah Dorman."

Georgiana was still puzzled. She had been sent away to school for a year after the death of her parents, and it was not a period of her life on which she reflected with any joy. James's eyes held a hint of anxiety. She knew he would have done his best to get rid of the couple. There was a touch of ruefulness in his well-trained voice.

"Mr and Mrs Mortimer are dressed in mourning, miss. I rather gained the impression they were related to Mr Polp."

Now Georgiana's interest was piqued. "I see. Very well. Where are they?"

"The small saloon, miss, They have not been served any refreshment. We were not certain how long you would be, or whether – "

"Whether I would wish to see them," she finished. "Quite right, James. I am not certain myself. Stay within earshot of the door, would you? It may be they will need to be shown out fairly promptly."

"Certainly, miss."

James opened the door of the small saloon. As Georgiana walked forward, she saw a man standing by the mantelpiece, examining an ornament. A young woman, seated in an armchair, was looking towards him uneasily. As they turned to face her, Georgiana stopped dead. She found herself staring at the couple who had been held up by the Crimson Cavalier.

The young lady rose hesitantly. Her face was pale against her black gown and the bonnet which adorned her dark hair.

"Miss Grey? Georgiana? I must beg your pardon for calling on you unannounced. I don't suppose you remember me. I was Sarah Dorman when we last met. At school." She gestured towards the man, who had come to stand beside her. "This is my husband, Adam Mortimer."

The man stepped forward, stretching out a hand. "I am very pleased to meet you, Miss Grey."

A shock of recognition shot through Georgiana as he

spoke. Now she knew where she had heard his voice before. He was one of the men she had encountered on the road, discussing the death of Boyce Polp.

She stood transfixed by the man in front of her, unable to speak for a moment. Then, pulling herself together, she smiled and accepted the outstretched hand. "How do you do? Please, won't you sit down?"

Mrs Mortimer returned to the seat she had occupied when Georgiana entered the room. Her husband waited until their hostess sat down before he took a chair himself.

"What can I do for you?" Georgiana asked.

"Oh, no, please, don't think we have come to ask anything of you," said Mrs Mortimer hastily. "Far from it." She paused and took a breath. "I should explain. We are visiting from Yorkshire. My brother has just died, that is, he has been killed."

James had been correct. Georgiana's eyes widened. "Mr Polp?"

Mrs Mortimer nodded.

"I'm so sorry," said Georgiana.

"Thank you," said Mrs Mortimer. "It was a dreadful shock, of course." She paused and gave Georgiana a small smile. "I had heard you were with him when he died, that you tried to save him. I wanted to thank you."

"Oh, no, please, I did very little. It was Mr Lakesby who made the real effort. I'm just sorry your brother couldn't be saved."

"Yes." Mrs Mortimer grew subdued.

Mr Mortimer was watching his wife, and Georgiana was watching Mr Mortimer. Had she misunderstood the conversation she had overheard on the road? Could this man, sitting in her home, gazing with concern at his wife, have been responsible for the death of her brother?

"Would you care for some refreshment?" Georgiana asked.

"Oh, no, thank you, we mustn't stay," said Mrs Mortimer.

"I do remember you from school," said Georgiana, "though I don't recall you visiting your brother from Yorkshire. Of course, it is a long journey for you."

"Yes." Mrs Mortimer looked down into her lap.

Her husband filled the ensuing silence. "You must forgive my wife, Miss Grey. We had the misfortune to be stopped by a highwayman when we were travelling yesterday evening. I'm afraid it has given her a rather poor impression of this part of the country."

"I see. I'm sure it is no wonder," said Georgiana. "I hope such an unfortunate experience will not colour your entire visit. I know this is a sad journey for you, but I'm sure you will find people very friendly. Your brother-in-law was certainly very well liked."

A shadow flickered across Mr Mortimer's face, and vanished as swiftly as it had appeared. "Yes, I know," he said. "Boyce had a gift for making himself agreeable."

Georgiana had the sense that this was not intended as a compliment.

"Tell me, is this your first visit to this area since you settled in Yorkshire?" she inquired.

"My husband has come down occasionally on business," said Mrs Mortimer, "But I have not been back since we married." She smiled up at her husband.

"I see," said Georgiana.

"We really should be going," said Mrs Mortimer. Her face, framed by her black bonnet, had an elfin quality. "We have taken enough of your time. However, I did want to thank you."

"It's very kind of you to take the trouble." Georgiana rang

the bell. "Ah, James," she said as her footman appeared. "Mr and Mrs Mortimer are leaving. Would you be good enough to show them out?"

"Certainly, miss. Mr Lakesby has just called. Would you care to see him?"

"Mr Lakesby?" Mrs Mortimer looked towards Georgiana. "Isn't that the gentleman you mentioned, the one who tried to help my brother?"

"Yes," said Georgiana.

"I should like to see him," said Mrs Mortimer, "to thank him. That is, if you don't mind."

"Of course," said Georgiana. "Show him in, please, James."

"Very good, miss."

As Lakesby entered the room, his confident stride checked at the sight of the Mortimers.

"Oh, I beg your pardon. I did not realise you had guests."

"No, please, come in, Mr Lakesby," said Georgiana with a welcoming smile. "May I introduce Mr and Mrs Mortimer? This is Mr Lakesby. Mr and Mrs Mortimer are from Yorkshire. Mrs Mortimer was at school with me, and is Mr Polp's sister."

"Oh, I see," said Lakesby, his expression as near to startled as Georgiana had ever seen it. "I am pleased to make your acquaintance, but I am sorry it should be under such sad circumstances. May I offer my condolences for your loss?"

"Thank you, Mr Lakesby," said Mrs Mortimer. "It is extremely kind of you. I understand you tried to help my brother after the… the incident which led to his death." She swallowed hard, but continued, "When I heard you had called to see Miss Grey, I wanted to take the opportunity to thank you."

"Really, there is no need, Mr Mortimer," said Lakesby. "Your gratitude is hardly deserved in view of the outcome. I am sorry I was not able to do more."

"Oh no, I am very grateful that you tried. It is not your fault that my poor brother…" Mrs Mortimer sat down again and began to search in her reticule for a handkerchief.

Her husband handed her his own. Mrs Mortimer thanked him in a watery voice as she dabbed at her eyes.

"It is time we left," said Mr Mortimer, supporting his wife's arm as she stood again. "It has been a pleasure meeting you, Miss Grey, Mr Lakesby."

Georgiana rang the bell again as farewells were said. This time James did show Mr and Mrs Mortimer from the room. Neither Georgiana nor Lakesby spoke until they heard the front door close.

"Would you like some tea or coffee?" Georgiana said.

"No, thank you. I didn't know you were acquainted with Boyce Polp's sister."

"Half-sister, to be perfectly accurate. To tell you the truth, neither did I. I knew Mrs Mortimer when she was still Miss Dorman. We were at school together, and I hadn't seen her since then, so I'm afraid I haven't thought about her in years. I certainly did not connect her with Mr Polp."

"I see. I gather you never met Mr Polp when you were at school with Mrs Mortimer?"

Georgiana shook her head. "Not that I recall. No, I am sure I did not. Mrs Milton mentioned to me that he had a sister, and only this morning my sister-in-law said Mr Polp's father had died and his mother had remarried."

"Ah." Lakesby looked around the room, as if suddenly becoming aware of something. "Where is your cousin?"

"At my brother's house." Georgiana hesitated, then decided to tell him the truth, albeit a minimal version. "I'm afraid we quarrelled and she left."

Lakesby raised an eyebrow. "You are here alone? I am shocked, Miss Grey."

Georgiana threw him a scornful look. "You needn't be. She will be back tomorrow."

"I see. Not a serious quarrel then."

Georgiana chose not to be drawn. "It's no matter. What can I do for you, Mr Lakesby?"

"I wondered if you would like to come for a drive."

Georgiana glanced at the clock on the mantelpiece. It was not as late as she had expected. Her morning had already been full, but the thought of a drive in the fresh air seemed appealing. "In your curricle?"

"Why, yes."

"I should like that," Georgiana said with a smile. "I shall just find a bonnet and pelisse. Please excuse me for a moment."

Lakesby nodded.

Georgiana was not many minutes before returning. When Emily had found the garments she sought, she paused only to tell the maid that she would need to speak to her later. When she descended the stairs, Lakesby was waiting for her in the hall, near the front door. He did not wait for James, but opened it for her himself. Georgiana preceded Lakesby out of doors; he tossed a coin to the lad he had engaged to hold his horses and assisted her into the waiting curricle.

"I assume the Bow Street Runner has been to see you again," he said as soon as the horses were moving.

"Yes," said Georgiana. "Have you received a visit?"

"I have. He asked me about Polp's final moments, and if

he said anything of consequence." Lakesby paused, looking thoughtful. "I rather gained the impression he was not convinced a highwayman was responsible for the killing."

"Yes, I thought that," said Georgiana. "My understanding was that he and my brother were looking for Mr Polp's killer when they set the trap on the road, but Mr Rogers did not seem wholly convinced that it would succeed."

"Hmm. Well, I suppose he has to explore all the possibilities," said Lakesby. "Did they catch anyone?"

"No," said Georgiana. She fell into a thoughtful silence.

Lakesby was watching her closely. "What is it, Miss Grey?"

Georgiana glanced at him, considering how to tell him what she knew without disclosing how she had come by the information. She decided his aunt was probably the best point at which to start.

"Your aunt's pearls," she said.

"What about them?"

"Well," she said slowly. "I have learned, through the good offices of my page, how your aunt's pearls came to be returned to her."

Lakesby looked towards her expectantly.

"It seems the highwayman who took them chose to return them because..." She moistened her lips. "Because they belonged to an old sweetheart."

"What? My Aunt Beatrice?" Lakesby burst out laughing. "My Aunt Beatrice, the old sweetheart of a highwayman? Oh, Miss Grey, please, this must be a joke."

"Not of my making," Georgiana assured him, a laugh in her own voice. "I found it as astonishing as you do."

"Are you certain your page is not funning with you?"

"No, he knows better than that."

"The person who told him, then?"

"Possibly, but for what purpose?"

Lakesby grew thoughtful himself. "Yes, I can see that. It's just the idea of my aunt, who hates highwaymen with a passion, having once been in love with one. It's a fantastical notion."

"Perhaps that is the answer," said Georgiana. "Suppose he broke her heart? She would be likely to carry that with her, and grow embittered. I beg your pardon, this is impertinent of me and you know Lady Winters far better than I do, but she does seem to me the type of person who would…"

"Carry a grudge? Yes, I have to admit she is," said Lakesby. "It would make a degree of sense," he admitted. "I'm assuming highwaymen are not usually given to making offers of marriage to well-bred young ladies?"

"I would not imagine so," she said dryly. "Even so, your aunt's parents would not have given their consent to such a match."

"Good grief, no."

"You had no idea?"

Lakesby shook his head.

"Can you honestly imagine my aunt telling me such a thing?"

"No, not really," Georgiana admitted. "But sometimes there are whispers within families, if someone has wanted to marry someone who would be met with disapproval."

"I have never heard any such thing," said Lakesby. "Have you spoken of this to Louisa?"

"No, I didn't think it was my place," said Georgiana.

"Assuming this supposed highwayman was the fellow who held up you and Louisa, one would expect him to lie low if he'd killed someone. The notion of him jaunting about the country not long afterwards to return my aunt's pearls seems either very daring or very foolhardy."

"Yes. Also, what mystifies me is how he knew the right carriage to approach," said Georgiana. "It suggests he has been following her ladyship's progress. Presumably he recognised the crest."

"It could be that it was the pearls he recognised, and that he subsequently went in search of their owner. We are assuming that he recognised the pearls, are we not?"

"It seems logical," said Georgiana, "but surely going in search of the carriage would be a time-consuming enterprise?"

"Yes; there would be no guarantee he would find it quickly, if at all. Time spent searching would hardly line his pockets."

This had already occurred to Georgiana. While she knew Harry had a good heart, she could not imagine that he would sacrifice potentially profitable activities for the sake of searching out some old love, simply to return her jewellery. A thought occurred to her. "I wonder, do you think someone could have told him where to find Lady Winters?"

"Who?"

Georgiana looked away, reluctant to meet Lakesby's incisive gaze.

"I don't know," she said quietly.

"It must be someone who knew my aunt's history," said Lakesby, "but I cannot imagine her discussing such a matter with anyone."

"I was not thinking of your aunt," said Georgiana, "but of the highwayman. Perhaps someone who knew of his history would also know how he would react were he to realise he had stolen property belonging to an old love."

"If that were the case, we have little chance of discovering who that someone might be," said Lakesby mildly.

Georgiana made no reply to this. After a few moments,

she said, "By the way, your cousin has introduced me to her acquaintance, Sir Charles Ross."

"What, the fellow who was betrothed to her friend?"

"Yes," said Georgiana. "He was distressed to learn that his dagger had been used to kill Mr Polp, and he certainly had no wish to entertain the notion that any of his house guests had stolen it."

"It is rather ironic," said Lakesby. "I came across another gentleman who told me a similar tale."

"Similar in what way?"

"He discovered something missing after an evening card party at which Boyce Polp was a guest."

"That seems strange. Was the party composed of the same people who attended Sir Charles's?"

"Some of them," said Lakesby. "However, in this case the host seems confident that Mr Polp stole the item."

18

Georgiana stared at Lakesby, dumbfounded.

"Mr Polp stole it?"

"That's what the fellow told me," said Lakesby. "Admittedly he does not seem to have liked Polp, which may have coloured his thinking."

"That in itself is unusual," said Georgiana. "I thought everyone liked Mr Polp, with the possible exception of your aunt."

"It is quite usual for my aunt to take a while to warm to people."

Georgiana studied Lakesby's profile as she considered how to broach her next thought. "Tell me, Mr Lakesby, are you acquainted with Frederick Barclay?"

Lakesby looked at her sharply. "Why?"

"I was told he was an intimate of Mr Polp."

Lakesby's eyes widened. "Was he now? Well, well. That is difficult to imagine."

Georgiana looked at him in innocent inquiry. "Why is that?" she asked.

Lakesby's expression remained hard, tinged with suspicion.

"He's an unpleasant bit of goods," he replied, "as well you know."

"Do I?"

"Come, Miss Grey, you are not so naïve. I'm sure you know full well that were it not for his excessive wealth, he would not be received. Even so, being as rich as Golden Ball does not mitigate his deplorable character sufficiently for him to be deemed an eligible party."

"Do you know him well?"

"A barely civil greeting on the rare occasions I encounter him, no more."

"I see. Well enough for you to introduce me?" Georgiana inquired.

"What? Absolutely not."

"That seems rather harsh," Georgiana protested.

"Have you taken leave of your senses?" Lakesby demanded. "Why the devil should you want to meet him?"

"Aren't you the least bit concerned about Mr Polp's murder?"

Lakesby's expression remained grim.

"Oh, very well," said Georgiana. "I've been told Mr Barclay and Mr Polp frequented some of the – less select gaming establishments."

"Have you indeed?"

"So Mr Polp might also have made some other acquaintances. Less than desirable ones."

"So he might. Do you also wish to move in those circles?" Lakesby asked sarcastically.

Georgiana chose to ignore this, and returned instead to the information he had proffered earlier. "Do you think Mr Polp stole from Sir Charles and his acquaintance?"

Lakesby pursed his lips. "I don't know. I suppose I could have imagined him doing something like that as a lark, a joke on some friends, but under present circumstances – " Lakesby shrugged. "I really don't know."

"If Mr Polp had lost money in a gaming hell, killing him would not help to get it repaid."

"No."

"Of course," continued Georgiana, "if his friend Mr Barclay is as rich as you say, he could have helped him out of any difficulties."

"No," said Lakesby firmly, with a shake of the head.

"It isn't the done thing to borrow money from one's friends, especially for a debt of honour."

"I see," said Georgiana. "But there is nothing wrong in taking one's friends to disreputable gaming hells?"

"Polp was an adult. It's not my idea of amusement, but there are people who do enjoy it, even find it exciting, perhaps because of its illicit nature."

Georgiana did not reply.

"I don't suppose his sister mentioned anything about it? No, of course she wouldn't," Lakesby continued, "especially if she lives in the north. She would have little idea of the kind of life he led."

"No," said Georgiana. "But I rather got the impression Mr Polp's brother-in-law was not fond of him."

"Oh?"

"Yes. He said something about Mr Polp having a gift for making himself agreeable. The way he said it did not sound as if he was paying a compliment."

"Indeed?"

Georgiana looked at him. She knew it sounded weak. Lakesby's expression suggested he thought there was something more. Georgiana was not sure how, or even if, she could tell him about the conversation she had overheard between the two men on the road. Whatever Lakesby might suspect about her relationship with the Crimson Cavalier, Georgiana had no intention of indulging him.

"Did the Mortimers mention where they were staying?" asked Lakesby.

Georgiana looked at him in some surprise. "I assumed they would stay at Mr Polp's house. Is there some reason they should not?"

"No, I'm sure not. It is just – " Lakesby hesitated. "I saw Lewis Brookstone coming from that direction, and wondered whether there was anything wrong."

Georgiana recognised the name of the 'vulgar banker' of whom Louisa had spoken.

"Was he not a friend of Mr Polp's?" said Georgiana.

"Yes, of course, that would be it. I daresay he went along to offer condolences."

Georgiana gave him a sideways glance as he turned the curricle back into Cavendish Square in the direction of her house. She was not convinced he believed this and wanted to know more.

"Are you acquainted with him?" she asked.

"I? No, I know him by sight only. We don't move in the same circles."

"How did he come to be a friend of Mr Polp?" Georgiana asked. Revelation dawned. "Ah! Mr Barclay."

Lakesby looked sternly at her.

"Have we not done with that subject?"

"Well – "

"I had something of more importance to tell you," said Lakesby, firmly taking the conversation away from Frederick Barclay. "Mr and Mrs Deacon's evening party: are you invited?"

"An evening party is more important than a murder? I beg your pardon, Mr Lakesby, but I hardly think – "

"I have heard a rumour," he said.

"Gossip?"

"Not that kind of rumour." Lakesby's tone was impatient. "This is connected to Mr Polp's death. Mr and Mrs Deacon are expecting a good attendance, and it seems, as the Bow Street Runner's trap failed to capture the highwayman, there are other gentlemen who think this will be a good opportunity to go after him."

"What?"

Lakesby nodded. "A large number in the same place. Volunteers will be sought."

Georgiana paled. She knew Harry had gone to ground, but even so this could be dangerous. If feelings were running high enough for such a suggestion to be put forward, what would happen if a large group of gentlemen set out together in pursuit of the assumed murderer? Georgiana had no doubt that courteous behaviour would be abandoned. For one thing, they would regard themselves as on a mission; for another, it was unlikely they would deem a highwayman worthy of any penalty short of hanging. Whether the highway robber they apprehended proved to be Harry or another, Georgiana was sure the rope would follow hard upon any questions a mob would feel inclined to ask – perhaps without even the formality of a trial.

"Miss Grey?" Lakesby's voice was gentle, concerned.

Georgiana roused herself. She knew she must have been abstracted for some moments.

"I beg your pardon," she said. "Do you mean to volunteer?" she added lightly.

"I would rather not," Lakesby replied. "I trust I am no coward, but I don't hold with taking the law into one's own hands. That is as much murder as the killing of Mr Polp."

Georgiana looked at him curiously. "I am quite sure you are no coward, Mr Lakesby."

She had certain knowledge that he was not. However, as this had been gained when she was in the guise of the Crimson Cavalier, she could not offer him any evidence to support her opinion.

"So," she continued as the curricle drew up in front of her door, "would you advise against attending Mr and Mrs Deacon's party?"

"It is hardly my place to advise you on your social engagements, Miss Grey," said Lakesby as he alighted and walked around the curricle to hand her down.

"It sounds so odd," she said. "What is the plan, to deprive Mr and Mrs Deacon of their male guests?"

"No, I don't believe so. I believe the intention is to set out when the party is drawing to a close. In any case, that is more likely to be the time when highwaymen are on the road, waiting for travellers returning home after their evening's entertainment."

Despite the serious nature of the situation, Georgiana sensed an element of teasing, as if he was seeking her confirmation that this was the practice of highway robbers.

"Will you be attending the party?" she asked.

"Yes, I thought I would. I feel obliged to try and talk the men out of this nonsensical scheme, though I suspect my chances of success are low."

"What about Lady Winters and Louisa?"

"I think they plan to attend, though I am not sure that – oh, yes, of course." Lakesby looked, suddenly enlightened. "Since your cousin is away from home, you will need an escort in order to go."

Georgiana looked at him in horrified embarrassment. "Mr Lakesby, I assure you that's not what I was thinking at all. Please do not think I was begging a favour."

"No, of course I imagined no such thing, Miss Grey. However, I beg you will permit me to offer my services."

No amount of protest on Georgiana's part would sway Lakesby, and before they parted company he insisted on arranging a time for him to call for her with his aunt and cousin.

As she mounted the steps, her mind cast about for an opportunity to avert the catastrophe she could see approaching. Like Lakesby, she was sure an appeal to the gentlemen to drop the scheme would fail to make an impact, and they would be even less inclined to listen to her than to him. She was considering other options as Horton opened the door. It was only as he looked oddly at her when she was about to ask for Emily that she realised he had spoken.

"I beg your pardon, Horton. My mind was otherwise occupied."

"Yes, miss. I only wished to say, miss, that Mr Rogers has called. He wanted to speak to young Tom."

"Mr Rogers. The Bow Street Runner. Yes, of course, the very thing."

"Miss?" Horton brow creased in puzzlement.

"Is Tom with Mr Rogers now?"

"No, miss. He only arrived a few minutes ago and – well, to be honest, Miss Georgiana, I think the boy is hiding. James went to fetch him a few minutes ago and he wasn't in his room, or in the kitchen."

"I see. Has anyone seen him leave the house?"

"I don't think so, miss. I have not left the door since Mr Rogers arrived and I'm sure Mrs Daniels or Richards would have noticed if he had gone out through the kitchen."

"Yes, of course. Is James searching on his own?"

"I believe Emily is helping him, miss."

"Very well. I would like to speak to Mr Rogers myself, but when Tom is found please have him brought straight in."

"Yes, miss."

Horton conducted her to the small saloon, where her visitor stood waiting patiently by the window. He turned as she entered and looked surprised to see the lady of the house. Georgiana walked forward with a smile on her face and her hand outstretched.

"Good day to you, Mr Rogers," she said.

"Good day, Miss Grey." Rogers shook the hand she offered. "I must apologise for disturbing you again. I wanted to talk to your page."

"So my butler told me." Georgiana thought it politic not to mention that her footman and maid were having trouble finding him. "However, I wanted to take the opportunity to speak to you myself. I understood that your attempt to find a highwayman on the road did not prove successful?"

Rogers hesitated. It was clear that his sense of duty and discretion made him reluctant to answer. As he faced her steady, intelligent gaze, Georgiana spoke again.

"Mr Rogers, I understand your wish to be discreet, but I do not ask out of idle curiosity. I have heard something which may be of interest to you."

Rogers became even more alert. "Oh? Very well, then, Miss Grey, you are quite right. I am afraid we were not successful."

"I see. In that case, Mr Rogers, I think you should know that some gentlemen are planning to take matters into their own hands, and go in search of the highwayman they believe to be responsible for Mr Polp's death."

"What? But... How...? They cannot possibly know who to look for; the description we have is so vague. In any case, we can't yet be certain that a highwayman is guilty. I don't doubt Mr Polp was robbed, but that doesn't mean to say the robber stabbed him."

"No, of course it doesn't. However, Mr Polp's death has caused a lot of unrest. He was a very popular man, and people are eager to see his killer punished."

"Yes, I understand that," said Rogers quietly.

"But this will not be justice," said Georgiana. "It will be a mob, seeking revenge. They won't trouble to ask whether or not the highwayman they apprehend is the one who held up Mr Polp. In fact, I doubt they will ask anything."

"No." The Runner looked thoughtful. "Thank you, Miss Grey. I must go. May I call back another time to speak to your page?"

"Yes, of course."

The Runner departed quickly. Georgiana followed him into the hall in time to see a surprised Horton let him out through the front door. Tom came through from the kitchen area, with James in his wake, propelling him in the direction of the small saloon. James and Tom looked equally surprised at the Runner's departure. Tom glanced at James with more than a hint of indignation at being herded along unnecessarily. Georgiana hid a smile as she told Tom he could go as something else had occurred which needed the Runner's immediate attention.

"However," she said, "Mr Rogers will want to speak to you. Please ensure you are available when he returns."

"Yes, miss," the boy mumbled.

James remained where he was as Tom departed into the kitchen regions. Georgiana caught Horton's barely perceptible shake of the head as he returned to his duties.

"Will there be anything else, miss?" James asked.

"I need to speak to Emily."

"I believe she has gone up to your room, miss."

"Very well, I shall join her there. Thank you, James."

Georgiana picked up the bonnet she had hastily discarded on the hall table when she had arrived home. She walked up the stairs as speedily as was commensurate with a ladylike demeanour, and found Emily tidying her dressing table.

"Did the Runner speak to Tom, miss?" Emily asked when

Georgiana had closed the door.

"No," said Georgiana. "There was something else in more urgent need of his attention. Emily, I shall be going to Mr and Mrs Deacon's party this evening. Mr Lakesby will be calling for me with his aunt and cousin at eight o'clock."

"Yes, Miss Georgiana."

"In the meantime," said Georgiana, "I shall have to make a visit to the Lucky Bell."

19

Emily stared at Georgiana in disbelief. "Are you serious, miss?" she asked after a moment of stunned silence.

"It's an emergency, Emily. Something dreadful is about to happen." Georgiana sat down on the bed, and removed her shoes as she spoke. She quickly repeated what Lakesby had told her about the plan to raise a mob to go in pursuit of the highwayman they believed responsible for Boyce Polp's death.

Emily was shocked, but remained uneasy about Georgiana's plan to visit the tavern at such an early hour. "Surely the Runner can deal with it, Miss Georgiana? It's his job, after all."

"He may not be able to persuade more than one or two gentlemen to help him," said Georgiana. "They would be vastly outnumbered. Feelings are running so high against Mr Polp's killer that these volunteers would not welcome any attempt to stop them. More than one person could be hurt. If I warn the patrons of the Lucky Bell, I could help to avoid that."

Emily's eyes were solemn. "Yes, I see," she said. "But wouldn't it be better to send Tom, miss?"

Georgiana shook her head. "No, not this time."

"But you have so little time. Suppose you don't get back before Mr Lakesby calls? Besides, it is not quite dark yet, and the risk of being seen…"

Georgiana knew Emily was right. She also had an uncomfortable feeling that if she hadn't returned by the time Mr Lakesby and his party arrived, he would have a good idea of where she had gone. She was sure he would not voice his suspicions, and might even cover for her, but it was nevertheless an undesirable scenario. All the same, imagining what could happen if she did nothing, Georgiana felt she had to act.

"I know. I will be careful," she promised. "Have something ready for me to wear to the Deacons' this evening. I'll leave it to you to decide. If it's all laid out when I get back, it won't take me long to change."

"Very well, miss."

Emily opened the chest in which the Crimson Cavalier's attire was stored and laid the shirt and breeches on the bed.

"There's something else I wanted to tell you, Emily. It's about those visitors I had earlier. Yes, I know," she added as Emily gave the clock a fleeting glance, "but this won't take long and it is important."

Emily nodded, giving Georgiana her full attention. "Very well, miss. James mentioned he thought the lady was someone you knew at school?"

"Yes, but I haven't seen her since. It's of far more interest that she is Mr Polp's half-sister."

Emily looked startled. "Good grief. You hadn't known that, miss?"

"No. She came to thank me for trying to help her brother."

"That was very civil of her."

"Yes, it was. I understand she lives with her husband in Yorkshire now. It was Mr Polp's death which brought them here."

"Yes, I expect there are things to sort out."

"No doubt," said Georgiana. "But there's something of more interest still; I think her husband was in this area a little earlier. I'm fairly certain he is one of the men I heard talking on the road."

Emily's jaw dropped. "You think Mr Polp was killed by his sister's husband?"

"Well, unless I mistook what I heard, it certainly sounded that way. I can't accuse him, of course; I don't have any evidence. Explaining that the Crimson Cavalier overheard their conversation would be difficult to say the least."

"Yes."

Georgiana was almost transformed into her alter ego; Emily handed her a boot.

"That's horrible, miss," Emily said. "To think he should have been killed by his own brother-in-law."

"Yes, I know." Georgiana tugged on the second boot and glanced at the clock herself. "I had better go. Emily, would you mind checking the back stairs?"

Emily slipped out and returned a couple of moments later to report that all was clear. Georgiana held her hat in her hand, with her mask folded inside it. The back stairs were quiet, and Georgiana listened at the kitchen door for a moment or two. Hearing Mrs Daniels go into the scullery, she slipped out through the back door with feline speed. Darkness was just falling, and Georgiana knew her groom's habits well enough to be certain that Richards would already have fed the horses. It was likely that he was washing, in readiness for his evening meal.

Princess was familiar with her mistress's unconventional routine, and made no startled reaction as Georgiana slipped the bridle over her head. She accepted Georgiana's attention at whatever hour she was taken out and, as no one else ever rode her, it was likely she would only make a noise if a stranger approached.

Georgiana was fortunate to encounter no one as she rode through the square and cantered to the edge of the town, her eyes alert in case she suddenly needed to move out of sight. Her luck held; it was likely that most residents of the neighbourhood were preparing for their dinner or an evening party. Georgiana knew this placed an even tighter limit on the time available to her. Once she was away from the houses and on the open road, she urged Princess to a gallop.

It was not long before Georgiana was tethering the mare outside the Lucky Bell. She entered quickly and her no-nonsense manner immediately attracted Cedric's attention. Casting her eyes around the taproom, she walked straight to the bar.

"Can we talk?" Georgiana said to Cedric.

He nodded, beckoning to his wife to take his place at the bar while he led the way into the small private parlour which she and Harry sometimes used to conduct business.

"What is it, lad?" Cedric asked without preamble. "Trouble, is there?"

"Remember that fellow Harry stopped? The one who was stabbed to death?"

Cedric nodded tersely.

"I've heard a group of gentlemen will be out looking for the killer."

"You mean for Harry."

"Is he still keeping out of sight?"

"He is," said Cedric. "No one seems to know where he is, and if they do they're not saying. He's probably safe – but a load of nobs on the hunt will be trouble enough even if they don't find what they're looking for."

"That was my thought," said Georgiana.

Cedric scratched his head. "I'll warn some of the lads," he said. "The Runners and narks know about this place – not that they've had any luck catching anyone, but that won't stop them coming here. Do you know when this is supposed to happen?"

"Later tonight." It occurred to Georgiana that he had not asked her how she knew about the plan. "Probably from eleven o'clock or so."

Cedric nodded. "Makes sense. Could cause a lot of trouble. They'll be angry, and wanting to take it out on someone – and Harry's the one in their sights."

"Yes."

"And if someone does have an idea where he is…"

"They might be persuaded to talk," finished Georgiana.

Cedric was nodding again, slowly, his frown deepening.

"Do you know if the Runners are involved? No, I suppose they wouldn't be," he said, answering his own question. "I'll put the word around, and do whatever I can, lad. Thanks for coming to tell me."

Georgiana gave a nod of acknowledgement and left the Lucky Bell as quickly as she had arrived. As she pulled the door after her, Georgiana's last image of the taproom was of Cedric leaning over a small table, speaking in a confidential way to a couple of his patrons.

Georgiana untied Princess, mounted effortlessly and turned the animal towards the road without delay. She returned home the way she had come, managing to avoid being seen, and arrived in her room to find Emily pacing the floor, chewing the tip of her thumb anxiously.

"Miss Georgiana! I thought you were never coming back."

"Surely I wasn't that long?"

"You've barely time to change."

As Georgiana had requested, Emily had laid a pale turquoise gown out on the bed; with stockings, jewellery and evening slippers also ready and waiting. Despite Emily's reservations, she was dressed and ready a few minutes before Mr Lakesby was expected. Emily was still dissatisfied, critically tweaking Georgiana's hair to the point where her exasperated mistress called a halt. Emily stopped, but it was clear she felt her work was incomplete, and her pride was wounded.

"It will do perfectly well, Emily. Fetch my evening cloak, would you? Mr Lakesby and his party will be here shortly."

Georgiana arrived downstairs just as James opened the door to Mr Lakesby. He was elegantly attired in knee-breeches and a well-tailored coat, finished with a cravat which was impeccably but not extravagantly tied. He offered his arm as they turned to leave.

As Lakesby helped Georgiana into the carriage, she recalled the first time she had gone out for the evening with him, his aunt and cousin. On that occasion, Lady Winters had been icily polite. While it would be too much to say her ladyship had thawed, she now seemed to have accepted her daughter's friendship with Georgiana. Louisa, for her part, had lost much of her original shyness, and greeted Georgiana warmly, chatting amiably about the events of her day. Her relaxed manner suggested she was not aware of the plan to go in search of Mr Polp's killer following the Deacons' party. Georgiana responded to her chatter in monosyllables; the matters which occupied her mind were unsuitable for sharing with a girl of Louisa's tender years. Lakesby was quieter than usual. Georgiana suspected his mind was on the manhunt proposed for later in the evening.

Mrs Deacon's welcome suggested she had nothing on her mind beyond ensuring that her guests were comfortable and her evening was a success. Her husband, after greeting the ladies, shook Lakesby's hand vigorously. Georgiana heard him beg the favour of a few words sometime during the evening. Lakesby agreed, and made no shift to satisfy his aunt's curiosity when she asked him what Mr Deacon had said.

Georgiana sensed an air of tense anticipation through-out the evening. At times she wondered whether it was merely in her imagination; none of the ladies present offered any indication that they knew what was in the wind. However, she noticed some of the men whispering to each other periodically. Lakesby's brief disappearance just before supper and the grim expression he wore on rejoining them told Georgiana she was not mistaken.

That something had disturbed Lakesby's equilibrium did not escape Louisa. "Is anything wrong, Max?" she asked as the company moved towards the supper room.

"No, nothing at all."

"Where did you go?" demanded Lady Winters.

"To the library, for a few words with Mr Deacon," he said curtly. "May I escort you to supper, Aunt Beatrice?"

Lady Winters looked inclined to pursue the subject of her nephew's mysterious conversation with their host, but Lakesby left her curiosity unsatisfied, instead offering her his arm and leading her purposefully towards the supper room. Most of the guests were moving in the same direction, but Georgiana noticed a small cluster beginning to collect in the entrance hall close to the front door of the house, Mr and Mrs Deacon among them. Louisa, too, had noticed, and sensed that something was happening; she craned her neck to see over the heads of the company and find out what was going on. Georgiana was surprised to see Mr Rogers, determinedly moving through what appeared to be a hostile reception party.

Mr Lakesby, equally determined, succeeded in seating

his party in the supper room, ignoring both the shrill demands of his aunt and the naïve curiosity of his cousin. As he held out Georgiana's seat for her, he said in a low voice, "Did you tell him?"

"Yes," Georgiana replied softly. "When I arrived home he was waiting to speak to my page. I thought I should take advantage of the opportunity."

"Excellent work." Lakesby moved towards Lady Winters. "Aunt Beatrice, let me bring you some supper. What would you like?"

"What? Don't be absurd, Maxwell. Sit down and let the servants attend to it."

Lakesby took no notice; instead he made his way to the tables and chose a plateful of delicacies for each of the ladies. Once he was sure they were settled he excused himself, and followed the majority of the gentlemen, who seemed to have followed the same course of action, ensuring their ladies' comfort at supper before going to join the activity in the entrance hall. Lady Winters and Louisa both began to nibble at their food in a distracted manner; Georgiana put down her plate, made her excuses and followed Lakesby out of the room.

The group around the door had filled out somewhat, and the atmosphere was certainly more heated. Georgiana eased a path through a crowd of rather surprised gentlemen until she found herself close to the centre of the throng. Lakesby threw her an exasperated look, but did not address or approach her. Close to him was Mr Rogers, who seemed to be the focus of most of the attention; he stood quietly, facing Mr Deacon, who seemed to have a great deal to say. Behind Mr Deacon, one or two other men were offering opinions. As far as she could see, Lakesby was not yet contributing to the discussion. Rogers himself maintained an air of dignity and determination, no easy matter when facing a group of gentlemen who clearly considered themselves his betters and entitled to exert authority over him.

"What's going on?"

Georgiana turned to face Louisa, who was on tiptoe behind her. "Louisa, what are you doing here? Surely your mother didn't allow you to leave the supper room?"

"I told her I was going to look for Max," came the reply. "I just came – I didn't give her a chance to stop me. What's going on?" she repeated. Her eyes widened. "Isn't that the Bow Street Runner?"

"Yes," said Georgiana. "I have the impression he is not being made very welcome."

"Why has he come here? Surely he doesn't think Mr Deacon is a criminal?"

"I don't think that for a moment – but he may think Mr Deacon has some information." A mischievous spirit spoke to Georgiana. "I daresay your cousin has a better idea of what has happened. Why don't you ask him when he returns?"

The two young ladies watched the scene develop before them. Georgiana knew more than Louisa of what was happening, but the conversation between Rogers and Mr Deacon was difficult to follow through the babble of other voices, and it took some effort to piece together the fragments she could hear. It became apparent that Rogers was trying to persuade Mr Deacon and the others that taking the law into their own hands was not a good strategy. Georgiana could not help but admire his calm demeanour in the face of an increasingly heated argument, in which only Lakesby did not participate. Everyone else reacted angrily, castigating the Runner for his interference, demanding justice yet insisting that they did not believe the law would provide it.

Finally Lakesby spoke up, raising his voice to ensure that he was heard. "Mr Rogers has a job to do."

"Then why doesn't he do it?"

Lakesby threw the speaker a contemptuous look. "It should be obvious that he cannot allow a rabble to pursue a man who may or may not be guilty of murder. The person in question needs to be apprehended by the proper authorities and tried before a judge."

"*Rabble*? How dare you, sir!"

"Well, of all the…"

"Withdraw that remark, Lakesby."

Lakesby folded his arms. Louisa's mouth dropped wide open, and even Georgiana found herself blinking. Mr Rogers's expression lay between gratitude and surprise.

Mr Deacon spoke quietly. "I would be grateful if you would withdraw that word, Lakesby."

Lakesby looked steadily at him, then at the crowd surrounding him. His eyes went back to his host.

"I regret, sir, that under the circumstances I find myself unable to do so."

"Oh, my goodness," whispered Louisa, still behind Georgiana.

An angry murmur emanated from the group of men congregated by the door. Georgiana heard someone exclaim, "Call him out!"

"In that case," said Mr Deacon, "I regret that I must ask you to leave." He glanced apologetically to where Georgiana and Louisa were standing. "Your party as well."

"Of course." Lakesby gave a small bow. "You'll be good enough to send for my carriage."

"Really, Mr Lakesby, there is no need," said the Runner.

"I shall leave."

Lakesby paid him no heed but turned and began to walk towards the supper room where he had left the ladies.

"Oh, no," said Louisa. "Mama will be so angry." She fled towards the supper room, determined to witness the wrath which she knew would descend on her cousin.

Georgiana remained where she was, and Lakesby came over to join her with a rueful smile. "Do you mind dreadfully?" he asked.

"Not in the least," said Georgiana. "On the contrary, I must compliment you on your courage."

Lakesby shrugged, and haughtily addressed a passing footman. "Fetch our cloaks, would you, please? Immediately."

Rogers was at the door, on the point of departure. Lakesby called across to him. "May I offer you a seat in my carriage, Mr Rogers?"

It was hard to tell who was more stunned: the assembled company or Rogers himself. He did not seem quite sure what to say.

"Thank you, Mr Lakesby. It is very kind of you, but I have my horse…"

"We will arrange something. My groom can ride it back for you if necessary." Deeming the matter settled, he turned back to Georgiana. "And now," he said, "I suppose I had better break the news to my aunt."

20

Lady Winters was incandescent with fury. The carriage ride home was accomplished in a frosty atmosphere which owed nothing to the open window of the carriage. Mr Rogers was plainly uncomfortable. Louisa kept her eyes trained upon her lap, apart from occasional furtive glances to one or other of her companions, apparently anxious to separate herself from the storm which was clearly brewing. The only member of the party who appeared relaxed was Lakesby.

For her part, Georgiana remained alert. She had not been surprised by Lakesby's defence of Mr Rogers, but his reference to the party of energetic gentlemen as a rabble had rather taken her aback. She had admired his courage in standing up to the crowd, and was sure it had taken took no less nerve, in fact probably more, to face his aunt, which he had done in an equally imperturbable manner.

It had been a strange evening. Georgiana was relieved to find that that the road was relatively quiet, at least so far, suggesting that Rogers's mission had been successful. However, when she warned the Bow Street Runner of what was afoot, she had not anticipated such a public scene, and certainly had not intended to bring upon herself and her friends the embarrassment of being asked to leave the Deacons' party. Though it was Lakesby's behaviour which had become the direct cause of the latter incident, Georgiana could not help feeling that it would not have occurred had she not made Rogers aware of what was afoot.

The chilly silence in the carriage made it easier to hear the occasional sounds which penetrated from outside. The noises gradually increased in both frequency and volume, until they came together into a constant, restless hum. An orange glow lit the road ahead, and seemed to be moving towards them. Dread filled Georgiana. Had the men gone ahead with their plan after all?

As the noise grew louder, the carriage slowly drew to a standstill. The shadows ahead came closer, and took on more recognisable shape. Eventually the road was blocked by men with lanterns in their hands; they spread out to surround the coach. Their manner was forceful, though oddly not threatening. Nonetheless, the atmosphere suggested it would not take much to turn them into an aggressive mob.

Looking out of the window, Georgiana realised that the crowd was not composed of Mr Deacon and his friends, but a collection of men from a rather different class. Some, though not all, were masked, and while she could not claim acquaintance with all of them, she recognised some of the customers of the Lucky Bell. Crowded together like this they looked far less amiable, and even she found the sight rather threatening. As well as the lanterns she could see club-shaped objects raised aloft, bright against the night sky.

Rogers was already starting to move from his seat. Lakesby's hand on his shoulder checked him. "Don't be a fool, man. They'll tear you to pieces."

"It's my duty, sir."

Rogers politely excused himself as he squeezed past the ladies and stepped down from the carriage.

"Well, really!" said Lady Winters. "If we can't avoid molestation from highwaymen when we have a Bow Street Runner with us, the least he can do is – "

"Please, Aunt Beatrice, I beg you will be quiet."

Lakesby alighted in Rogers's wake, leaving her ladyship sputtering; Georgiana suspected she was controlling herself with difficulty, determined as always to maintain her dignity. Louisa's eyes were lowered; she appeared uncertain as to where her mother's furious disbelief would be vented.

Georgiana slid along the seat to get a better view through the window. It appeared to her that Mr Rogers was trying to reason with the crowd, much as he had in Mr Deacon's entrance hall. It was difficult to judge how successful his attempt would prove. They seemed to be giving him their attention, but Georgiana sensed that they had no intention of allowing the travellers through without ensuring that their case was heard. They did not appear to be interested in robbery; so far there had been no request for any valuables. Georgiana peered into the crowd, wondering if Harry could be among them.

"You will gain nothing by harassing innocent travellers," came Rogers's calm, reasonable tones. "Let these people go on their way. They can do nothing for you."

"Maybe, maybe not," responded a voice Georgiana thought she recognised; it sounded like one of Harry's friends. "A mate of ours is in trouble, and for something he didn't do. Seems all the gentry is against him. We're not about to let him be taken and hanged. Hardly fair, that."

"No one will be hanged without a fair trial," said Rogers. "In any case, these are ladies, travelling home. They can't help your friend, and this talk of hanging will be distressing to them."

"Oh, I don't know about that," said the other man, who appeared to have appointed himself spokesman for the crowd. "There's often ladies attending a hanging. If one o' them dropped a word in the right ear it could help no end."

The speaker approached the carriage window, one hand holding up his flaring club, the other removing his hat. "Good evening, ladies," he began respectfully.

His eyes took in all the occupants. They rested longer on one than on the others – and Georgiana was relieved, though not a little surprised, to find that she was not the object of his special attention.

"Begging your pardon, my lady," he addressed Lady Winters. He drew back and bowed, sweeping his hat in front of him flamboyantly. "Move aside, lads," he instructed his companions. "There's no need to hold these up ladies any longer. Let 'em go through." He turned to Rogers and Lakesby, who were exchanging surprised looks. "On your way, gents. We'll not bother you further."

"But – " Rogers began, only to find Lakesby's hand on his arm, pushing him towards the carriage.

"Let it go," whispered Lakesby. "We must get the ladies home."

"Very well," said Rogers, allowing himself to be led back to the carriage.

As the two gentlemen took their seats, the highwayman graciously closed the door behind them and signalled to the coachman to move on. The crowd behind him parted to allow them a path. Even Georgiana, who knew something of highwaymen, was bemused by the incident.

"I don't understand," said Louisa. "I thought they were going to rob us."

"They clearly thought better of it," said Lady Winters. "I daresay it was the presence of a Bow Street Runner which deterred them," she said, inclining her head towards Mr Rogers in stately fashion.

Rogers shook his head, clearly at a loss for words.

"Perhaps," said Lakesby, his eyes fixed on his aunt.

The remainder of the journey was accomplished without incident and in a silence very different from that of the first part. Everyone seemed occupied by their own thoughts, and when Lakesby asked Rogers where he wished to be put down there was no reaction from Lady Winters. Indeed, she wished him a polite good night as he alighted at his lodging in a part of town she would not normally think of frequenting.

"You and Louisa both look tired, Aunt Beatrice," said Lakesby. "I think we should take you home first, and then I shall escort Miss Grey to her house."

Louisa almost protested, but caught sight of her cousin's expression and held her peace. Lady Winters, quite unexpectedly, said nothing about the impropriety of her nephew being alone in the carriage with Miss Grey. "If that is what you think best, Maxwell," she said, almost meekly.

When they arrived at the Winters residence, Lakesby descended from the carriage first, then assisted both his aunt and cousin to alight. Georgiana looked at him in puzzlement as he turned and held his hand out to her.

"But Mr Lakesby – "

He beckoned her into the house with a slight movement of his head. She demurred no further, but, assuming he had some purpose in mind, accepted his hand and alighted, following Lady Winters and Louisa into the house at Lakesby's side. It was Louisa who looked surprised; her ladyship did not seem to notice, and went so far as to ask her butler to bring some refreshment.

"You'll take a glass of wine, Miss Grey?"

"Yes, thank you, Lady Winters, that would be most welcome."

Louisa looked more puzzled than ever and cast a look towards her cousin. "I think I shall go to bed," she said.

"Very wise," commented Lakesby.

"Goodnight, Mama," she said, bending to give her mother a dutiful kiss on the cheek.

"Goodnight, Louisa." Her ladyship returned her daughter's embrace more warmly than was her wont.

Louisa's surprise seemed to increase and she kissed Georgiana on the cheek as she wished her goodnight.

"Goodnight, Max," Louisa said, walking past her cousin.

"Goodnight, Louisa. Sleep well."

As Louisa reached the door it was opened by the footman bearing the tray of wine. Lakesby told him they would help themselves, so he set it down and departed.

Lakesby handed his aunt a glass of wine, watching her closely. She thanked him almost absently, then took a sip in much the same fashion. Georgiana felt as if she was watching a different person. Lady Winters seemed to have forgotten she was there; it was Lakesby who bade her be seated and brought her a glass of wine. Both Georgiana's and Lakesby's eyes were fixed on her ladyship. It was Lakesby who eventually spoke.

"It appears, Aunt Beatrice, that we have you to thank for our deliverance from that band of highwaymen who blocked the road."

"I beg your pardon?" said her ladyship.

"They were highwaymen, were they not?" Lakesby asked Georgiana.

"I assume so."

Lakesby's attention went back to his aunt.

"It appeared to me that it was when their leader saw you were in the carriage that he decided to let us pass. I had no idea you had such influence in the highwayman community."

"Don't be absurd, Maxwell."

"Absurd?" Lakesby glanced at Georgiana before continuing; she schooled her features into an expression of polite interest. "The leader of that group appeared to recognise you when he approached the carriage. It was then that he decided to let us through."

Her ladyship sat a little straighter in her chair. "I daresay the Bow Street Runner persuaded them it would be foolish to pursue their actions," she said.

"In what way would it have been foolish?" said Lakesby. "We were vastly outnumbered, Rogers, the coachman and I. We could not have overpowered them."

Lady Winters said nothing, but sat gazing into her glass.

Lakesby looked at Georgiana, raising an eyebrow in inquiry. They were clearly of the same mind; Lady Winters must be made aware of Georgiana's discovery about the pearl necklace. But it was not her place to raise the matter. Lakesby appeared to be asking her permission to continue; she nodded assent.

"Aunt, I'm sure you recall that Miss Grey's page is the young man who attempted to hold us up on the road a few months ago. Miss Grey took pity on him when he was shot by my groom."

"What? Oh, yes. What about him?"

"I understand he still has friends in – er – certain quarters. He has obtained a rather interesting piece of information."

"What is that?" asked Lady Winters, toying with her wine glass.

"It concerns the manner in which your pearls were returned after the recent robbery." Lakesby's tone was relaxed, conversational. "Correct me if I am mistaken in this, Miss Grey: the lad was told that the pearls had been returned to you because the person who had stolen them recognised them as the property of a former sweetheart."

Her ladyship looked up, her eyes alert. She carefully placed the wine glass on the table beside her, but made no reply.

"Is that what young Tom told you, Miss Grey?" said Lakesby, his eyes fixed on his aunt.

"Yes, it was."

"I see," said her ladyship quietly.

It was the first time since Georgiana had known her that Lady Winters had failed to appear confident to the point of arrogance. Her ladyship invariably carried about her an air of superiority, as if she considered herself better than most people with whom she came into contact. Yet at this moment she was sitting quietly, her head lowered, gazing into the depths of the fire as if it could provide an answer to Lakesby's question.

"Aunt Beatrice?"

"Yes, Maxwell?" Lady Winters looked at him, her manner almost submissive.

"Is something wrong?"

"No. That is – I…" She glanced towards Georgiana.

"Perhaps I had better leave." Georgiana rose and moved to set down her own glass.

Lady Winters sighed. It was an incongruous sound. "No. That will not be necessary." Her ladyship sighed again. "You seem to know much of the tale already."

"I would not say that, Lady Winters. And certainly, if it is a personal matter, I would not wish to…"

"It was all so long ago," said her ladyship in an oddly dreamy tone. "I have not thought of it for years."

"Thought of what?" said Lakesby.

Her ladyship looked scornfully at him, her manner suddenly more in keeping with the Lady Winters they knew. "My first love, of course."

"A highwayman?" said Lakesby.

Lady Winters nodded. "His name was Harry. Harry Smith, he told me, though I daresay that was assumed."

"Very likely," said Georgiana, feeling as if she was about to choke on a biscuit crumb.

"He was quite dashing. I was not much older than Louisa is, and I must confess my head was turned."

"I see," said Lakesby.

Lady Winters sighed again and looked at her nephew. "No, Maxwell, I don't think you see at all. I'm sure you think I experienced the same sort of empty infatuation as Louisa has for that Crimson Cavalier."

Georgiana dared not look at either of them.

"I would not presume to make any such assumption, Aunt."

"Very well," said her ladyship. "It was before I met your uncle, of course. It was the year I came out. He stopped our carriage on the way home from some party or other."

"Rather as the Crimson Cavalier did you and Louisa," said Lakesby.

"Yes," said her ladyship baldly, looking at her nephew.

Lakesby begged pardon and asked his aunt to continue.

"He did not take anything," said Lady Winters. "It was the oddest thing. He bowed his head, paid me a compliment and rode away."

Georgiana and Lakesby exchanged puzzled glances.

"Surely there must have been more than that?" said Lakesby.

"Not then, but later," Lady Winters admitted. "It seems he followed the carriage and discovered where I lived."

"Did he approach you at home?" asked Georgiana.

"Not immediately. He stopped us several more times on

the road, yet never took anything from us." Lady Winters paused, her expression far away. "Each time he ignored my mother, or whoever was accompanying me, and spoke only to me. It was as if he wanted to become properly acquainted with me."

"But Aunt Beatrice, how well acquainted could he become merely by stopping your carriage, even if he did so on a regular basis?"

Her ladyship looked at her nephew wryly. "I am aware that this was not a conventional situation, Maxwell."

Georgiana could resist no longer. "I beg your pardon, Lady Winters, but... you encouraged this man?"

A shadow of guilt and embarrassment flickered across her ladyship's face. "I was young, Miss Grey, and he was... intriguing." Lady Winters gave a small smile which lit her face into uncharacteristically soft lines. "After a while he came to the house. He said he had waited and watched for my parents to leave for the evening."

"And no doubt called at the front door," said Lakesby sardonically.

Lady Winters ignored him. "I was never sure how he managed it, but he sent me a note. Against my better judgement, of course, I went to the side door where he was waiting."

Lakesby looked stunned. "And then? You met him regularly?"

Lady Winters nodded.

"But, Aunt Beatrice, if Louisa were to do such a thing – "

"I should lock her in her room. Of course I should. I am familiar with the dangers." Her ladyship rose and went to stand by the mantelpiece. As her recital progressed, she seemed to retreat further into her own world and become less aware of her listeners. "Yes, we met regularly. It was not

197

difficult to slip away. He was quite charming, and very different from the young gentlemen of my acquaintance."

Like mother, like daughter, Georgiana thought with some surprise, recalling that this had been Louisa's reaction to the Crimson Cavalier.

"He went so far as to ask me to run away with him," said Lady Winters. Her nephew's jaw dropped, and she acknowledged him with another wry smile. "It was impossible, of course. All the same, I was flattered. But we had to part. Before we did, he made me a gift."

Georgiana was hard pressed to maintain a bland expression. Her ladyship's tale did not ring true. Even allowing for Harry's bluff good nature, it sounded too civilised, the parting too amicable. As for Lady Winters: to accept with dignity that she could not enjoy a future with Harry after endangering her reputation by engaging in clandestine meetings, but then to give way to the impropriety of accepting a gift... It all seemed rather implausible.

"Lady Winters," said Georgiana, "may I ask what was the nature of the gift?"

Lady Winters looked hesitantly at Georgiana for a moment, then sighed. "I suppose you may, Miss Grey. He gave me the pearls."

21

For a few moments Lakesby seemed incapable of speech.

"The pearls," he said at last. "You accepted a string of pearls as a gift from a highwayman."

"Pray do not judge me, Maxwell," said Lady Winters in a voice more like her own. "I was young and it was before I married your uncle."

"But Aunt, did you not stop to consider where those pearls must have come from?"

"No, I regret I did not," said Lady Winters, her voice rising. "I was young and of a romantic turn of mind, and I was, I admit, rather taken with the man. Why would I have questioned the origins of a gift he offered?"

"I wonder who they belonged to?" said Georgiana, almost to herself.

"It is all too long ago now to be wondering that," said Lady Winters.

"But Aunt, you of all people... You who are so opposed to highwaymen... To behave in such a manner." Lakesby was clearly taken aback.

"Yes, Maxwell, I. And now you have the whole of it." Her ladyship reached for the bell pull. "I am rather tired, and should like to retire to my chamber if you have no objection, Miss Grey. Maxwell, you offered to escort Miss Grey home."

Georgiana and Lakesby made their farewells and left quietly. They had been settled in the carriage for several minutes before either of them spoke.

"I can hardly believe it," said Lakesby.

Georgiana looked at him. "Are you shocked?"

"I don't know," he said, shaking his head slowly. "Astonished, I think, is the word."

"Yes."

They fell silent again. After a few minutes, Lakesby spoke. "Do you think we'll be stopped by any more highwaymen?"

"They seemed otherwise occupied," Georgiana said.

"Ah, yes, of course." Lakesby shook his head again. "Aunt Beatrice, of all people."

"Yes. You know her better than I do, of course, but this does not match what I have discerned of her character."

"Astonishing."

"It would explain her antagonism towards highwaymen," said Georgiana, "if her heart was broken by one. Her hostility has always been somewhat… fiercer than most."

"Did my Aunt Beatrice look like someone whose heart had been broken?" said Lakesby.

"No," Georgiana acknowledged. "However, it was all a long time ago. She has been married for many years, and has a daughter who is now grown up."

Lakesby grinned. "I would question that."

"You know what I mean." She hid a smile; her own feelings about Louisa were not so very different. "Even so, your aunt was quite – composed about it all. The thought of a noble leave-taking, with no acrimony on either side – "

"And a parting gift from the highwayman," said Lakesby. "Yes, it does sound curious, even if she was young and fascinated by the man, as she would have us believe."

"Yes," said Georgiana. "What is more, your aunt does not seem to have given a thought as to where the pearls came from. If she has always worn them so openly, it is to be wondered at that their original owner has never recognised them."

"Perhaps the original owner was dead, or lived in another part of the country."

"Yorkshire, for instance," murmured Georgiana.

"I beg your pardon?"

"Nothing. A mere thought. It is a long time since it all happened – too long, perhaps, to discover where the pearls came from."

"Especially if Aunt Beatrice herself has never considered the matter."

"A memory of a lost love," said Georgiana.

"Which the highwayman was himself sentimental enough to recognise and return," said Lakesby. "My aunt has never appeared to me to be the sentimental type."

"People are not always as they appear," said Georgiana.

"Very true," said Lakesby, with a long look at her.

They arrived at Georgiana's front door and Lakesby escorted her up the steps, waiting only until James opened the door and admitted her to the house before taking his leave.

Georgiana's mind was full as she prepared for bed. Unusually, she said little to Emily. After wishing the maid goodnight and blowing out the candle, it was a long time before she fell asleep.

She was no less preoccupied when she awoke next morning. She was already out of bed and searching for something to wear when Emily came to wake her. The maid set down the tray holding the chocolate pot and bade her mistress sit down while she took care of things. But Georgiana was too disturbed to sit still. Too much had happened in the last few days.

"Isn't Miss Knatchbull returning today, Miss Georgiana?"

Georgiana hadn't given a thought to her cousin's return. She had spent much of the night trying to disentangle the abundance of things which had taken root in her mind. Not least of these was the problem of how to prove that Boyce Polp's murderer was indeed the person she thought it was. When Emily mentioned Selina, it occurred to her that her cousin could be an unwitting ally in this.

"Emily…"

The maid looked at her warily. "Don't tell me you're planning to take afternoon tea at the Lucky Bell."

"That is an interesting prospect," said Georgiana, "but perhaps one for another day. No, I was only thinking that it would be a gracious gesture to welcome my cousin home in some way."

Emily looked more wary than ever.

Georgiana told her of Miss Knatchbull's mention of her acquaintance with Miss Trent.

"That's interesting, miss. I, um, got myself invited to tea in Lady Winters's kitchen. I managed to speak to Miss Winters's maid and the cook."

"Well done, Emily. Did you learn anything useful?"

"Sort of," said the maid, sounding uncertain. "You were right about that young gentleman we saw being a relative of Miss Trent's. He's her nephew. Apparently he works for that banker – Mr Brookfield? Brookmere?"

"Lewis Brookstone?"

Emily nodded. "Seems it brings him into contact with all sorts of people, including members of the quality."

"Which could include Mr Mortimer."

"It could. It seems he made a point of mentioning he had some fancy friends to try and impress Miss Winters's maid."

Georgiana grinned. "I gather he didn't succeed?"

"Afraid not, miss. She doesn't like these show-off types any more than I do."

"Nor I," said Georgiana. "What else?"

"Well, Miss Trent's nephew was invited along to card games and the like with these people he'd met."

"Gaming hells?" asked Georgiana.

"Maybe," said Emily. "Anyway, the play was more than he could afford. He got in quite deep. Then he had a bit of luck."

"Oh?"

"Won some piece of jewellery that someone pledged. He was showing it off to Miss Winters's maid. She thought it was quite valuable."

"Was she impressed by that?" said Georgiana.

"No," said Emily. "Until he told her he'd won it at play, she thought he might have stolen it. The thing was, he was accused of stealing it."

"What?"

"He'd tried to sell it but couldn't get enough to cover his debts. Didn't really know what he was doing, I expect."

"That's possible," said Georgiana. She had learned that negotiations of this type were a delicate business.

"He thought it was worth more and decided to try some other merchant, but ended up wearing the thing, to impress his fancy friends, I suppose."

"One of them recognised it?"

"In the bank where he worked," said Emily. "It caused quite a scene, and he lost his position."

Georgiana's eyes narrowed. "He didn't tell that to Louisa Winters's maid."

"Oh, no," said Emily, vigorously shaking her head. "But someone heard him tell Miss Trent he'd been discharged. It was the talk of the kitchen." Emily paused. "They enjoy a good gossip, and now she's a bit distant from the house-hold, miss, not really being one of them, at least not any more, there's no love lost, you might say. I don't think they'd have told me so much otherwise. In fact, I don't think they'd have said so much at all, only with you being such a good friend of Miss Louisa."

"Of course. Emily, do you know who pledged the piece that this young man won?"

"No, miss. But I do believe Mr Polp and Mr Barclay played with him, as well as the banker."

"I suppose they wouldn't welcome him at the table after his discharge from the bank," said Georgiana, half to herself, "even in a disreputable gaming hell."

"No, that they wouldn't," said Emily. "They'd still want paying, though, if he'd lost."

"Yes, of course," said Georgiana. "Emily, this is the fourth time I've heard of some item being where it shouldn't have been, and Boyce Polp somehow connected to it."

"You think he stole them?" asked Emily.

"I think it is rather suspicious," said Georgiana. "In fact, Mr Lakesby mentioned an incident with an acquaintance of his. There was cause for believing Mr Polp had stolen something."

For once, Emily did not offer an opinion.

Georgiana decided it was time for a change of subject. "Regarding my cousin," she said briskly. "Some flowers in her room would be a pleasant touch."

"I'll speak to the housemaid, miss."

"Thank you."

"Will there be anything else, miss?"

"No, I don't think so." Georgiana's eyes fell on the pale green morning gown Emily had laid out for her. "Thank you, Emily."

"Were you planning on going out this morning, miss?"

"No. I am not sure what time my cousin will be home

and I think I should be here when she arrives. Quite apart from any reconciliation, I should like to speak to her."

"About Miss Trent?"

"Yes, though whether she'll be willing to speak to me on the subject is another matter." Georgiana thought for a moment. "It might be better if Tom is out of sight," she said. "Not that I have any intention of pandering to her whims over the boy, but it might be prudent to avoid any immediate potential for disruption."

"Yes, miss. I'll see if James can find him something to do which will keep him out of sight."

"Well, there is one thing," said Georgiana, "but it could be difficult to arrange."

"Harry, miss?"

Georgiana nodded, eyeing Emily speculatively as she considered how best to explain what had happened on the previous night. "We had an interesting experience last night. Mr Rogers arrived at the Deacon house, to try to reason with Mr Deacon about the plans to hunt down Mr Polp's killer."

"Did he succeed?"

"Not entirely. Mr Lakesby joined in the discussion in support of Mr Rogers and we left early."

"I see."

"The truly interesting aspect of the matter," said Georgiana, "is that we didn't see Mr Deacon and his friends on the way home but we did see a number of patrons from the Lucky Bell, in a crowd on the road."

Emily's eyes widened. "When you say 'in a crowd', do you mean…?"

Georgiana nodded. "Waving clubs, some of them."

"Good grief. Was anyone hurt?"

"No. Believe it or not, Lady Winters was recognised and

205

we were allowed to go on our way."

Emily slowly shook her head, her expression more and more dumbfounded. "Lady Winters?"

"Yes. Odd, isn't it?"

"That it is, Miss Georgiana. Lady Winters recognised by a highwayman? Was it your friend Harry?"

"No. Harry was not among them," Georgiana said. "I daresay he is still in hiding."

"Did the Runner try to take any of them?" Emily asked curiously.

Georgiana shook her head. "No. He seemed more concerned with trying to disperse the crowd, to avoid further trouble. That in itself was brave enough."

Emily nodded agreement.

"I don't think he has given up," said Georgiana. "However, we were not robbed, or attacked." She spoke again, solemnly. "I feel responsible. Had I not told Cedric… I did not expect anything like that. I just thought the men would stay off the road."

"Well, it could have been nasty if they'd met the gentlemen. At least *they* were stopped."

"Yes," said Georgiana. "For the moment at least. But Mr Deacon and his friends made it very clear that they were running out of patience. If Mr Polp's killer is not caught soon, I'm not sure they can be prevented from taking action themselves. When Selina comes home, I will speak to her and see if I can find out any more about Miss Trent and her nephew. Though you have done well, Emily – very well indeed. After that – " She paused, knowing that the maid would find what she had to say unpalatable. "After that, I really would like to make the acquaintance of Mr Barclay, to find out what he knows about Mr Polp's activities."

Emily pursed her lips. "I'm not sure that's wise, miss."

"No, neither is Mr Lakesby. In fact, he completely refuses to introduce me."

"Well, I can't say that's a surprise, miss."

"Perhaps not. In any case, this is simply a means to an end. I certainly don't propose to build a lasting friendship with the man." Georgiana had not told Emily about her idea for obtaining Barclay's purse. However, it occurred to her that there was one person who would not judge her actions in the same harsh light. "Send Tom to me as soon as I have finished breakfast, would you, please, Emily?"

Tom made no comment about Georgiana's request, but he did look surprised by it. In fact, he repeated her words back to her, to ensure he had understood them correctly.

"You want me to go the Lucky Bell to find you a pick-pocket, to – to teach you how to do it?"

"Yes, that's right."

"Beg your pardon, miss, but the lads might be a bit fearful. They might think it's a trap."

"Yes, I understand that," said Georgiana. "The fact is, it is to do with the murder of that man at the party. Mr Polp."

Tom looked at her attentively, his face creased in concentration.

"I have discovered that someone who was friendly with Mr Polp may know why he was killed. I have learned they went to gaming hells together."

Tom's eyes took on a horror-stricken expression. "Miss, you ain't going to…?"

"Visit one of these establishments? Good heavens, no. However, I should like to know more, so I want to get hold of his purse and see if it contains visiting cards, or any other papers related to the matter."

Tom's brow cleared. "I can do that, miss."

Georgiana looked doubtfully at him. "You?"

Tom nodded. His expression darkened suddenly, as if he realised such knowledge did him no credit.

"It's something you've done before?" Georgiana asked.

"Well… yes, miss. In me younger days," he added weightily, as if he were a man burdened with years rather than a lad of thirteen or so.

"Tom," Georgiana spoke deliberately, "your attempt at highway robbery was less than successful. I'm really not sure that – "

"Oh, I was good at picking pockets, miss. Could have a man's watch out of his pocket and be clean away long before he wanted to know the time." He stopped and blushed. "I – I don't do it any more, miss."

"I am glad to hear that."

"Only if it would help, I'll do it for you," Tom said. "Those aren't the sort of places a lady like you should go."

"I must admit, it would make things easier for me," said Georgiana. "In fact, Mr Lakesby has refused to introduce me to the gentleman concerned, and I can't suppose that my brother would be any more obliging."

"There you are then," said Tom. "He must be a wrong 'un."

Georgiana was still hesitant. If Tom were caught, Selina would have just the excuse she wanted to hand him over the law.

"Very well," she said. "If you can get it, I'll find some way of returning it to him. If you'll teach me how."

Tom seemed disposed to argue until Georgiana pointed out that while he might successfully filch the item, it was likely he would be spotted if he were seen in the man's vicinity a second time. Furthermore, she said, the purse's return would be more difficult to explain, and, she suggested, rather embarrassing. This secured his co-operation immediately, and an agreeable few minutes passed during which Tom taught her the basic skills required to get close to a potential target and open a pocket without putting him on his guard. By the time they parted company, Georgiana had begun to think she had underestimated her young protégé.

They agreed that Georgiana would ask either James or Emily to find some way to identify Mr Barclay to him. She knew neither of them would like the proposed scheme, but would accept it and likely welcome it in preference to her original idea. She still had no idea how to surmount the problem of an introduction to Mr Barclay, but she hoped that the plans she had laid with Tom would allow her to avoid the need for that.

As Tom left the room, Georgiana heard a rush of activity in the hall, signalling her cousin's return. She took a deep breath. She would be glad when this first meeting was over. Her instinct told her that Selina would not let her forget that it was Georgiana who had made the first approach and asked her to come back. Although she had made it clear through the incident over Tom that she would not allow her cousin to take advantage, the situation was still fragile; this was not the moment to set out rules of behaviour. She went into the hall with a smile of welcome pasted on her face.

"Good morning, Selina. I am pleased to see you back."

"Georgiana. Thank you." Selina came forward and offered an unexpected embrace. "I am very pleased to be home. I was just giving James directions about my luggage. I trust that is permitted?"

"Certainly." Georgiana hoped that her cousin would not now go the extreme of checking every little detail with her before speaking to a servant. "Come and have some tea."

"Thank you. That would be very welcome."

Selina followed Georgiana into the breakfast room, her docile demeanour reminiscent of her behaviour when she had first moved in. Georgiana wondered how long it would last. She requested some tea, and the two women passed the time until its arrival in mundane conversation about family matters no more contentious than how much Edward's children had grown and the talents of the new cook Amanda had engaged. So far Selina's homecoming was proving fairly smooth. Neither made reference to their quarrel, and it appeared the matter was closed. Georgiana could only hope her cousin would not attempt to raise any of the issues further once she felt a decent interval had passed.

As the tea was brought in, Selina started to look more settled and comfortable. Georgiana knew she ought to ease carefully into the information she required from her cousin, but time was of the essence. Harry could not remain in hiding forever. Not only was he in danger of hanging for a murder he did not commit, but there was no saying when another group of men in search of vengeance might take to the roads. Last night's good luck would not necessarily hold.

"Tell me, Selina, have you seen anything of Miss Trent since she has been staying with Lady Winters?"

Selina looked at her in some surprise.

"I rather got the impression she was a friend of yours," Georgiana explained. "Is that not the case?"

"Well," said Selina uncertainly, "we have had tea together once or twice. Why do you ask?"

It was clear Georgiana had roused her cousin's suspicions. However, she had no time for subtlety. "Louisa and I saw her talking to a young man when we were out walking a few days ago. I heard somewhere that he was her nephew, but I had seen him elsewhere, in some questionable company."

Selina's eyes grew round. Suddenly she looked as if she had a guilty secret. "Oh, dear," she said. "Is everything known then? Oh, poor Delia!"

"Is what known?"

Selina's flush deepened. She set down her cup and saucer. "It is rather embarrassing for Delia. She told me in the strictest confidence."

This was difficult. How could Georgiana press her to break the confidence of a friend, even if it could hold the key to a murder? She was hardly in a position to explain the truth in the hope of influencing Selina. Perhaps there was another way.

Georgiana smiled. "Then, of course, you must not tell me. I beg your pardon, Selina, I had no idea it was a sensitive matter. I daresay it is nothing and what I heard was an exaggeration."

"What did you hear?" Selina leaned forward anxiously.

"Well, perhaps 'hear' is not the right word," said Georgiana with deliberation. "Please don't think there are any rumours attached to your friend's relative."

Selina looked dubious but relaxed a little. Her eyes remained fixed on her cousin.

"Delia has had a very difficult time," she said at last.

"Oh?" said Georgiana. "I am very sorry to hear that. When I saw her at the Winters house she seemed very strong and capable."

"Well, yes, she is," Selina acknowledged. "One does one's duty, after all."

Georgiana wondered whether her cousin was referring to Miss Trent or herself.

"She has had some difficult charges," commented Miss Knatchbull.

Georgiana suppressed a sigh. Surely that was part of the life of a governess.

"Oh, I would not wish to suggest that Miss Winters was among them," Selina added quickly.

Georgiana smiled. If she was to hear nothing more than schoolroom anecdotes, it would be better to excuse herself and find a way to make the acquaintance of Mr Barclay, or even Mr Brookstone.

"She was trying to support her nephew, you see," Selina continued in an earnest tone, leaning forward again.

Georgiana looked at Selina in some puzzlement. "Oh? Was he left to her guardianship?"

"No, not that, though I believe she is his only relative."

"In any case," said Georgiana, "surely he is now of an age to support himself?"

"Well, yes, but he has had... difficulties. He had hoped to borrow money from Delia to relieve them."

Georgiana could not imagine that Miss Trent was in a position to lend her nephew money, even if she had saved prudently throughout her career. If the 'difficulties' were gaming debts, as Georgiana was certain they were, she suspected the amount would shock Miss Trent.

"Have you ever met the nephew?" Georgiana asked.

Miss Knatchbull shook her head. "No. Delia told me about him when we were having tea one day. It was preying on her mind, and she needed someone to talk to."

"I see." Georgiana grew abstracted.

Miss Knatchbull looked in her in curiosity, a frown beginning to crease her features. "Is something wrong, Georgiana?"

"I beg your pardon? Oh, no, Selina. I'm sorry, I was just

thinking what a worry this must be for Miss Trent."

"Indeed," said Selina. "You can have no idea."

"Of course not," said Georgiana.

"There is one thing," said Selina. "He is fortunate to count a wealthy man among his friends. Mr Barclay."

22

For a moment Georgiana was speechless. It was clear her cousin knew nothing of Mr Barclay's reputation.

"Are – are you acquainted with Mr Barclay?" she asked at last.

"I have met him once," Selina acknowledged in a confidential tone. "I found him quite charming, I must say."

"But if you have not met Miss Trent's nephew…"

"Well," said Selina, in the same confidential tone, "it was quite strange, really. We were taking a walk to the circulating library and met Mr Barclay in the street. He was obviously acquainted with Delia, and stopped to wish her good day. She was kind enough to introduce me."

Georgiana hoped she succeeded in masking her shock, and thanked all the divine forces she could think of for this unexpected bolt of good fortune. She wondered what Edward would say if he knew their cousin had made the acquaintance of a man he clearly did not wish his sister to know.

"Strange that he should not be married," Miss Knatchbull mused. "However, I daresay it is difficult for him. There must be a great many fortune hunters in pursuit of his wealth."

"Yes," said Georgiana, not venturing to remark on the indelicacy of such an observation, nor on the fact that such a condemnation was generally applied to men in search of heiresses. When a lady married a man of considerable means, it was generally considered that she had made a good match. Neither did she think it necessary to mention that wealth alone was insufficient cause for regarding

Mr Barclay as a desirable bridegroom. "Was it just on the one occasion that you met him?" she inquired.

"That's right," Selina nodded. "However, he was very agreeable, and showed a great deal of interest."

Interest in what, Georgiana was itching to ask. She was not at all sure what to make of that remark, or what Selina wanted her to make of it.

"In fact," said Selina, "I believe he is going to Almack's this evening."

This surprised Georgiana even further. The strict patronesses of Almack's drove terror into the hearts of every young lady launched into society. The smallest hint of anything improper could mean a refusal of the vouchers which allowed entry into that sacred establishment; such a rejection inevitably brought with it social failure. Georgiana was astounded to hear that Mr Barclay had persuaded the patronesses that he was a suitable person to allow across Almack's threshold. She wondered who had introduced him; only one name came to mind. But whatever the circumstances, she saw an opportunity too good to ignore.

"Perhaps we should look in at Almack's this evening," said Georgiana. "What do you think, Selina?"

Pleasure suffused Selina's face.

"Why, yes, that sounds an excellent idea, Georgiana."

Georgiana wondered whether Selina would consider her next idea quite so excellent.

"I think, if you don't mind of course," Georgiana said in a placating tone, "that it might be useful to have Tom ride on the outside of the carriage, to escort us."

Miss Knatchbull stiffened.

"Now, Selina, please. In view of how exacting Almack's is, I think an escort is appropriate."

"What about James?" Miss Knatchbull asked.

"James has other duties."

Selina grudgingly acknowledged the truth of this with a curt nod.

"It is a more suitable task for a page," said Georgiana. "Besides, it would also be the perfect opportunity to put an end to the recent unpleasantness, and demonstrate accept-ance of him as a member of the household."

"Very well," said Selina. To Georgiana's surprise, she sounded sincere.

Miss Knatchbull proved as good as her word when they were preparing to leave for the evening. She had little to say, but, there was no evidence of acrimony in her manner when she saw the boy. Tom glowered briefly when he saw her. However, having received a sermon from Georgiana earlier in the day about the importance of getting along with her cousin, it appeared that he too was on his best behaviour: clean, with neatly combed hair, and spruced up in his finest livery, right down to pristine white gloves. Georgiana had no doubt that Harry and his other acquaintances from the Lucky Bell would be hard pressed to recognise him as the grubby urchin they knew.

It appeared that Selina's pleasure at their expedition over-rode her innate suspicion of Tom. Once they were settled in the carriage with the boy perched up on the box outside, her manner became relaxed and loquacious, and they whiled away the drive to Almack's with idle pleasantries.

Tom stepped down nimbly when they arrived, and stood straight-backed at the side of the coach as Georgiana and Selina alighted. He followed a few paces behind them as they entered, and although Miss Knatchbull gave him an odd look she made no comment, and no one else gave him a second glance. As the door swung shut behind them Georgiana whispered to the boy and handed him her pelisse.

He nodded and turned to Miss Knatchbull, holding out a hand to take hers. With only a brief hesitation she handed it to him, and followed just a step behind Georgiana.

Georgiana's hopes were realised almost as soon as they were properly over the threshold. An unfamiliar voice greeted her cousin, and she turned her head to see a gentleman bowing low over Miss Knatchbull's hand. Selina was not only blushing but tilting her head with the coyness of a schoolgirl, compounding this image with a sound something between a giggle and a titter. It embarrassed Georgiana sufficiently to make her wish she could flee and disclaim all knowledge of Miss Knatchbull. However, she remained resolutely a pace or two away, waiting patiently as her cousin exchanged greetings with the fashionably dressed gentleman who was complimenting her appearance. After a few moments he glanced towards her curiously, and Georgiana smiled and shook hands politely when her cousin made the gentleman known to her.

As Mr Barclay expressed himself charmed to meet her, Georgiana had leisure to observe him. His attire did not go to extremes of fashion, but met the stringent rules for attendance at Almack's. It was clearly of the highest quality, and Georgiana had the impression he wanted others to know it.

"Your cousin has spoken of you, Miss Grey," said Mr Barclay.

"Has she?" said Georgiana with a look towards Miss Knatchbull.

The gentleman nodded. "Oh, nothing but good, I assure you," he said with a smile which did not reach his eyes.

Georgiana acknowledged the compliment, and complied with her cousin's eager acceptance of Mr Barclay's offer to escort them into the Assembly Room. Miss Knatchbull took hold of his right arm proprietorially, and Georgiana laid her hand lightly on his left for form's sake. The man made her skin crawl, but she fought to ignore the unpleasant sensation. As they entered the main Assembly Room Georgiana noticed Lakesby. As he caught sight of her his expression turned to thunder, and he moved away almost immediately, apparently deep in conversation with some venerable matron.

It seemed the arrival of her little party created surprise in more breasts than Lakesby's. Georgiana noticed a hint of anxiety, and not a little puzzlement, in the gaze of a lady of her acquaintance as she approached to greet them. Lady Oliver had been a friend of her mother and Georgiana knew they had been girls together. She had kept a friendly eye on Georgiana since Mrs Grey's premature death, happily without the cloying suffocation such a relationship often carried with it. Georgiana knew her ladyship would at the very least have been aware that Mr Barclay had been granted vouchers to this imposing establishment; yet the look in her eyes suggested that she was surprised to see him. Her welcoming words did not lack warmth, however, although her curious eyes followed Mr Barclay as he led Miss Knatchbull off in search of refreshment.

"Georgiana, I did not know you were acquainted with Mr Barclay," Lady Oliver said softly.

Georgiana felt obliged to defend herself. Lady Oliver was one of the few people whose good opinion she valued. "Not precisely acquainted; I have only just met him. My cousin introduced us almost as we arrived. I understand she encountered him through a mutual acquaintance."

"I see," said Lady Oliver. "Your cousin seems very taken with him." Her eyes again followed the progress of Miss Knatchbull and Mr Barclay to the supper room.

"Well – "

Lady Oliver turned back to face Georgiana. "May I offer a word of warning, Georgiana? Mr Barclay's reputation is not of the highest. You and your cousin might not do well to encourage too close an acquaintance."

Georgiana nodded. "Thank you, Lady Oliver. I will bear that in mind. If you don't mind my asking, do you know how he comes to be admitted here?"

Lady Oliver frowned. "I heard he was introduced by a friend. As you can see, he is most charming." She smiled. "It's not often one of the patronesses makes such an error of judgement."

"No, indeed," said Georgiana warmly. "Do you know who introduced Mr Barclay?"

"I believe it was Mr Polp."

As Lady Oliver moved away to greet another acquaintance, Georgiana cast her eyes around the room. Many of the usual faces were present. Edward and Amanda were not among them, however, and neither did she notice Lady Winters and Louisa. In their absence it seemed odd that Lakesby should have come on his own. Gentlemen often complained Almack's was too respectable and more than a little slow. Those of more dashing tastes considered it had little to offer in the way of entertainment or refreshment. If they were to be found there, it was usually at the behest of some female relative.

Tom had disposed of the wraps, and hovered a few feet away from Georgiana, his saucer-like eyes taking in the elegance around him. Georgiana was proud to see that his appearance fitted in as well as any of the other servants. She was hopeful that this would both assist her to carry out her plan and offer a measure of protection if anything went wrong.

"I see Mr Barclay has not left you completely without a chaperon."

Georgiana turned to see Mr Lakesby had approached from behind her. His manner was stiff and his tone disapproving. However, she sensed an element of relief as he glanced towards Tom. The boy himself looked puzzled. He was usually rather wary around Lakesby, as if he expected that at any moment, that gentleman might think better of the decision he had made some months earlier, and hand Tom over to the law for holding up his carriage.

"Where are your aunt and cousin?" Georgiana asked.

Lakesby raised an eyebrow. "Not here. I am not always dancing attendance on my Aunt Beatrice's whims."

"I was not suggesting that you were." Georgiana's tone was casual.

"So you achieved your introduction." Lakesby's voice had an edge.

Georgiana turned to her page. "Tom, would you get me something to drink, please? Some lemonade, I think."

"Yes, miss."

"Would you care for something, Mr Lakesby?" she asked.

"No." Lakesby spoke curtly, then looked at the boy's upturned face. He relented. "No, thank you."

Tom trotted off on his errand. Georgiana turned back to Mr Lakesby. "Yes, I made Mr Barclay's acquaintance just a few minutes ago, as we came in. My cousin introduced me."

"Your cousin?" Lakesby's astonishment put paid to his chilly manner. "How on earth does she come to know him?"

"Through Louisa's governess."

"What? Miss Trent? That pillar of respectability? How

on earth could she be acquainted with a character like Barclay?"

"Through her nephew, apparently." Georgiana paused, then decided to take the gamble. "I believe he is also acquainted with Mr Mortimer."

Lakesby gave her a sharp look. "Polp's brother-in-law? Good grief." His eyes narrowed. "How do you know that?"

"I don't remember. Someone mentioned it."

"Do you remember who?"

"Not really."

Lakesby offered no further comment. She was certain he did not believe her but thought it best to brazen it out.

"So, your cousin is acquainted with Miss Trent. Are they close friends?"

"I'm not sure I would go as far as that," replied Georgiana, "I believe they take tea together occasionally."

"I see."

Georgiana's gaze took in the rest of the room, passing with interest over those who had chosen to attend this evening's Assembly. She noticed that her cousin was still in the company of Mr Barclay; they had not yet progressed as far as the supper room. There was no sign of Tom.

"Taken with him, is she?" came Lakesby's voice.

Georgiana turned. "I beg your pardon?"

"Miss Knatchbull. Is she taken with Mr Barclay?"

"I don't think she knows him well enough to make a judgement of that nature," said Georgiana dryly. She began to make her way slowly towards the centre of the room.

Lakesby followed. "Perhaps a word of warning might be in order. I should hate to see your cousin taken advantage of."

"Thank you, Mr Lakesby. I'll bear that in mind."

Lakesby frowned. "That page of yours is the devil of a

time getting your lemonade."

"Is he?"

"Perhaps I should go and see what's keeping him?"

"No, please don't concern yourself, Mr Lakesby," said Georgiana. She had a fair notion of what was keeping Tom. She looked back towards Miss Knatchbull and Mr Barclay. She still could not see her page.

"Would you like me to fetch you something?"

"No, thank you. I'm sure Tom will return shortly."

Lakesby did not reply, but she was aware that he was watching her closely. Georgiana thought she detected suspicion in his expression.

"So where are your aunt and cousin this evening?" she asked.

"How the devil should I know?"

Georgiana's cool green eyes appraised him. "If you are disposed to be unpleasant, Mr Lakesby, perhaps you would have done better to have followed their example and stayed away." She turned and started to walk away from him.

Her pace was quick for the decorous atmosphere of Almack's and Lakesby had to move quickly himself to keep pace with her. He caught her arm, and one or two people glanced at them. Georgiana looked down at his hand grasping her arm, then raised her eyes to meet his.

Lakesby hastily released her and begged her pardon with a hint of embarrassment: something he had never before exhibited in her company. She did not speak and, when he drew a breath, she sensed he was about to apologise again.

Whether or not this was the case Georgiana did not get the opportunity to discover. A ripple of alarm and disruption ran through the sedate gathering. Both Georgiana and Lakesby turned to look towards its source.

Standing before one of the patronesses, voicing a

complaint in as stern a tone as he dared, was Mr Barclay. Next to him, with Mr Barclay's hand gripping his shoulder tightly, was Tom.

23

Georgiana felt Lakesby's gaze upon her as she took in the scene. From the corner of her eye she saw that he had raised his quizzing glass.

"Dear me," was all he said.

Georgiana moved forward to the little group. "Is there a problem?"

"Nothing for you to be concerned about, Miss Grey" said Mr Barclay, his tone a honeyed combination of condescension and a suggestion that she should mind her own business.

"But indeed there is," said Georgiana. "This boy is my page. I am responsible for him. Now, may I ask again, is there a problem?"

Mr Barclay looked taken aback at Georgiana's words. "I see," he said. "In that case, Miss Grey, I am sorry to have to tell you that this boy tried to rob me."

"Indeed?"

There was just enough scepticism in Georgiana's voice to trigger startled expressions on the faces around her. Even Tom's eyes widened.

Mr Barclay recovered himself. "Yes," he said. "He tried to steal my purse."

"Indeed?"

Barclay glanced from Georgiana to Tom. The gentleman was beginning to look uneasy. His voice had lost some of its honeyed quality when he replied. "Most certainly he did. I am sorry, Miss Grey, but if you are responsible for this boy, it falls to you to take some action."

"So, Mr Barclay," said Georgiana slowly, "you are suggesting that I am harbouring a thief in my household?"

"Well…"

"I know this boy," came Lakesby's voice.

A flicker of anxiety crossed Tom's face, and Barclay's eyes narrowed in suspicion.

"Do you indeed?"

"Yes," said Lakesby. "You may accept Miss Grey's assurance that he is not a thief."

Barclay glanced down towards Tom again, his irritation evident.

"If you choose to question Miss Grey's word," said Lakesby haughtily, "perhaps we should discuss it in another place?"

Lady Oliver came forward, smiling at the horrified patroness. "I'm sure this is simply a misunderstanding," she said. "There is no need for a dispute."

Lakesby bowed towards the ladies and begged pardon.

Georgiana seized the opportunity Lady Oliver was providing. "Mr Barclay, my page went to fetch me some refreshment. I daresay he passed a little too close, and brushed against you. He is relatively new to his post and not very experienced, I'm afraid. Please accept my apologies."

Barclay's expression suggested he wasn't fully satisfied, although Georgiana's apology appeared to mollify him to some extent. An exchange of looks with the more mature ladies seemed to persuade him it would be wise to let the matter drop. But his outward calm fooled nobody. It was common knowledge that anyone involved in the merest hint of a brawl within Almack's hallowed walls need not expect further admittance; after tonight his vouchers would be withdrawn.

Barclay's jaw tensed. He bowed stiffly, agreed he had probably been mistaken, and apologised for his error.

The look he cast in the direction of Lakesby and Tom burned with barely suppressed hostility. After a quick, uncertain glance at his employer, Tom cast down his eyes.

As the group dispersed, Georgiana turned to Lady Oliver. "Thank you, ma'am. I am very sorry for any embarrassment this unpleasantness has caused," she said.

Lady Oliver waved a hand. "Please, don't concern yourself. It was not your fault." She looked towards Tom. "However, it might be better if the boy were to wait outside with your carriage. That is, if you can manage without him."

"Yes, of course."

The general disapproval of Mr Barclay appeared to have worked in Georgiana's favour. Thankful for that, and for Lady Oliver's support, she put a hand to Tom's shoulder and directed him towards the door. Lakesby made to follow them; to prevent him from doing so she asked if he would be good enough to fetch her the refreshment the boy had failed to obtain. Lakesby's eyes remained fixed on her, unmoving as she and Tom walked towards the bright area of the entrance. The plentiful candles lit their path to the front door, and once outside they walked past the torches which helped the elegantly dressed to identify the more hazardous areas of the road. They attracted curious glances from a couple of grooms who were idling the time away as they waited for their employers; Georgiana led Tom a few yards from them, safely out of earshot.

"What happened?"

"Dunno, miss."

"Well, that's very helpful," said Georgiana. "I thought you said you were good at this?"

"I am," Tom said hotly. "On me life." He frowned. "To tell the truth, miss, I didn't get near him."

"How could he have caught you if you didn't get near him?"

"I dunno, miss. Maybe it were someone else, or maybe he just thought I was going to do something. I swear I didn't go near him."

Georgiana frowned thoughtfully. "I wonder… Was my cousin anywhere near him?"

"I didn't see her, not then," Tom said. He tilted his head slightly and looked up at her. "Do you think she might have said something to him?"

"She might."

"But she don't know – " Tom looked perplexed.

"No, but I'm afraid that won't necessarily stop her talking," said Georgiana. "Don't worry about it. I daresay she is feeling aggrieved."

"What shall we do, miss?"

"You had better wait out here," she said. "There was too much attention drawn to you. I shall have to do it myself."

"In there?" he said in awe. "Lor' miss, what if you get caught as well? There'll be the devil of a stink."

"I know." Georgiana nibbled her bottom lip.

"Then there's that friend of yours," Tom pointed out. "He's got his eyes on you like an 'awk."

"True, but I don't think he would give me away. The thing is, I may not get another chance. Mr Barclay and I – er – don't generally move in the same circles."

"Well, jolly good thing if you ask me, miss," said Tom.

"I didn't."

Tom begged her pardon, clearly embarrassed that his employer's confidence had so far prompted him to forget they were not on equal terms. He stammered an apology, which turned into an increasingly tangled explanation that he thought the gent was a smoky cove and generally unworthy of his mistress's notice. Georgiana interrupted him before it grew garbled beyond understanding; she recognised the admiration which lay beneath his behaviour, and had enough sympathy for him to spare him further embarrassment.

When she went back inside Lakesby was waiting near the door, a glass of wine in his hand and a shadow of suspicion in his eyes.

"Is everything all right?" he asked smoothly, his voice at odds with his expression.

"Oh, yes," Georgiana said, accepting the glass from him with thanks. "It was just a misunderstanding. Uncomfortable to be sure, but nothing which can't be settled. Thank you for vouching for Tom, by the way."

"You are most welcome." Lakesby looked at her intently. "Do you believe him?"

"Whom?" she asked with almost convincing naivety.

"Your page."

"Of course. Why shouldn't I?"

Lakesby looked thoughtful. "It is just that, in view of his – ah – history, I would have thought a certain amount of scepticism might be prudent."

"Would you?"

Lakesby gave a small smile and shook his head ruefully. "Well, he is a member of your household. I am sure you know your own business best."

"Thank you. I do."

Lakesby appeared rather amused. Georgiana relented; he had, after all, given her his support in a potentially difficult situation. "Tom knows better than to attempt anything of such a troublesome nature. I have certainly not had any problems of that kind in my household." She smiled. "However, whether I can afford to go on feeding him is a debatable question."

"Yes, boys of that age have a healthy appetite."

Lakesby fell into step beside Georgiana as she began to walk back to the Assembly Rooms.

"May I escort you in to supper, Miss Grey?"

Georgiana hesitated momentarily, her eyes in search of her cousin. Seeing Miss Knatchbull rise from her chair and accept the arm of Mr Barclay, Georgiana suppressed a sigh of resignation. At least this was one place in which Selina would no longer be able to pursue that acquaintance after tonight.

She turned back to Lakesby with a smile. "Thank you, Mr Lakesby. I shall be pleased to go in with you."

Lakesby followed the direction of Georgiana's gaze. "I do not think your cousin will come to any harm here."

"No, but she is raising comment." Georgiana shook her head, a rueful smile on her face. "I never thought to say that of her."

"I do not imagine she is aware," said Lakesby. "I rather get the impression she does not realise Barclay is less than reputable."

"No," said Georgiana.

They walked into the supper room and Lakesby held out a chair for her.

"So," he said, "having achieved your own ambition to meet Mr Barclay, how do you intend to pursue your acquaintance with him?"

"I'm not sure I would call it an ambition, precisely," said Georgiana. "Curiosity, perhaps."

"Ah." Lakesby's tone suggested he was not convinced this was the full story.

"I am intrigued by his connection with Mr Polp," Georgiana continued, "someone of whom everyone speaks well. Yet it seems Mr Barclay is barely tolerated. The more I hear, the odder it all sounds."

"Yes, it is incongruous," agreed Lakesby. "What do they say, these people who speak well of Mr Polp?"

Georgiana furrowed her brow. "I can think of nothing specific, but a picture seems to emerge, from talk by different people. Some of what has been said is rather unsavoury, and yet…"

"He was generally well liked."

"Yes," said Georgiana.

"I know. It makes no sense."

"You mentioned a friend of yours?"

Lakesby nodded. "Yes. Something went missing from his home when Polp was a guest there. He was convinced Polp had taken it. I believe he mentioned it to his wife, who was horrified that he could even suggest such a possibility."

"She didn't believe it?"

"No. My friend's reasoning was that if his own wife refused to believe it, he would have little chance of convincing anyone else."

"Yes." Georgiana was thinking about what she had learned from her less law-abiding acquaintances. It certainly appeared that Mr Polp had a talent for collecting items which had other rightful owners, a talent which raised comment even among the clientele of the Lucky Bell.

"Miss Grey?"

Lakesby's voice was gentle. Georgiana realised she had fallen silent for longer than was polite. "I beg your pardon, Mr Lakesby."

"What is it?"

"I wonder," she said, "whether anything – else – was found among Mr Polp's possessions."

"Which did not belong to him," said Lakesby. "A difficult

question to ask. His sister might not even know."

"No. But I wonder whether his brother-in-law would."

"That too seems unlikely," said Lakesby.

"Perhaps," said Georgiana, mulling this over. A thought occurred to her. "Polp's valet would know."

"Yes, he would," said Lakesby. "Excellent thinking, Miss Grey. However, there remains the difficulty of how to question the valet on the subject."

"I shall speak to James," said Georgiana. "Or perhaps Emily..."

"I suspect that would be more effective."

"In the meantime..." said Georgiana, looking towards Mr Barclay, conscious that her task wasn't completed.

Lakesby followed the direction of her gaze. "In the meantime, try not to worry too much about it this evening. Your cousin's choice of companion for the evening has already attracted attention. If you were also to seek him out the tongues would rattle for days."

Georgiana acquiesced; if Barclay's suspicions had been raised, there was little to be gained in approaching him just yet. Looking up from her plate, she noticed Miss Knatchbull's head bend as if she was listening intently to something Mr Barclay was saying. She began to giggle, and Barclay threw back his head and laughed. The situation made Georgiana uneasy; she had no wish to see Selina duped by a scoundrel.

"Would you prefer your cousin was not in Mr Barclay's company?" asked Lakesby.

Georgiana looked at him in surprise. Could the man read her thoughts?

"Is that why you were so eager to meet him?"

"No," said Georgiana. "Besides, I would hardly say eager, Mr Lakesby. Merely interested."

"Very well."

The subject was dropped, though it did not fade from Georgiana's mind. She suspected it also remained in Lakesby's, and saw him occasionally glancing in her cousin's direction. Selina was clearly enjoying Mr Barclay's company. They continued to attract notice from those around them, and Georgiana sensed a degree of pride in Selina's manner at having claimed so much of the gentleman's attention.

As they were finishing their supper, Lady Oliver approached and pleasantries were exchanged. Her manner was agreeable, but Georgiana could not miss her glance towards Miss Knatchbull and her companion. Georgiana sensed her ladyship's disapproval and, while nothing was said, she felt she was expected to drop a word of warning in her cousin's ear.

Georgiana and Lakesby returned to the main hall a few moments after Miss Knatchbull and Mr Barclay. Georgiana's gaze kept returning to them, and her cousin met her eye and came towards them, hands clasped in front of her and an uncharacteristically pert smile on her face. Mr Barclay was a few steps behind her. His earlier unpleasant demeanour had disappeared, but Georgiana almost preferred that to this simulated friendliness. There was something disagreeable in his beaming pink face and red-rimmed eyes.

"That was a very pleasant supper, was it not, Georgiana?" said Selina.

"Yes, certainly." Georgiana looked at her cousin curiously. She had expected some mention of the earlier incident involving Tom, and could only assume Selina was not aware of it. Georgiana had no doubt that her cousin would seize any opportunity to crow over anything which she thought would support her opinion of the boy and prove her judgement correct.

Georgiana turned to Mr Barclay, hoping the smile she offered him did not look too forced. "Did you enjoy your supper, sir?"

"Indeed, I did," Mr Barclay said, "though I must say, I enjoyed the company a great deal more."

Selina blushed and tittered in a fashion which Georgiana found highly embarrassing. She felt an impulse to flee, and was grateful when Mr Lakesby came to the rescue.

"Perhaps I may be permitted to escort you and your cousin home, Miss Grey? Shall I fetch your cloaks?"

"Oh, well…" Miss Knatchbull cast a hopeful look towards Mr Barclay.

"Thank you, Mr Lakesby. That would be very kind," said Georgiana.

Georgiana's firm tone put paid to any plans Miss Knatchbull and Mr Barclay might have considered for extending the evening. As Lakesby bowed and departed in search of their wraps his manner suggested nothing other than ordinary courtesy. However, as he caught Georgiana's eye, she detected a hint of amusement.

Mr Barclay was still with the two ladies when Mr Lakesby returned. His own simply cut black cloak was over his shoulders and the two pelisses hung over his left arm. As he lifted Miss Knatchbull's to help her put it on, Barclay stepped forward and took it from him, the abruptness of his manner causing even Lakesby to look at him in astonishment. He shrugged and turned towards Georgiana, holding up her pelisse to place it over her shoulders.

Suddenly, Georgiana saw her chance. As soon as her pelisse was secured she dropped her reticule. Lakesby looked a little surprised, but before he could retrieve it she bent down herself. Her foot slipped and she caught hold of her cousin's arm. Selina looked at her in surprised concern, which turned to annoyance as Georgiana's efforts to regain her balance tipped her against Mr Barclay. His purse was out of his pocket and buried in the folds of her pelisse in an instant. He grasped her elbow and helped her to her feet, dismissing her profuse apologies with a smile she found nauseatingly smug.

24

The suspicion in Lakesby's eyes did not escape Georgiana's notice. However, she sailed out of Almack's calmly and stepped into her carriage with a smile of thanks which implied she was blissfully unaware that there was anything wrong. Selina, for her part, was looking very cross. Georgiana suppressed a desire to laugh; surely her cousin could not be harbouring the notion that she was trying to steal the interest of the man who had made Miss Knatchbull the object of his gallantry for the evening.

Georgiana had managed to slip the purse to Tom as they approached the carriage, taking advantage of a moment when Lakesby's attention was taken up with instructing his groom to send his own carriage home. Of course he would not have committed the impropriety of searching her, but it would only have taken a jolt of the carriage for the purse to slip out of her hand and into plain sight – and Lakesby was far too observant.

Tom had looked at her with surprise and admiration, and immediately secreted the purse in the pocket of his own coat, nodding at her whispered instruction to wait for her in the small saloon when they arrived home.

There was an odd atmosphere on the journey home. Miss Knatchbull was stiff and silent, and while she did not precisely glare at Georgiana, it was clear she was not in charity with her. Lakesby was largely silent, though he responded to the occasional polite remark; his eyes remained fixed on Georgiana. She saw unasked questions there, and though she knew Miss Knatchbull's presence would prevent him from voicing his concerns, she also knew he would be unlikely to forget them.

"Thank you for your kindness in escorting us home, Mr Lakesby," Georgiana said formally as the carriage drew up in front of her home.

She saw Tom jump down from the box. He waited at the side of the carriage; a flicker of a glance into its interior was the only suggestion that he was not yet fully trained. Miss Knatchbull stepped out unusually quickly, bidding Mr Lakesby a cursory goodnight as she went.

Lakesby alighted and assisted Georgiana down. He declined her offer of the use of the carriage to take him home.

"It is a fine evening. I shall be glad of the walk," he said.

Georgiana felt his gaze still upon her as she mounted the steps; it was some moments before he began to walk away. Tom, a few steps behind her, gave the departing gentleman a nervous glance, clearly recognising the signs of suspicion. As Georgiana went indoors, she found James helping her cousin to take off her pelisse. As he turned to assist Georgiana, Miss Knatchbull bade her a chilly goodnight, peeling off her long white gloves as she ascended the stairs.

Tom stared after her. "Lor', miss, what's wrong with her?"

Georgiana quelled this with a look.

"Beg pardon, miss," Tom said, abashed.

"Please wait for me as I told you," she said.

Tom went off obediently and if James was surprised to see him open the door of the small saloon, he did not show it.

"Have Emily come to me in ten minutes," Georgiana said to James.

"Yes, miss."

As Georgiana entered the small saloon, Tom stood waiting,

hands folded behind his back, as if he was making an effort to behave more correctly than usual.

"You have it?" she said.

The boy nodded and held out Mr Barclay's purse on the palm of his hand. Georgiana smiled.

"Thank you, Tom." She was about to put her hand inside the purse and extract a coin to give him, but she stopped herself in time, remembering that while no one would question such an action from the Crimson Cavalier, it would certainly provoke comment in Miss Georgiana Grey.

"You going to give it back, miss?"

"Certainly," she said, "once I see what it has to tell me." Hesitating for just a moment, she sat down and bade him lock the door. When he had done so she beckoned him forward.

Georgiana tipped the contents of Mr Barclay's purse on to a small round table next to her chair. Under Tom's astonished gaze, she sorted through the items one by one. Most were fairly ordinary, things one would expect a gentleman to have about his person. Georgiana's eyes lingered for a moment on a pearl-topped snuff box. She opened it, curious to see if it fulfilled its intended purpose. A few grains of snuff spilled on the table – and so did a little bundle of paper, carefully folded. She closed the box, set it down and picked up the paper.

Tom swept the snuff from the table without taking his eyes off her. Georgiana gave a little frown when he brushed his hands together, scattering snuff over the carpet, but she made no comment.

There were three pieces of paper folded together. They were too small to be letters, and Georgiana had never previously seen anything like them, but from the numbers written on them she suspected they were vowels pledged at play. None bore a full signature, but there was a set of initials on each. Georgiana stared at these, trying to determine who had promised them. She did notice that none of the initials were Boyce Polp's. They were not written clearly, and she struggled to decipher an initial which could have been N, M or even H. She sighed in frustration, but supposed that when a gambler was reduced to offering vowels, his handwriting was the least of his worries.

She picked up a card which lay on the table beside the snuff box. At first she thought it was a visiting card, but closer inspection revealed the name of one of the less salubrious gaming establishments, inscribed in an immaculate copperplate hand which was incongruous given the reputation of the club. The card was creased across the middle in a manner which suggested that it was frequently consulted. Something about its well-thumbed appearance increased Georgiana's distaste for its owner.

Tom looked with great interest at the items which remained on the table. Georgiana found herself wondering whether his curiosity would offer up some useful observation, or if he might even have some shred of knowledge which could answer the questions in her own mind.

"Do you know this place, Tom?"

He nodded. "Heard of it, miss. Never been there, mind," he said, as if he sensed that she would disapprove and was anxious to reassure her.

Georgiana smiled. "No, I'm sure you haven't. You've heard something about it, though?"

Tom hesitated. "Well, miss, it's a bit low, but full of nobs. Don't understand it myself."

"Go on."

"From what I hear, they all lose money. They win when

they first go, once or twice like, but then they start losing – a lot." He shrugged. "Can't see why they keep doing it myself, but it's their money."

"Yes," said Georgiana, "except that perhaps it's not. I suppose if they are in debt to the place, or to another player there…"

"Waiting for the luck to turn, miss?"

"It could be. It could also be that they are expected to keep on going there until the debt is paid."

Tom frowned at this. "That don't seem right, miss."

"No."

The boy shrugged again. "Well, I've heard say it's a nasty place."

Georgiana had picked up the vowels again. Studying them told her very little, except that the sums they represented were high. She wondered how many men had left one of the tables only to shoot themselves before the night was out. She also had a suspicion that a good many faced someone else's pistol, with paces measured out on the damp grass in the light of the sunrise after a particularly acrimonious session.

Tom was still watching her, waiting to be told whether she needed him to do anything else. She smiled.

"Thank you, Tom. I appreciate all your help this evening. We'll keep this between ourselves."

She dug her fingers into her reticule and produced a couple of coins which she handed to him. He looked surprised but thanked her warmly before trotting off to bed.

Georgiana remained for a few moments after he had gone, turning the vowels around between her hand and the table. She felt she was missing something. Frustration pressed down on her as the candle burned low in its socket. She went through the items again and again, to no avail, until Emily came in search of her.

"Miss Georgiana?"

Georgiana looked up. "Emily," she said with a smile. "What time is it?"

"A little after two."

Georgiana looked again at the little collection of items on the table. Emily glanced at them uneasily as she approached.

"Mr Barclay's?"

Georgiana nodded.

Emily shook her head slowly.

"I can't believe you did this."

Georgiana sighed. "It hasn't helped a great deal, except to prove a connection between Mr Barclay and – " She looked at the card again. "Clockton's Select Rooms." She gave an ironic smile. "It sounds as if it is anything but select."

"Please, miss, tell me you haven't been there?"

"No, but Tom has heard something about it."

Emily's eyes widened and her face paled. "You've discussed this with Tom?"

"He was rather helpful." Georgiana's finger traced a carving on the top of the snuff box.

Emily was looking at her intently. "Did he take the purse?"

Georgiana rose and collected the items on the table, putting them back in the purse. She picked up the candle Emily had put on the table.

"It is time we went to bed, Emily."

The two went upstairs quietly, the silence continuing until they were in Georgiana's bedroom. As she prepared for bed, Georgiana remained in a brown study.

"What is it, miss?"

"I'm sorry, Emily. My mind was elsewhere."

"So I see."

Mr Barclay's purse lay on the nightstand. Georgiana wandered over to it and picked it up, turning it round and round in her hand as she sat on the edge of her bed. Now she told Emily everything that had taken place at Almack's. The maid's bland expression did not deceive her. As Emily moved around the room putting clothes away, Georgiana found herself fingering the snuffbox again. She didn't know what drew her to it.

"Are you going to keep that?" Emily asked.

Georgiana shook her head. "No. It would be too easy for Mr Barclay to discover who was responsible. He accused Tom before he had even tried to take the purse."

"But how will you get it back to him?"

"I don't know. I'll think of something. Perhaps I'll suggest he dropped it when I stumbled."

Emily looked unconvinced. "How are you going to get to speak to him?" she asked. "You can hardly just call on him, especially if he's a wrong 'un."

"No, that is true," said Georgiana.

Emily looked at her apprehensively. "You're not thinking of stopping his carriage?"

"What? No, of course not. Have you any idea how odd that would look, holding him up to return his purse?"

Emily nodded, relief in her eyes.

"Returning the purse is probably the smallest difficulty," said Georgiana. "What I really need to know is what goes on in that club."

Emily grimaced. "You'll not get in there," she said, "either as yourself or the Crimson Cavalier."

"No," said Georgiana. "I don't think I need to. Maybe I just need to talk to the right people."

Emily pointed at the snuff box. "What is it about *that* that has you so interested?"

"I don't know," said Georgiana, looking at the trinket in her hand. "I wonder where he got it."

"Well, he's rich, isn't he? Perhaps he just bought it."

"Yes," said Georgiana. She sighed. "And perhaps this whole business will make more sense after a good night's sleep." She tapped the nightstand with her fingers. "There is one other thing which worries me. Nothing's been heard of Harry for a while. I hope he's all right."

"I'm sure he can take care of himself," said Emily, turning down the bed covers.

Georgiana agreed, but found herself unable to put the matter out of her mind. She slept fitfully, and had a mixture of disjointed dreams which left her feeling anything but rested.

At breakfast, she found her cousin full of plans for the day. Selina had recovered her good humour; her manner was brisk and cheerful. Even Tom's arrival at the door bearing a note failed to unsettle her. She did look curiously at the paper he handed to Georgiana, but made no comment; instead she suggested more tea and offered to ring for it. Georgiana wondered with unease whether this sunny side of her cousin's disposition had been aroused by the Mr Barclay's attentions the previous evening. Georgiana was certain Selina had received little, if any, notice from prospective suitors, and situated as she was, she would no doubt welcome an offer at this unlikely stage in her life. Georgiana was not certain of Miss Knatchbull's age, but now that she considered the matter, she realised her cousin could be no more than ten or twelve years older than herself, though her generally dull appearance and manner made her appear older. Suddenly she was sorry for Selina.

Even if Mr Barclay was not Boyce Polp's killer, he was a wholly ineligible match. Georgiana dared not imagine Edward's reaction were he to learn his cousin was encouraging such a man's attention.

Georgiana became aware of her cousin's voice and smiled. "I beg your pardon, Selina. My thoughts were far away."

"So I see," said Selina crisply. "I declare, Georgiana, you seem to be more and more in a daydream these days. I don't know what is the matter with you."

Georgiana was still listening with only half an ear, frowning over the note she was reading.

"Georgiana!" Selina's voice had a sharp edge.

Georgiana looked up. "I'm sorry, Selina."

"It must be a very interesting note," Selina said pointedly.

"I must go out. I beg your pardon, but I'm afraid something has happened."

Selina was immediately all contrition. "Oh, dear. I hope it is not bad news?"

"Well, yes, I'm afraid it is." Georgiana had already risen from the table and was pulling the bell. "Ah, James," she said when the footman appeared. "Would you please ask Emily to fetch my pelisse? I will also need the carriage brought around. I must go out right away."

"Yes, miss."

"Would you like me to go with you?" asked Selina solicitously.

Georgiana smiled in appreciation. "Thank you, Selina, but this is something I must attend to alone."

"Very well."

Georgiana had the impression this was not the answer Selina wanted, but she seemed disappointed more than displeased. In any case, she could not worry about her cousin's feelings at the moment. She went quickly up the stairs, the note still in her hand, surprising even Emily with her hurried, incommunicative manner. The maid knew better than to question her but was determined to ensure her mistress looked fit to be seen, despite her haste to be gone.

Within a few minutes, Georgiana was settled in her phaeton, reading the note again, trying to take it in. She had been unable to believe the truth of it. Yet the words were clear, if incongruous, in Louisa's copperplate hand on the elegant pale rose notepaper.

Georgiana,

Please come quickly. Something dreadful has happened. The house is in uproar. Miss Trent is in hysterics. Her nephew has been killed.

> *Yours ever,*
> *Louisa.*

25

Georgiana's arrival did not find the house precisely in uproar but certainly not in a state of normality. The footman who opened the door to her was outwardly calm but Georgiana thought she detected a hint of a flush. He seemed taken aback to see her, and hesitated fleetingly when she asked to see Miss Winters. But he recovered his composure quickly and asked her to step inside.

Georgiana had not been waiting many minutes when Louisa appeared. She came down the stairs as quickly as her slippered feet could carry her, and hurried over to greet her visitor, her expression one of serious concern. Georgiana thought she heard someone sobbing; the sound seemed to come from upstairs. It was a husky noise: not gentle, lady-like weeping but loud and strident, almost like an animal in distress.

"Oh, Georgiana, I'm so glad you're here," said Louisa. "It's been horrible. I would never have believed Miss Trent could cry so much. Or so loud," she added as another wail sounded. "Mama is beside herself."

"But what has happened?" asked Georgiana, not at all sure that Lady Winters would welcome her presence.

"It was the oddest thing," said Louisa. "Mama and I were having breakfast and Miss Trent just burst in, exclaiming that her nephew had been killed. Mama has been trying to calm her down ever since. It was so strange. She has always seemed so serious, so proper and correct."

"It's not improper to grieve for a relative."

"No, but – " Louisa paused. "I didn't think they were as close as all that."

"What happened to Miss Trent's nephew?" asked Georgiana.

"That Bow Street Runner came to see Miss Trent," said Louisa. "He said her nephew had drowned. Oh, Georgiana, it sounded horrible."

Georgiana followed her friend up the stairs to a small sitting room, and asked the footman to arrange for some tea. Miss Trent was still crying, in a room not far away; she closed the door on the sound, persuaded Louisa into a chair, and gradually coaxed the story out of her.

"It is certain that it is Miss Trent's nephew?" she asked, taking a seat opposite Louisa.

"It seems so," said Louisa. "He had some document on his person which appeared to belong to him." She chewed her underlip, looking very childlike. "They think he killed himself."

"Really?"

Louisa nodded. "Apparently he had gaming debts, quite enormous ones, which he couldn't pay."

"So have many young men," said Georgiana. "They don't all kill themselves."

"No, but it was not as if he was a duke's son and could expect to inherit a fortune," Louisa pointed out. "His position…"

"Yes, of course." Georgiana was thoughtful. "Do you know what happened?"

"Only that he was found face down in the river." Louisa suddenly broke down. Tears began to roll down her cheeks. "Oh, Georgiana, it sounded quite horrible."

"Yes, of course." Georgiana began to make soothing noises to calm her friend. She suspected Louisa's distress had been lingering under the surface since she witnessed the death of Boyce Polp.

"The Runner asked if Miss Trent could go and – and

246

s-see him, to confirm who it was."

"Oh dear."

Louisa nodded vigorously. "Indeed. I do not think she is up to it."

"It will be very upsetting for her." Georgiana stared ahead as she spoke; this had triggered a thought of which she could not let go.

Louisa watched her, sniffling as her tears abated. "What is it, Georgiana?"

Georgiana shook her head. "Nothing."

The door opened and Lady Winters entered, looking more fraught than Georgiana had ever seen her.

"Here you are, Louisa. Oh, Miss Grey, I did not know you were here."

Her ladyship's tone was not welcoming. Georgiana took the hint and rose.

"I asked her to come, Mama."

"Really, Louisa, I hardly think…"

"I wanted a friend to talk to, Mama."

There was a sliver of determination in Louisa's voice which took both Lady Winters and Georgiana by surprise. Lady Winters drew a breath. "Louisa, this is a matter best kept within the family."

"I don't see what difference it makes, Mama. To be sure, it is very tragic but it's not a scandal."

Lady Winters said nothing but looked at her daughter meaningfully. Georgiana glanced from one to the other.

"Indeed, I have no wish to cause difficulties, and I really should be going," she said.

Louisa was crestfallen but any further discussion was prevented by a knock at the door. Lady Winters glared at it in some irritation before bidding the person outside to enter. The door was opened by a footman whose well trained expression betrayed just a shadow of uneasiness.

"I beg your pardon, my lady, but Mr Rogers has returned."

Lady Winters's irritation deepened.

"What can he want with us? Surely his business is with Miss Trent."

"Miss Trent has gone to lie down, my lady. She took some sal volatile with her."

Lady Winters pressed her lips together. "I see. Very well. I suppose you had better send him in."

Mr Rogers entered with his usual respectful air, though Georgiana noticed he gave a small start at the sight of her. However, this did not impede his professionalism. His cap held in his hands in front of him, he addressed Lady Winters.

"I am sorry to intrude, your ladyship. I understand Miss Trent is indisposed?"

"Yes, I'm afraid so. What can I do for you?"

Georgiana wondered if Lady Winters's failure to afford Rogers the courtesy of addressing him by name was deliberate, a way of reminding him of his inferiority of station.

"I had hoped Miss Trent would be able to identify the young gentleman we found," Rogers said. "I would be glad to spare her such an ordeal, but we must be certain that he is who we think."

"No, certainly not," said Lady Winters. "Miss Trent is not up to facing such a distasteful task. You will have to ask someone else to do it."

Rogers looked perplexed, but was not to be deflected from his duty. "Miss Trent appears to be his only relative. However, if you are able to direct me to some other person…"

"I could do it," said Louisa, "if Georgiana will accompany me. We saw him talking to Miss Trent."

Everyone stared at Louisa in surprise. It was her mother who spoke.

"Don't be ridiculous, Louisa. I never heard such a foolish notion, quite apart from the impropriety of it."

"Impropriety?" Louisa looked puzzled.

"Why, yes, of course," said Lady Winters. "You were not introduced to the man, were you?"

"No, Mama."

"Well then," said her ladyship. "It's an absurd notion, Louisa."

"But, Mama, Georgiana and I did see Miss Trent talking to her nephew. If Miss Trent is not up to seeing him, surely it would help her."

Georgiana was impressed with this new strength of mind Louisa was displaying towards her mother. Lady Winters looked a little taken aback herself, and unsure how to respond to such unusual behaviour in her daughter. Looking from one to the other, Rogers interposed.

"If Miss Trent is indisposed, it would be helpful if Miss Grey or Miss Winters could recognise the gentleman," said Rogers.

Lady Winters drew a breath and spoke slowly, as if endeavouring to make herself clear to an idiot. "He was not a gentleman."

Mr Rogers immediately begged pardon. His tone was tactful, and his manner made it clear that he was aware he did not satisfy this criterion himself.

"It would be an unpleasant experience for the young ladies, I'm afraid," said Rogers. "Perhaps it is best that they do not become involved. Indeed, I would never have suggested such a thing had Miss Winters not been kind enough to offer."

Louisa smiled at Rogers in a manner which showed her

approval of his words. Despite this, Georgiana noticed a mulish glint in her eyes which tended to appear when Louisa did not get her own way. She wondered at the girl's willingness to identify the body of Miss Trent's nephew, whom she had seen on only one occasion. In fact, despite Louisa's good nature, Georgiana was not fully convinced that her eagerness was merely a desire to do Miss Trent a good turn.

"May I ask, Miss Winters, if you have no objection," said Rogers, "where did you see the young man?"

"On the street, a few days ago," said Louisa. "Georgiana, that is, Miss Grey and I had gone for a walk – Oh! Charlie!"

"I beg your pardon, Miss Winters?" said Rogers.

Louisa looked up at the Runner, ignoring her mother's disapproving stare. "Sir Charles Ross. He was with us. We all saw Miss Trent talking to her nephew, at least I think it was her nephew. He did look a great deal younger than she is."

"I see. Perhaps you could give me Sir Charles's direction?" Rogers asked.

With a glance at her mother, Louisa nodded and told the Runner where the young gentleman lived.

"One moment," said Lady Winters, "I believe I have a visiting card somewhere."

Rogers thanked her solemnly for her help and the three waited in silence for Lady Winters's return. When her ladyship entered the room, she wordlessly handed Mr Rogers the card and gave an equally silent nod of acknowledgement as he thanked her.

"I'm not sure he knows Miss Trent's nephew, though," said Louisa. "He may not remember."

"That's no matter, Miss Winters. It may still be helpful for me to speak to him."

During this dialogue between Louisa and the Runner,

Georgiana had been considering the additional knowledge she herself had of Miss Trent's nephew and of someone who might know rather more. Yet how could she bring it to the Runner's attention without raising curiosity?

"Was nothing found on his person which could help?" inquired Lady Winters, showing an unexpected interest.

"No, my lady," said Rogers. "There were one or two documents which might have been helpful, but of course they were soaked and impossible to read."

Lady Winters nodded her head slowly, resignation on her face.

"I will not detain you any longer," said Rogers. "I am very grateful for your assistance. Perhaps…" He looked from Louisa to her ladyship and back again. "Perhaps you would be good enough to contact me at Bow Street if you think of anything which may be helpful, or if, that is when, Miss Trent recovers her composure?"

"Very well," said Lady Winters.

Louisa gave him a small smile as she rose to pull the bell. This did not escape Lady Winters's notice. Georgiana thought it might be wise to take her leave, but before she could do so, the servant who answered the bell announced yet another visitor.

Mr Lakesby looked surprised at the sight of the assembled company but rapidly recovered, offering a bow and greeting everyone as if it was nothing out of the ordinary to see a Bow Street Runner in his aunt's home.

"Are you here on your inquiries into Mr Polp's death, Mr Rogers?" he asked.

"No, sir," said Rogers. "It's about another matter. An accident."

"An accident?"

Something about Lakesby's tone caught Georgiana's

attention. Louisa looked towards him curiously. "Miss Trent's nephew has drowned," she said.

"I see. I am very sorry to hear that." Lakesby's eyes were alert, and even more attentive than usual. His gaze rested slightly longer on his aunt, who seemed to have withdrawn into her own thoughts. "How is Miss Trent?" he asked.

Lady Winters made no reply, and Louisa gave her mother an appraising look.

"Very upset," she told her cousin. "She is lying down."

Lakesby's eyes were fixed on the Runner. "You are looking into this?" he inquired.

Rogers nodded. "It would be helpful to know what happened."

"So you are not certain it is an accident?"

"I would not like to say, sir," replied Rogers. "Little is known as yet."

It was clear Mr Rogers was not disposed to share any more. He departed, pleading the call of duty.

Georgiana rose to follow his example. "I must be on my way as well," she said. "You have enough to occupy you; I should not take up any more of your time."

Louisa looked disappointed at her friend's departure but bade her farewell. Lady Winters took her leave absently, to the surprise of everyone else in the room. Lakesby offered to escort Georgiana home if she would wait a few minutes. She thanked him but declined; she had a great deal on her mind and wanted some time to herself to consider everything she had learned in the past half-hour or so. She found herself wondering about Lady Winters's abstraction; was her only concern for Louisa's offer to identify the body of Miss Trent's nephew, or had what had happened revived her memories of Harry in some way? Her ladyship was usually so proper; that she had behaved in such a manner was in itself odd.

As for Louisa's somewhat reckless offer, she was certainly an impulsive girl. Georgiana was not certain whether she was acting from genuine eagerness to help, or from a macabre interest and thirst for adventure. In either case, it was likely she had not fully thought through the implications of her suggestion.

As she pondered all this during the carriage ride home, a sudden thought occurred to Georgiana. She leaned forward to attract her coachman's attention, and asked him to drive to Boyce Polp's residence.

26

Standing outside the front door of Boyce Polp's erstwhile home, her eyes level with the black wreath which hung there, Georgiana raised her hand to the knocker. She was still not certain what she was going to say.

"Is Mrs Mortimer at home?" she asked the footman who opened the door.

"Yes, miss, but I am afraid she is not receiving anyone. She is in mourning, you know."

"Yes, I know," said Georgiana. "However, Mr and Mrs Mortimer called on me when they arrived in London. I hoped she would consent to see me."

"Very well, miss. I will check. Would you please wait here?"

Georgiana stood in the hall, looking around her. The décor of the hall reflected the degree of good taste she would have expected of Mr Polp. As she waited for the footman to return, she wondered where he had come by the items she saw.

"Excuse me, miss. Mrs Mortimer would be pleased to see you. Would you care to follow me?"

Georgiana walked behind the footman to a small room which seemed to reflect the mood of its solitary, black-clad occupant. Mrs Mortimer rose and came forward to meet her, offering a small smile of welcome which seemed sincere if melancholy. There was no sign of her husband.

"Good morning, Miss Grey. It is very kind of you to call. May I offer you some refreshment?"

"No, I thank you," said Georgiana. "How are you?"

"Oh, well enough," Mrs Mortimer said, gesturing to a

chair. "Adam, that is my husband, has been a great help. He has been taking care of my brother's business affairs."

"That must be a comfort."

"Yes." Mrs Mortimer smiled and nodded her head in a rather childlike manner. "My brother's friends have also been very kind, those I have met. There was one gentleman, a Mr Barclay, I think. He called to offer his condolences, and was very kind."

"I am sure he was. You have not met previously met Mr Barclay?"

"No, I know very few of my brother's friends. Living in the North, you know, the opportunity does not present itself. I believe my husband is acquainted with him."

"Has your husband visited London often?" Georgiana asked.

"Occasionally," said Mrs Mortimer. "I suppose men travel more, don't they? Business matters and so forth."

"Yes, I suppose so," said Georgiana, wondering what business matters she could mean. "Is your husband in trade?"

The question was not asked with any disdain but Mrs Mortimer hastened to deny it.

"Oh, no," she said. "But I believe there are always things for a gentleman to do; at least that is what my husband says."

"Does he? Then I suppose it must be true. He does not tell you anything about what he does?"

Mrs Mortimer looked surprised. "No. Why should he?"

Instead of answering the question, Georgiana asked another of her own. "Was he friendly with your brother?"

"Yes, I think so. They were civil enough to each other. However, as I said, we did not see much of poor Boyce." Mrs Mortimer paused for a moment then spoke hesitantly, in a confidential tone. "My husband lost his own brother, you see. He was killed in a duel."

"I am so sorry."

"I think my husband found it difficult to spend time with my brother without being reminded of his own. I don't think Adam ever recovered from his brother's death."

"It must have been dreadful," Georgiana sympathised. "What happened?"

"Some sort of misunderstanding. He was mistaken for someone else, someone who owed money. His name was signed on a vowel and there was… some unpleasantness."

"That was unfortunate."

"It was quite tragic," said Mrs Mortimer. "He would not pay it, of course and he took such abuse. He was actually called a cheat! Can you imagine?"

"Quite shocking."

"That was as much as my husband would tell me," said Mrs Mortimer, "but I believe things took quite an ugly turn. Of course, my brother-in-law could not accept such an insult."

"No, indeed."

Mrs Mortimer was shaking her head. "Imagine signing another man's name on a vowel. Who could have done such a thing?" she said.

"It does seem quite dishonourable," said Georgiana, turning over a thought in her mind.

"By the time the gentleman who held the debt realised the mistake, it was too late," Mrs Mortimer said quietly.

"Who was he?" asked Georgiana, not really expecting an answer.

"I don't know. My husband wouldn't tell me. I believe he left the country."

"Yes, of course. He would have to do that." Georgiana looked towards Mrs Mortimer. "Your husband is not at home?"

"No. He is dealing with some business of my brother's." She looked around the room. "I shall be sad to leave here in a way." Suddenly she smiled at Georgiana, and the childlike quality reappeared. "It would have been agreeable to have a home in London."

"You are not keeping your brother's house?"

Mrs Mortimer shook her head. "No, my husband tells me it must be sold. It is something to do with property terms. I don't understand it at all, but he is taking care of everything."

"I see." Georgiana was unsure if Mr Mortimer was genuinely trying to spare his wife further distress, but she was beginning to suspect that there were other motives for the sale of Mr Polp's house than the legal issues he had implied.

She rose to take her leave. "I should not take up any more of your time. Please present my compliments to your husband."

"Thank you. It is such a pity we had to meet again under these circumstances."

"Yes, it is." Georgiana felt unable to say anything more. It was clear Mrs Mortimer depended upon her husband, and would be crushed to hear of the suspicions her guest harboured. There was no saying how she would react.

Georgiana passed the short carriage ride to her home thinking what to do next. She had no proof that Polp was responsible for the forged vowel though, in view of the conversation she had overheard on the road, she could not help believing it to be a strong possibility. Under the circumstances it would certainly give Mortimer reason enough to kill him.

Georgiana considered the Runner would be best placed to judge the situation. She determined to send him a note as soon as she arrived home, and spent a few moments considering how best to word it so that she did not sound fanciful. She was certainly glad to have the information about the duel, since it left her no longer dependent on the conversation overheard by the Crimson Cavalier.

Georgiana's arrival home brought more surprises. James opened the door, and informed her that Miss Winters was waiting for her in the small saloon. She found an anxious Louisa pacing the room.

"Oh, Georgiana."

"Louisa, what on earth has happened?"

Louisa clasped her friend's hands tightly; the strength of her grasp was incongruous beside her fragile looks.

"It's Mama. She has disappeared."

"What?"

Louisa sat down and burst into tears. "I don't understand. It's been such a horrible day. Why would Mama go away?"

"Disappeared? Gone away? Whatever do you mean?"

Louisa sniffed and dabbed her eyes with the corner of her handkerchief. "You know how she seemed when you were there? As if she had something on her mind?"

Georgiana nodded.

"Well, when you had gone, she said something about needing to lie down. But she didn't."

"No?"

Louisa shook her head vigorously. "No. She went to the stables and asked for a horse and – and rode away."

Georgiana stared at her friend in astonishment. The mental image of Lady Winters on a horse was one she found difficult to comprehend.

It was clear that Louisa could see this. "Mama was an accomplished horsewoman when she was young," she explained. "It is just that she has not ridden for a number of years." She twisted the handkerchief between her hands. "Georgiana, I don't know where she would go. Or why. And without telling anyone."

"Was your cousin still there?"

"He has gone to find Mr Rogers, to see if he can help. Where can she have gone, Georgiana?"

In the light of Louisa's current panic-stricken state, it seemed futile for Georgiana to point out that she was less likely to know what was in Lady Winters's mind than her own daughter. Or was this really the case? As far as Georgiana was aware, Louisa knew nothing of her mother's history with Harry Smith.

A thought occurred to her. Having calmed and settled Louisa with some refreshment, Georgiana went in search of Tom.

"Have you heard anything of your friend Harry?" she asked without preamble.

"No, miss," Tom replied. "He might still be lying low but I'm afraid he could be in trouble."

Georgiana was thinking along similar lines – and there was a possibility that the same thought could have occurred to Lady Winters. She glanced out of the window. The sun was low, but it was still too light for the Crimson Cavalier to set forth from the house without attracting attention. She thanked Tom and before returning to Louisa, she asked the page to stay within call in case she needed him.

"How are you feeling?" she asked her friend.

"Better." Louisa managed a smile. "But I am so very worried about Mama. This is so unlike her. You know how proper she is; something must be very wrong to make her act like this."

Georgiana squeezed Louisa's hand. "I know." She hesitated, then smiled in what she hoped was a reassuring way. "Why don't I send Tom out to look for her? He knows the area well, and could look in places where you and I could not venture, or which Mr Rogers might not consider."

Louisa looked up at this. "Oh. Yes. Thank you. Would it be all right? I mean, in view of – what happened – you know, when he held up Max's carriage. He might not want to help."

"Don't worry about that. Tom will do as I ask."

The door opened, taking both young ladies by surprise. Miss Knatchbull stood on the threshold, a book in her hand, looking awkward as she realised she had interrupted.

"Oh. I beg your pardon. I had not meant to intrude."

Selina turned to leave but Georgiana stopped her. For once, her cousin's appearance was timely; she was the very person the situation required.

"Please don't go, Selina. I'm afraid Louisa is a little distressed by something which has happened at home. There is something I must do rather urgently. Would you be good enough to sit with her?"

Selina could not have demonstrated more obliging concern as she came into the room. Louisa seemed glad enough of her company.

Georgiana slipped out through the door and asked James to fetch Tom back to her. The two returned quickly, and Tom looked intently at her as Georgiana explained the errand she had for him. He looked dubious about searching for Lady Winters and it took all of Georgiana's powers of persuasion to convince him that her ladyship would not set the law on him. Eventually he agreed, but still with an air of reluctance. However, this was swallowed by astonishment as she suggested he also look for his friend Harry.

"Her ladyship gonna put the law on him, miss?"

"I don't think so," said Georgiana. "I am just concerned. About both of them. Be as quick as you can, please, Tom."

"Yes, miss."

Georgiana watched the boy scamper off, then went lightly up the stairs to her bedroom. Emily found her pacing, one hand against her chin, the other twisting her hair, as if it would provide inspiration.

"James told me you'd sent Tom to look for her ladyship."

"Yes, but I think I ought to try to find her myself."

"Beg pardon, miss, but where do you mean to start? If her daughter doesn't know where to look."

"Louisa doesn't know everything about her mother." Georgiana glanced out of the window. Shadows were lengthening, and she could only hope Louisa and Selina were not keeping a close enough watch on the time to realise how long she had been gone. An idea occurred to her. She gave Emily brief instructions and told her she would be back shortly, then went downstairs to the small saloon.

"I beg your pardon," she said with a smile as she entered the room. "That took rather longer than I expected. How are you feeling, Louisa?"

"Oh, well enough," said Louisa. "I am just so worried."

"Yes, I know," said Georgiana sympathetically. "Perhaps you would like to lie down?"

Louisa looked at her uncertainly. "No. No, thank you. I don't want to impose. Perhaps I should go home?"

"Whatever you wish, Louisa," said Georgiana. She looked towards her cousin. "Selina, if you wouldn't mind, if it's not too much trouble, perhaps you could accompany Louisa?

I don't think she should be alone, and it may be I can be of more use here. I could try to make some discreet inquiries through the servants."

"Oh, yes. Yes, of course," said Selina, bowing her head and clasping her hands solemnly. "I should be glad to do so."

"I don't wish to give you any trouble," said Louisa.

"Nonsense, Louisa, you are doing nothing of the sort," said Georgiana.

"Not at all," said Selina. "I shall just get my pelisse."

"Ask James to send for Louisa's carriage, would you please?"

The situation was arranged to Georgiana's satisfaction. She bade her two companions farewell, and her last sight of them was of Selina solicitously offering Louisa a blanket for her knees.

Georgiana ran back up the stairs. As instructed, Emily had laid out the Crimson Cavalier's wardrobe. Little speech passed between them as she helped Georgiana to change.

"Where do you mean to start, miss?" Emily asked, holding the tricorne hat as Georgiana straightened her cravat.

"I thought I'd ride towards the Lucky Bell. Anyone Harry would trust is more likely to be there than anywhere. Unless – "

Emily handed her the hat and waited for her to continue. Georgiana did not answer immediately, but pondered a thought which had just occurred to her.

"I wonder… Perhaps the place where she used to meet Harry all those years ago."

"But do you know where that is, miss?"

"No, though there can't be many places where a young lady could meet a highwayman discreetly, and where Harry would have felt safe too, even in his younger days."

"Somewhere on the highway?"

"It would have to be. A highwayman would find it difficult to remain out of sight in a residential area."

"As you know," murmured Emily.

"He would certainly attract attention if he were seen, particularly if Lady Winters's parents noticed him. Besides, if her ladyship was anything like Louisa when she was young, there would be no adventure in meeting him near her home."

"No, I suppose not."

"Emily, would you please check to see if there's anyone in the hall?"

"What about the kitchen, miss? Mrs Daniels will be preparing dinner."

"Yes. I think I should use the front door."

Emily looked horrified. "Miss Georgiana, you can't go out through the front door, straight on to the street. You're sure to be seen."

"Not necessarily," said Georgiana. "There aren't so very many houses in the square. I expect those of our neighbours who are at home will be preparing for their own dinner."

"There's always one or two curious ones, liable to look out a window."

"It is still less risky than walking through our busy kitchen."

Emily had to acknowledge the truth of this, but she still looked uneasy as she checked the corridor and reported to Georgiana that all was clear. Emily walked down the stairs ahead of her mistress, pausing near the bottom of the staircase as a shadow crossed the hall. Georgiana waited a few steps behind her, pressing against the wall, holding her breath. She heard Emily give a sigh of relief and saw her step forward. Georgiana watched as James came to the staircase to speak to his sister. He looked up the stairs, his eyes widening in surprise.

"Are there many people in the square, James?" Georgiana asked.

"No, miss, it's always just about deserted at this time of day. But surely you're not thinking…" James's eyes ran up and down Georgiana's attire.

"She is," said Emily.

"Would you at least allow me to bring your horse to the front of the house, Miss Georgiana?" said James.

"If you think you can do so without provoking Richards into asking questions. Thank you, James."

She and Emily remained silent as they waited; Emily kept watch in the hall, and Georgiana remained in the shadows on the stairs. As they heard the soft clip clop of hooves outside, Emily moved slowly to the front door, peering cautiously around it as she opened it. With a quick glance about the hall, she beckoned to Georgiana.

She managed to slip out of the front door without sight of anyone else, and she saw no prying eyes at neighbouring windows. James held Princess, and Georgiana mounted quickly. She asked James to make some excuse if she were late for dinner, and Emily to speak to her cousin if Miss Knatchbull returned before she did. Both nodded, and Emily asked if there was anything else she should do if Georgiana were delayed.

Georgiana shook her head. "No, thank you, Emily. I don't know how long I will be but I really do want to locate Lady Winters."

"It might take you a while," said Emily.

"Yes, but I hope nothing exceptional will occur."

"Is there anything I can do, miss?" asked James.

"Only what I have asked, James. Thank you. Thank you

both for your help with this."

Georgiana urged Princess into a brisk trot with the anxious eyes of her two servants following her. She moved to the narrow, less populated streets as soon as she could, and was relieved to see an increasing number of trees as she left the residential area behind.

Georgiana found herself wondering what was in Lady Winters's mind when she had left her home. She realised she was making a huge assumption in believing that her ladyship was looking for Harry; it was equally possible that she had simply felt the need for some fresh air – though if this had been the case, Lady Winters would surely have said something to a servant, if only to order a carriage. Since she was not in the habit of riding, something out of the ordinary must have prompted her to take this decision today.

As she neared the road, Georgiana's sharp eyes scanned the terrain on either side, trying to pierce the gloom and spot the most effective hiding places. She was not at all certain what, or whom, she expected to see. As she gazed about her from the comparative safety of Princess's back, she pondered on the possible whereabouts of Harry Smith and Adam Mortimer as well as Lady Winters.

Her answer to one of the questions came sooner than she expected. The sound of raucous laughter mingling with the familiar rattle of carriage wheels a short distance away along the road sent her into the shelter of the trees. She backed Princess behind a tangle of branches and undergrowth, moving carefully to make as little noise as possible. Peering through the leaves, she could see dust rising in the distance, and after a few moments, saw the vehicle appearing around a bend in the road. The laughter grew louder, interspersed with snatches of male conversation.

As the carriage approached, she saw it was a curricle, containing two men. One was Mr Barclay, the other Mr Mortimer. As Georgiana watched, another figure appeared from behind a tree on the other side of the road. A familiar gruff voice demanded that the travellers hand over their gewgaws.

27

Georgiana was shocked at Harry's appearance. His face was pale, his cheeks gaunt and sunken, and the usual grizzled stubble on his chin had grown to a full, untidy beard. She watched him carefully; he must have become desperate to come out of hiding in order to stop a carriage, particularly in view of how early in the evening it was.

"Well, look who's here," came Barclay's voice. "I believe it's the highwayman who killed your brother-in-law, Mortimer."

"So it is," said Mortimer.

Georgiana could see that Harry looked startled. Nevertheless, he stood his ground and kept his composure.

"You're mistaken about that, gents. Now, if you'll just hand over your trinkets, I'll be on my way and let you go on yours."

"No, I don't think I could do that," said Mortimer, so quietly that Georgiana had to strain to hear him.

"You'll not be passing through until you do, sirs. Come, it's a fine evening, you'd not wish to spoil it. I'll even leave you a few coins so you can play a game or two of cards."

"Most kind but quite impossible," said Mortimer.

"Good grief, Mortimer, what are you doing?"

Georgiana detected genuine shock in Barclay's voice, and it was easy to see why. Mortimer had produced his own pistol and held it levelled at Harry. His voice was still quiet, but now held a note of threat.

"As you say, this is the man who killed my wife's brother."

"In that case, hand him over to the Bow Street Runner. There's no need for bloodshed on the road."

Mr Mortimer seemed not to hear his companion. The

two armed men held each other's stare. Barclay looked uneasy.

Harry gave a crack of laughter. "It's a long time since I've had to shoot anyone. Do you really want blood on that natty waistcoat of yours?"

"A threat?" said Mortimer. "Did you threaten my brother-in-law before you stabbed him?"

"Now, you look here…" said Harry.

"Don't argue with him, Harry." Georgiana spoke softly to herself. She drew her own pistol, checked it and looked around to determine the best course of action.

"What's wrong with you, Mortimer?" said Barclay.

Mortimer glanced at his companion. "The man's a menace, Barclay. He's killed once; it's likely he'll do so again. Why not save the courts the trouble?"

"Why not just give him your purse so we can be on our way?" said Barclay.

"Give him your own," said Mortimer.

"I would if that wretched boy hadn't stolen it last night," said Barclay. He removed a ring and threw it towards Harry. "Here you are, fellow. Let us pass, will you?"

"Glad to, sir, though your friend will need to put his pistol away."

"You heard him, Mortimer. Put the damned thing away."

Georgiana began to move Princess around the small thicket, picking a way carefully through the branches and leaves covering the ground. A few yards away, the two men continued to stare each other down in silence.

"What are you doing? Put away that pistol."

The voice was familiar, but completely unexpected. Georgiana paused and blinked, unable to believe her ears. She had the distinct impression that her incredulity was shared by the three men, Harry in particular.

The highwayman lowered his pistol a fraction, and stared in disbelief as a horse emerged from the trees. Upon its back sat Lady Winters.

Neither Barclay nor Mortimer moved.

"Well, I'll be…" Harry gulped.

"There is no need for profanity." Lady Winters rode towards the men.

Georgiana had to admire her ladyship's seat. She rode with great dignity, and commanded the trio's attention. Georgiana was relieved to hear the customary imperious note in her voice; it had been sadly lacking at their last meeting.

Harry begged her ladyship's pardon, and, to Georgiana's surprise, removed his hat respectfully. Mortimer looked annoyed, and a sheen of sweat appeared on Barclay's face; he seemed be to growing increasingly nervous.

After a moment, Mortimer bowed towards Lady Winters. "I am so sorry you were drawn into this unpleasantness, ma'am. Permit me to introduce myself. I am Adam Mortimer. You were probably acquainted with Mr Polp, Boyce Polp; he was my wife's brother. This gentleman is Mr Barclay."

Barclay looked oddly at his companion, but bowed to her ladyship as if they were in a drawing room.

"And this," Mortimer gestured towards Harry with his pistol, "is the highwayman who killed my brother-in-law. I had in mind to turn him over to the Bow Street Runners."

"Did you?" said her ladyship loftily. "I gained the impression you had it in mind to shoot him."

"Of course, if he were to give us any trouble…" said Mortimer.

"So that's your plan, is it?" said Harry. "Well, the *trouble* is, I didn't kill the cove. Not my style."

269

"It is generally known that he was killed by a highwayman," Mortimer pointed out.

"You seem very anxious to put the blame on this one," said Lady Winters.

"That he does," said Harry, looking closely at Mortimer. "I wonder why that can be."

Pistol in hand, Georgiana judged it time to intervene. She rode forward.

"Because he killed the gentleman himself."

All eyes turned towards her. Harry and Lady Winters looked astonished; Barclay's expression said that he would have liked to be anywhere but there. Mortimer looked towards her with a sneer on his face.

"Another highwayman? Protecting your own kind, I suppose." Mortimer shook his head. "However, you are mistaken. Why would I kill my brother-in-law?"

"I imagine your friend could tell us. The young fellow I heard you talking to on the road one evening," said Georgiana lightly.

Barclay stared at Mortimer, looking more and more horrified.

"What does he mean?" Barclay asked.

"I have no idea," said Mortimer. "He's lying."

Harry shook his head. "No. I know this lad. He's not a liar."

"Oh, of course we will take the word of a couple of highwaymen," Mortimer sneered.

Lady Winters looked from Harry to Mortimer and back again, apparently considering the information that had been put before her. For the first time since making her acquaintance, Georgiana had the impression that she was inclined to trust the highwaymen, and believe that they were the ones who were telling the truth.

"What friend?" Barclay pursued. "You mean that Trent lad? Why, he's – he's dead."

Harry gave a low whistle. "Is he now?"

Barclay looked sickened. "He was found in the river this morning. Mortimer, you don't mean that you…" He tumbled unsteadily out of the curricle and lurched towards the side of the road. He barely reached the edge before he started retching.

It was clear that Mortimer did not mean to tell them anything. He flung a contemptuous, disgusted glance at Barclay and looked at Georgiana with fury in his eyes.

Georgiana lifted her chin and tilted her head slightly. Her smile was not visible because of her mask but the flutter of the red scarf fastened to her hat seemed a taunt in itself.

"You had to kill him," said Georgiana. "He knew what you had done."

"I've done nothing," said Mortimer.

"No?" said Georgiana. "Then why were you speaking with Mr Trent on the road a few nights ago about what you had done to Mr Polp? As I said, I heard you."

"You are mistaken. I could not have done anything to Mr Polp. My home is in Yorkshire. My wife and I came to London after her brother's death, to make arrangements."

Georgiana was shaking her head. "No. Mr Trent did not want you to kill Mr Polp."

"Mr Polp!" said Mortimer. "Mr Polp! The darling of society. Oh yes, everyone liked Boyce Polp." He paused, and gave an oddly disturbing grin. "He couldn't do a thing wrong, could he? Oh, yes, Boyce Polp, so amiable, how much he'll be missed."

"Couldn't say," said Harry. "Didn't know the cove."

"Which makes you the perfect one to take the blame for

his killing," said Mortimer.

Harry shook his head. "Not sure as I'd like to do that. Why don't you give me the gun? Let's forget the whole thing. Shouldn't think the Runner's that swift. He'll never imagine it's you that did it."

Mr Mortimer seemed to have lapsed into his own little world. "Missed by so many," he said, in a low, almost sinister voice. "Not like my brother."

Georgiana's ears pricked up. "Your brother?" Mrs Mortimer's story came back to her.

"Yes, my brother. A good lad, never harmed anyone. Then one day he was accused of cheating at cards and defaulting on a debt of honour. It wasn't even his debt, though it was his name on the vowel."

"Oh?" Georgiana watched him closely.

"He was challenged to a duel by the fellow who held it. Never had a chance, was dead within the hour."

"I'm sorry," said Lady Winters.

"Mortimer, this won't bring him back," said Barclay. "Stop all this. Go home to your wife."

"And tell her what?" Mortimer said in a mocking tone. "How proud she should be of her brother for what he did?"

"Polp signed your brother's name on a vowel?" said Barclay.

Mortimer nodded. "That's right. He had no money of his own, but he never let that stop his pleasure. If he wasn't cheating he was stealing, trinkets and ornaments from some place or other he'd been invited to. A snuffbox here, a candlestick there, not enough to be noticed immediately. People generally thought the thing had been lost or broken."

Georgiana recalled how she herself had pieced together

various things she had been told, and arrived at the same conclusion about Boyce Polp.

Mortimer was still speaking. "And he did it all with that nauseating charm that made everyone think what a wonderful fellow he was. He killed my brother, as surely as if he had shot him himself."

His audience was silent, all eyes fixed on him.

"This is quite outrageous," said Lady Winters at last. "Really, Mr Mortimer, if you have any regard for your wife, you will cease this spectacle." She turned towards Georgiana. "And I suppose you mean to rob us?"

Georgiana realised her ladyship was trying to convey a message. She bowed. "Such had been my intention, but as my friend here was before me – "

"Don't let that worry you, lad. We could share the booty," said Harry.

"Really!" said Lady Winters indignantly. She put her hands behind her neck, removed her pearls and threw them to Harry. "To be subjected to such indignity!"

The distraction was all Georgiana needed. As Mortimer stared at Lady Winters in disbelief, she urged Princess forward. The sudden movement startled the two horses at the curricle, and they shied. Georgiana's pistol was still in her hand; she brought it down on Mr Mortimer's wrist. He gave a shout and dropped his own.

Harry was already down from his own horse; he kicked the weapon away, climbed into the curricle and landed a well aimed blow on Mortimer's jaw. Georgiana slid from Princess's back and went to his aid; she pulled off Mortimer's cravat and handed it to Harry, who was better positioned to tie the man's hands. Barclay had recovered enough to move to the horses' heads, and was endeavouring to calm them.

Once the captive was tied, Harry stepped down and picked up the pearls, dropped in the scuffle. He held them out to Lady Winters.

"Yours, I believe, your ladyship."

As Lady Winters accepted the pearls from Harry's extended hand, Georgiana detected the ghost of a soft smile on her ladyship's face. A twinkle of acknowledgement flickered in Harry's eyes before he turned back to Mortimer.

"Well, what shall we do with him, lad?"

"Let the law have him," said Georgiana promptly. "If he's publicly tried, there'll be no reason for anyone to think you killed the man."

"Good point." Harry nodded slowly. He mounted his horse and stretched out his hand. "Thanks for your help, lad."

Georgiana knew he was not only referring to their subduing of Mortimer. She accepted the hand he held out to her then turned to face Barclay.

"Perhaps you could see that this – gentleman – is handed over to the Runners, and ensure the lady gets home safely?"

Barclay nodded, clearly bemused by what had taken place.

There was one final thing to be done. Georgiana reached into her black velvet bag, pulled out Barclay's purse and tossed it over to him.

"I came across that. I understand it belongs to you."

Barclay stared at the purse and at Georgiana, quite stunned. Before he or the surprised onlookers could ask for an explanation, a voice sounded in the distance.

"I thought I heard something along here."

It was Tom. Georgiana and Harry exchanged looks.

"Time we were off," said Harry, turning his horse around.

He touched his hat briefly towards Georgiana in a salute of farewell.

As Georgiana returned the gesture, Harry glanced in the direction of Lady Winters, and blew her a kiss before he rode off. Still mounted, her ladyship nodded as the voices grew nearer. Rogers was approaching with Tom, apparently leading a search party which seemed to include Lakesby as well. Georgiana turned Princess towards the trees and rode away in the opposite direction to Harry. The last thing she heard was Lady Winters calling.

"Over here, Maxwell!"

28

The following day Georgiana sat in the drawing room of the Winters residence, taking tea with an astonished Louisa and a remarkably calm Lady Winters. Her ladyship fingered her pearls absently, almost with affection. Lakesby stood near the fireplace.

Lady Winters had asked that her daughter not be made aware of her old friendship with Harry Smith. Both Georgiana and Lakesby had agreed to respect her request and, while Louisa was not at all satisfied with the explanation that her mother's sudden disappearance was down to an urgent need for fresh air, no one seemed disposed to enlighten her.

"I still can't believe Mr Polp's brother-in-law killed him," said Louisa. "Did Mr Polp really sign Mr Mortimer's brother's name on a gaming vowel?"

"Apparently," said Lakesby. "It appears he was not the only one either. Because Polp was gaming at some – er – less than respectable places, he was able to conceal his true identity."

Georgiana felt Lakesby's glance flicker towards her.

"And sign other people's names for his gaming debts," she finished.

"But why did no one else complain?" asked Louisa.

Lakesby shrugged. "It was not worth the humiliation. No one wants to be known for defaulting on a debt of honour. A denial could create the deuce of a stink. For most people, it was easier simply to pay. Unfortunately, the younger Mortimer couldn't. He was very unlucky to encounter someone who demanded satisfaction."

"It is quite shocking," said Louisa.

"It is deplorable," said Lady Winters.

"I have to agree," said Georgiana. "To think that he cheated so many people, and that it should have led to a death. In fact, judging by the way he behaved, always so bright and cheerful, seeking to be the centre of attention, one must assume he cannot have felt any remorse."

"I suppose such behaviour is not something one would wish to make public. However, I am sure you are right; there would have been something in his manner if he had a thing like that on his conscience."

"I wonder if he had a conscience," Georgiana mused.

"Very likely not," said Lakesby. "Have you seen Mortimer's wife?"

Georgiana nodded. "Yes. She came to see me last night, after her husband was taken. She was looked quite ill, and was unable believe any of it. I believe Mr Rogers was searching her brother's home and found various pieces Mr Polp had stolen. Including those items your friend lost," she added to Lakesby.

"He never really believed they were lost. I daresay he'll be glad to get them back – but two deaths and two other lives destroyed." Lakesby shook his head.

"I have asked Sarah Mortimer to stay with me for a few days," said Georgiana. "It has all been quite dreadful for her: her brother dead and her husband taken up for his murder. She is at my house; Selina is taking good care of her."

"Do you think Mr Mortimer will hang?" asked Louisa, looking around at the others.

Lady Winters shuddered.

"If he is found guilty," said Lakesby.

"Which he should certainly be," said Lady Winters. "The

way he carried on in front of Mr Barclay and myself! Disgraceful!"

Georgiana noticed with gratitude her omission of any mention of the Crimson Cavalier and Harry Smith. She also detected Lakesby's gaze on her again; something in it suggested that he had an idea that the Crimson Cavalier had been involved in some way.

Setting down her cup, Georgiana smiled at her hostess.

"I am glad you are none the worse for your experience, Lady Winters. Now I must be going. I'm sure you will want to rest, and I must see how Mrs Mortimer is."

To Georgiana's surprise, Lady Winters rose and came towards her, hands extended. "Of course. Thank you so much for calling. Maxwell, do you mean to escort Miss Grey home?"

Lakesby looked at his aunt in surprise, but agreed willingly enough. He went to summon his curricle as Louisa took leave of her friend.

To Georgiana's further astonishment, Lady Winters accompanied her to the front hall where a footman waited with her pelisse. Her ladyship clasped her hands between her own.

"Good day, Lady Winters, and thank you."

"No, Miss Grey. Thank *you*."

Meet Georgiana Grey again in

CRIMINAL TENDENCIES

a diverse and wholly engrossing collection of short stories from some of the best of the UK's crime writers.

**£1 from every copy sold of this
first-rate collection will go to support the
NATIONAL HEREDITARY
BREAST CANCER HELPLINE**

She lay on her face, as if asleep. I turned her over and saw the deep wound on her brow...
– Reginald Hill, *John Brown's Body*

...she was shaking badly. Terror was gripping her; the same terror she previously experienced only in her dreams...
– Peter James, *12 Bolinbroke Avenue*

His lips were thin and pale. "She must be following us. She's some sort of stalker."
– Sophie Hannah, *The Octopus Nest*

When he thought he was alone, he squatted down and opened the briefcase. I was interested to see that it contained an automatic pistol and piles and piles of banknotes.
– Andrew Taylor, *Waiting for Mr Right*

Avengers, that's what we are. We're there to avenge the punters who pay our wages.
– Val McDermid, *Sneeze for Danger*

The job was a real peach. Soft, juicy, ripe for plucking.
– Simon Brett, *Work Experience*

ISBN: 978-09557078-5-8   **£7.99**